JUSTICE BITES

A LEGAL THRILLER

JAMES CHANDLER
LAURA SNIDER

SEVERN RIVER
PUBLISHING

Severn River Publishing
www.SevernRiverBooks.com

ISBN: 978-1-64875-616-0 (Paperback)

ALSO BY THE AUTHORS

Smith and Bauer Legal Thrillers

Justice Bites

Bodies of Proof

By James Chandler

Sam Johnstone Legal Thrillers

Misjudged

One and Done

False Evidence

Capital Justice

The Truthful Witness

Conflict of Duty

Course of Conduct

By Laura Snider

Ashley Montgomery Legal Thrillers

Molly Sand Must Die

To join the reader list and find out more, visit

severnriverbooks.com

"To our spouses, Ann Phillips and Chris Snider, for their support of this insane hobby of ours."

PROLOGUE
MARKO

Everything hurt. It was a pain so deep that relief through death seemed far closer than through life. Every second, Marko slipped closer to that inevitability, that release. He hadn't lived a good life, but he had lived an acceptable one. Or at least that was what he would argue to whatever waited for him at the other side. He was a lawyer. Argument had served him in life. He hoped it would serve him in death.

"Lie still," a woman hissed into his ear.

He couldn't see her. The room was pitch black with no windows. What time was it? Was it day or night?

"What happened?" Marko said. Speech inflamed the already excruciating pain.

"You've been stabbed," she said, her voice barely a whisper. "In the stomach, I think."

"By you?"

"No."

He fell silent. The pain didn't subside, but it began to grow muffled. His brain was protecting him from the worst of it. He was getting cold. He wasn't fighting his end, but it wasn't coming fast enough.

"I hear something," the woman whispered.

Marko couldn't bring himself to care.

"Someone is here."

He wondered how much blood he'd lost. Was it pooling around him?

"I'll take care of them."

Marko sensed the woman's presence as she left his side. She wasn't someone he'd considered a friend. She was more of an acquaintance. But he felt the loss of her nearness almost as a new kind of pain. She'd mattered more than he had allowed himself to believe.

He should have told her when he'd had the chance.

1

MARKO

One Month Earlier

He wasn't late. Marko was never late. He was delayed. It wasn't his fault.

"I got stuck behind a combine. It was going thirty miles per hour. I couldn't get around it," Marko mumbled to himself as he opened the front door to the courthouse and hurried inside.

"My mother's sick. I had to take her to the doctor," he said as he ran up one flight of stairs. His mother was dead, but they didn't know that. Or did they?

Sweat sprang to his brow; his breathing grew labored. *I need to start working out*. But who had time for that? He was the best attorney in the state of Iowa. He wouldn't waste his energy on exercise.

The courtrooms were on the third floor of the Wyandotte County Courthouse. It was an old courthouse, one of those beautiful buildings with marble floors, crown molding, and intricate, gold filigree banisters. A building meant to make its occupants feel small. They ought to tear it apart and sell it brick by brick, build something less ostentatious, less expensive, and squirrel away the cash. That's what Marko would do if he were in charge.

"Road construction. I had to go an alternate route," he said, trying out the words, tasting them in his mouth as he ran up the second flight of stairs. He paused, placing his hands on his knees, panting to catch his breath. A bead of sweat threaded its way down his cheek. Was there actually road construction between his home office in Ostlund and the courthouse in Franklin? It was June, so construction was going on everywhere—the window of weather was quite small in northern Iowa—but he didn't know where, exactly, it was happening.

He finished the hike up the last flight of stairs and found the court attendant standing at the very top, arms crossed, tapping the toe of her bargain-brand, mouse-brown kitten heels.

"Good afternoon, Delilah," Marko said between heavy breaths. "I—"

Delilah put up a hand. "I don't want your excuses, Mr. Bauer."

"But I—"

"Your client is waiting for you." She nodded toward a bench at the other end of the hall, where a young man in his early twenties sat next to a woman who was a good fifteen years older. She wore her hair in a bleach-blonde, almost white, pixie cut. The younger man wasn't looking at Marko; his head was down as he gazed at a cell phone. On the other hand, the woman glared at him, her eyes a washed-out blue, hard and sharp as a scythe. He knew her, he'd represented her, but he couldn't remember her name.

"Get on with it," Delilah said. "The judge is tired of waiting." She turned on her heel and marched toward a door that read *Judge's Chambers.* When she opened the door, Marko could see a reception-like area where Delilah's desk sat perfectly positioned to gatekeep access to the judges. She closed the door behind her with a sharp *thwack.*

Straightening his tie, Marko gripped his briefcase and approached his client. In the otherwise silent courthouse, his steps echoed off the high, domed ceiling, bouncing over the balcony and off the marble flooring three stories below. He saw nobody else. He was alone with his client and—who? His sister? A friend?

"Nathaniel," Marko said as he approached the duo.

His expression unreadable, the young man looked up. "Nate."

"Nathaniel Michael Jonathon Shore?" This was Marko's first meeting with his client in person. While they had exchanged a few emails and one phone call to discuss Nathaniel's arraignment, this was their first look at each other. That wasn't unusual; the pretrial conference was frequently the first time Marko saw his clients. He preferred to keep contact to a minimum.

"Nate Shore," the kid said.

"And..." Marko's gaze shifted to the woman.

"Allee. You represented me, remember?"

"I remember your face and your case. I have a, uh, little trouble with names, what with meeting a, uh, lot of clients," he stammered. "And you've been...*gone* for a while." He swallowed hard.

"Five years," Allee said. "You didn't age well."

He ignored the insult. "Has it been that long?"

"I paroled a week ago."

"Oh. Congratulations." Marko readjusted his tie. "I guess," he added. He never quite knew how to deal with former clients like Allee. Her case was one of his failures. They'd walked into her sentencing hearing—a delivery of methamphetamine charge—with Marko (unwisely, it had turned out) assuring her that she'd walk out the same way she'd come in, with supervision by the Department of Correctional Services, except it would be on probation rather than pretrial release. Unfortunately, the judge had a different fate in mind.

He recalled fighting to maintain his composure as the judge pronounced the imposition of a ten-year prison sentence. Allee hadn't even tried to fake her understanding or acceptance of the consequences imposed for her actions. Back then, she had looked and acted like the poster child for meth addiction: thin as a rail; a pasty, acne-scarred complexion; empty, drawn features; and thinning, unkempt dishwater-blonde hair featuring purple highlights. He remembered that upon hearing the sentence, she had scoffed and dropped into her chair, oblivious to the judge's command to remain standing and his subsequent threat to hold her in contempt. Marko had tried to gain her compliance, but she had resisted his efforts; she was already going to prison.

She'd apparently served five years before being released on parole—more than the usual for a non-violent narcotics crime.

Looking at her, Marko now recalled the situation in detail. The presentence investigation had recommended probation. The prosecutor had recommended probation. Marko had recommended probation. But the judge had started taking a hard line with methamphetamine charges. He was up for retention election that year, and he'd decided to make drugs, which were *a scourge upon the community*—his words, not Marko's—his pet project. The judge ultimately retained his position, and Allee suffered the consequences.

"Nate's pretrial was at one o'clock," Allee said pointedly, bringing Marko back to the present.

"Right. Sure, sure," Marko said. His gaze shifted toward the judge's chambers. A face stared out at him from the window, but it didn't belong to Delilah. It was a man close to Marko's age—mid to late-thirties—who was holding his arm up and purposefully tapping the face of his watch. Marko also wore a watch, a gold Timex that had once belonged to his father. It had ticked its last tock years ago, the hands now permanently indicating nine minutes after two.

Marko scoffed. "Daniel McJames. What a clown."

McJames was the prosecutor that Marko dealt with most often. There were five attorneys in the Wyandotte County Attorney's Office, but McJames held a grudge against Marko, and he took over any case assigned to Marko. Which was bullshit. He didn't deserve the hassle. Marko had to admit he'd skirted the rules at times, but that was criminal defense. He didn't worry about justice, that was McJames' job. Marko was there to win.

"You can talk shit, but at least *he* was on time," Allee said.

Marko looked at the large, ornate clock hanging above the staircase. The small hand pointed at the two while the large hand pointed at the twelve. *It's fast.*

"You're late," she added unhelpfully.

"And you're on parole," Marko said, flashing a quick smile that didn't reach his eyes. *It's my opinion that matters here,* he thought, before turning his attention to Nathaniel. "Shall we have a chat?" Marko motioned to a nearby attorney-client room.

"I'll come with you." Allee stood and motioned for Nathaniel to do the same.

Marko stopped and looked at Allee. Tattoos lined most of her visible skin—shaky, hand-inked words, souvenirs from her time inside the Mitchellville prison. Marko's eyes dropped to read the phrase on her right forearm. "You are mine; you shall be mine; you and I are one forever." It was an oddly possessive phrase—a stamp of ownership. *Why would she let someone put something like that on her body? It might as well say, "Property of," followed by a name. Something butch like "Barb" or "Sam."* Marko looked pointedly at her. "I'd like to speak to Nathaniel alone."

"It's Nate," Nathaniel said, rising to his feet.

"I'm coming," Allee said, undeterred.

Marko took a breath, then released it. "No, you're not." This wasn't his first rodeo.

They stared at each other in silence, each willing the other to break the gaze. Then they heard footsteps. Heavy steps in quick succession, amplified by the marble flooring—the sound of someone running.

Marko turned his head in time to see a young man approaching them at a dead sprint. Marko could see the stairs, and the elevator hadn't indicated anyone arriving. He must have come from a shadowed corner of the third floor. The young man was running at full speed, directly toward them.

"What the—" He raised his briefcase like a shield to protect himself, expecting an assault.

But instead of an assault upon the three of them, the man ran past them, then leapt atop the gold handrail, where he paused for a moment and glanced back at the little group. "You will own me no more!" he shouted, before leaning forward and plummeting over the rail like a diver into the deep end of a swimming pool.

2

MARKO

There was a beat of silence.

Nate was the first to respond. "Holy shit!" he screamed. "What the hell? Did he just—?" It was the first time he had uttered more than two words. His cadence was staccato—a burst of words followed by a pause, like the rat-a-tat-tat of a machine gun.

Then the screaming began—eardrum-bursting screeches emanating from a horrified onlooker two floors below. The sound of someone who would never be the same.

Allee covered her ears as Marko watched, exposing another tattooed phrase running along the bottom of her left arm: "I am the chief of sinners, I am the chief of sufferers also."

He ran to the railing and looked down. He had recognized that voice, but he wanted to be sure. People were coming out of their offices, intrigued by the noise. Curiosity and cats and all that. But only one person was near the body. A woman with long, Barbie-blonde hair. As always, she wore a form-fitting dress, one that hugged her ample curves a little too tightly. Nikki Price, the Wyandotte County Registerer. If she looked away from the mangled body and up toward him, Marko knew he would see full lips and intelligent green eyes assessing him.

Accusing him.

The only thing Marko disliked more than prosecutors and cops was Nikki Price, formerly Nikki Marker. If Wyandotte County had a queen, she'd be it. Her parents were juggernauts in the ethanol business. The money, power, and influence behind the Marker name weren't limited to the local area; rather, they had spread across Iowa like a Purslane weed.

It was time to go. Marko swung around just in time to see Allee scoop something off the ground and tuck it into her pocket. She straightened and stood. He studied her for a moment, then decided some things were best left unknown. *Don't ask the question unless you want to know the answer.* Whatever she'd picked up was not his business, and he had no intention of changing that.

"Get in there," he ordered, indicating the attorney-client room. "This place is going to be crawling with cops in seconds."

At the mention of cops, Allee and Nate hurried toward the small room in the corner. Marko followed, closed the door, and took a deep breath, listening and considering the situation. Downstairs, it seemed Nikki had stopped screaming—apparently satisfied she'd sufficiently dramatized the situation. But things were far from over, of course. Cops would be coming, and if they thought Marko or his clients had anything to contribute, they'd be tied up in interviews for hours. Or worse, they could be accused of pushing the guy.

"If anyone asks, we were in here the whole time," Marko said. His gaze met Nate's, then Allee's. "Got it?"

"If anyone asks, we were in here the whole time," Marko repeated. "Got it?"

Nate nodded.

"Fine," Allee said, crossing her arms.

"Now, we're here for a pretrial conference," he reminded them. "We ought to get to it. Sit," he commanded, then pulled a chair from under the table and sank wearily into it. The room was closet-sized and furnished only with a rickety table and three chairs. There wasn't space for anything else. After motioning for Allee and Nate to join him, he placed his briefcase on the table, popped it open, and removed his laptop to access the electronic files saved on his drive. He had considered electronic client-management software, but the cost was exorbitant.

It took him a few moments to boot up the computer and find Nate's case file. He reviewed the file briefly, then began his spiel, reciting the words he'd memorized after hundreds of pretrial conferences.

"Nathaniel, you've been charged with possession and burglary, a class D felony," he began. "That carries a maximum of five years in prison."

"All he had was residue," Allee said.

Marko gave her a hard look. He did not appreciate the interruption. "Allegedly."

"Right. Allegedly...And he didn't know it was there."

Marko took a deep breath, held it, and then slowly released it. This was exactly why he hadn't wanted her to sit in on the meeting. She was disrupting him. She was the typical jail-house lawyer type, knowing just enough to get in the way, spouting buzz words like *Miranda, reasonable doubt,* and *probable cause,* but not knowing enough to recognize real legal issues.

"Oh, I'm sorry, Allee, I didn't realize you'd gone to law school," he said sourly. "When did you graduate?"

She grunted, sat back, and folded her arms.

"I thought so," Marko said snidely. "Now, back to business." He turned his attention to Nate. "You're a drug addict—"

"It takes one to know one," Allee said.

Marko froze. He was not a drug addict. He'd never volunteer for a drug test—who knows what the results of that would be—but he was around drug addicts all the time. That was it. If he tested positive, it would be because he spent time around people like *them*, people like Nathaniel and Allee. Not because he sometimes, on very few occasions, dabbled in a recreational bump or two. "Likewise," he said at last.

"I'm clean," Allee said.

For now, Marko thought. Incarceration forced sobriety. Two to one she'd be back to familiar playgrounds with familiar playmates by next week.

A siren pierced the momentary silence, quick and sharp, like a needle puncturing skin. Allee had better quit challenging him if they wanted to get out of the courthouse anytime soon.

"Good for you. Now, if you don't shut your mouth, you're gonna have to go. You can deal with the cops out there." He nodded to the door. "I'm trying to help you out of that mess by allowing you to stay in here, but I'm a lawyer, not a saint. I'll cast you out into hell in a heartbeat and I'll enjoy doing it. Do you understand me?"

Allee crossed her arms, exposing a crude tattoo on her left forearm: "It is one thing to mortify curiosity, another to conquer it." Marko read it, then shook his head. What was with her tattoos? Most prisoners tattooed themselves with prison gang symbols or imprinted letters of words like *truth* above the knuckles of one hand and *pain* on the other. Those kinds of tattoos, while cliché, made sense. They insinuated strength, something needed in prison. Allee's were odd, unstable, bordering on psychotic.

"Do you understand?" Marko repeated.

Allee didn't respond.

That was all the acknowledgement he would get. He turned back to his client. "The prosecutor wants you to plead to possession as a class D felony. I couldn't get him down to a misdemeanor, but he is agreeing to a suspended sentence with probation."

The truth was that Marko had yet to respond to McJames about the offer he'd received by email the day before. The offer would require Nate to reside at the Residential Correctional Facility—the so-called "RCF," a halfway house—for one hundred and eighty days before he was placed on probation. Marko thought he could get Daniel to drop that condition, so he didn't bring it up with his client. Besides, bringing it up—especially with Allee here—would only lead to a pissing contest. No client wanted incarceration—which was the point of incarceration. But arguing with Nate (and Allee) would take time, and they didn't have time.

"How can you ensure he doesn't go to prison?" Allee asked.

So much for keeping your mouth shut. "Well, as you know, judges don't always go along with the plea agreements," Marko admitted. "But there are things we can do that will help encourage the judge to grant probation. Things *you* wouldn't do the first time around," he said to Allee.

"Such as?"

"First, get a substance abuse evaluation," Marko began, turning his attention to Nate. "Then, get into treatment. Find a job. Start attending Narcotics Anonymous meetings. Go to church. Join a Bible study." He studied Nate, who seemed amenable. "Do stuff to show the judge you are serious about changing."

"So much for separation of church and state," Allee harumphed.

"For someone who is supposed to be shutting up, you have an awful lot to say." She shrugged insolently, but didn't say anything else, so he continued. "But yeah. In theory, there is separation between church and state. You are free to stand on those principles if you'd like." He focused intently upon Nate. "But you also could end up going to prison like your—" He paused, turning his attention back to Allee. "What are you to him, anyway?"

"I'm his cousin."

Marko turned back to Nate. "You could end up sitting in a cell, playing double-deck pinochle and tatting yourself up like your *cousin* here. Assuming you don't want that, you should consider following my advice."

Nate nodded his understanding, so Marko slid a business card across the table. "This is the contact information for the manager at The Yellow Lark."

The Yellow Lark was a chain restaurant. Its flagship location was in Franklin. The owner was none other than Nikki and her husband, city councilman Benjamin Price.

Nathaniel picked up the card. "Adam Price?"

"He's Nikki and Benjamin Price's son. He manages the Franklin restaurant. You should contact him for a job. They hire people on probation and parole. 'Everyone deserves a second chance' is their motto. Nikki is a real Bible thumper. Hence the church recommendation." She was also a controlling attention-seeker who always had an ulterior motive, but Marko kept that bit to himself. "You both could use a job, I'm sure," he continued, looking pointedly from Nate to Allee. "The Yellow Lark will make you wear ridiculous uniforms, but what the hell. Money is money, right?"

Allee didn't touch the card, but she didn't disagree.

"So, you want the deal?" Marko said.

"Is that the best deal I'm gonna get?" Nathaniel asked.

"Yes." Marko was the best defense attorney in the state. He knew a good deal when he saw it. "You were arrested on the premises," he began. "You had a baggie of meth in your pocket. Your criminal history is what it is. McJames knows his witnesses will show. You were in the garage without authority. They have the drug testing results from the crime lab. You can argue you didn't know the baggie was in your pants—you can even argue they weren't your pants"—his gaze shifted to Allee as he spoke—"but no one will buy that. This is as airtight as a case can get."

Nate shrugged. "Okay. I'll do it. Tell the prosecutor that I'll plead."

"Good man," Marko said, standing. Now all he had to do was convince the prosecutor to drop the halfway house bit and they were golden.

3

MARKO

Marko wasn't even through the door before McJames intercepted him. "What's going on out here?"

"How am I supposed to know?" Marko replied. "I was meeting with my client."

"You're kidding me, right? With all that screaming, you didn't even hazard a look over the railing?"

Marko shrugged. "I mind my business. You should try it sometime."

McJames' face reddened to a shade that nearly matched his fire-red hair. "I didn't know if I should be worried about courthouse security. We have women working here," he said, indicating Delilah, who was typing at her computer, pretending she wasn't listening to their conversation.

"Delilah can take care of herself," Marko said. Delilah didn't look away from her computer, but Marko thought he saw a small smile turn up the corners of her prim mouth. "She's as tough as owl hide," he added. This time he was sure he saw a smile.

McJames wasn't amused. "I thought I heard a man shouting something, and then that screeching wail."

One of Allee's tattoos said something about ownership, didn't it?

Marko shrugged again. "Sounds like you know more than I do." He clapped McJames on the shoulder—an awkward gesture, given McJames was almost a foot taller. "You should definitely talk to a cop."

"Officer."

"Potato, patahto." Marko had employed the word *cop* intentionally, knowing McJames objected to it, claiming it cheapened the profession. He pulled out his notepad and studied it. "Should we get to this pretrial conference?"

"Does your guy want to take my offer?"

Marko shrugged with practiced nonchalance. "He won't go to the RCF."

McJames studied Marko briefly. "Did you even talk to him about it?"

"Are you insinuating that I don't fully discuss offers with my clients?" Marko feigned offense. "Because that would be unethical."

McJames sighed heavily. "No, I'm not. I just...Well, why the hell not?"

"Because it doesn't make sense," Marko replied tersely. "It's burglary, and his priors—including this charge—are all simple possessions. He's never hurt anyone other than himself. You wanna insist on a felony, fine. But drop the drugs and let the poor guy be. The RCF is overkill."

McJames crossed his arms, but he was thinking. *Anything other than an immediate no is a yes in progress.* He just needed one final push. "My understanding is that there was only a trace of residue in that bag. Is there anything left for us after you finished testing? 'Cause, you know, if we're going to trial, I'd have to ask for an independent test, and if there isn't a sufficient amount of the alleged drug available..."

"I don't know..."

Marko had him. "And what are you going to do with what you've got at trial, anyway—wave an empty baggie around and shout about the danger posed to society by my client's possession of traces of white powder?"

McJames gave in. "Fine, fine. I'll drop the possession and the RCF, but your guy better get into treatment," he threatened, trying to save face.

"Already done," Marko lied. He was reasonably confident that Allee would impress upon her younger cousin the importance of following a lawyer's instructions. She knew from experience how quickly things could go south for a client who failed to comply with her attorney's advice.

"Fine," McJames said, probably pleased he'd extracted a concession from Marko he could pass on to the judge. "Let's go talk to the judge."

4

MARKO

A long hallway led past a desk reserved for Natalie, Judge Connor's court reporter, and ended at an open door. Natalie sat at the desk, her head turned to the side as she studied her computer, ignoring them. She was middle-aged and probably best described as homely. Rail thin, she wore clothing that was always too something: too large, too long, too loose, too young, too old. She was in desperate need of a makeover, but no one would dare suggest it. Makeovers had died after the '90s, when every other movie was about a nerdy girl who got hot after changing her clothes and popping in a pair of contact lenses.

"Good afternoon, Natalie," McJames said to her.

She didn't look away from her computer. "He's waiting for you."

"Should we go in?"

"You might as well."

McJames turned and glared at Marko, as if to say, "This is all your fault," then made his way to the open door. Marko hung back, allowing McJames to lead the way into the judge's chambers. Marko knew better than to interrupt a judge—especially one like Connor—so if the judge was busy, he wanted McJames' face to be the first he saw. Reaching the threshold, McJames knocked.

"What is it?" It was both a question and a demand.

"Your Honor," McJames began doubtfully, "we are here to discuss the Shore pretrial."

Connor put down his pen impatiently. "It's about time. Get in here."

McJames motioned for Marko to follow, and they entered Connor's chambers.

"What the hell was the holdup?" Connor asked. He was in his late sixties and peered at them through rectangular black plastic frames. His hair was thick for his age and still surprisingly dark, albeit streaked with telltale gray.

McJames was looking at Marko, who had plenty of excuses for his tardiness prepared, but none that he wanted to try. Lying to a court attendant was one thing, but a judge, well, that could lead to some problems. "I... there was some, uh, commotion, in the courthouse today."

"I heard. What is going on out there?" Connor's piercing gaze settled on McJames.

"I don't know exactly," McJames replied uncertainly.

"Don't you work for the prosecutor's office?"

"Yes, but I haven't been back to the office. I've been here. Waiting on Marko."

Connor's attention swung back to Marko.

"He could call to try and find out," Marko suggested. "I'm as curious as you are, Your Honor. I was meeting with my client at the time."

"Do it," Connor said to McJames. Judges came in all sizes, genders, and temperaments, but one thing they all had in common was the desire to know all, including gossip—especially if the gossip involved attorneys or courthouse staff.

McJames' expression did not change, but his lips dipped into a slight scowl. He would have preferred to watch Connor ream Marko for his tardiness.

Not today, buddy, Marko thought. It was a close one, he knew—but *close* wasn't *caught.*

McJames reluctantly removed his phone from his pocket, mumbled, "Give me a few minutes," then stepped into Connor's outer office.

Marko remained where he was. "About Nathaniel Shore's pretrial," he began. It was unethical to have private conversations with a judge without the presence of opposing counsel, but McJames was right there, and he knew that Marko was still in chambers. If it ever became an issue before an ethics board, Marko could argue that this wasn't a true *ex parte* communication. Besides, if it came up with the ethics board, it was more Connor's problem than his.

"Yes?" Connor asked, his thick eyebrows raised doubtfully.

"We are settled," Marko said. "Mr. Shore will be pleading to burglary in return for probation. The State will move to dismiss the possession charge. But I wanted to make sure that you will go along with the recommendation."

"You want me to bind myself to your agreement," Connor said. He picked up his pen and examined it. Under Iowa law, attorneys could ask the judge to agree that he or she would not diverge from the joint sentencing recommendation of the parties. It was often called a "Rule 12 agreement." Because judges preferred their autonomy, they didn't like them.

"If you will, Your Honor. I don't know that my guy will plead without that assurance." This was a bald-faced lie, but Connor didn't know that.

The old judge leaned back in his chair, rubbing his chin.

Anything other than an automatic no is a yes in progress. "I know the trial calendar is packed," Marko continued. "The public defender has at least three trials set for the next trial date. Only one can go, of course, and the other two are up against their speedy trial deadlines." Marko was court-appointed to represent Nate, but the Franklin area was also covered by the Public Defender's Office, which handled the major crimes coming through the system. While Marko generally ended up with misdemeanors and minor felonies, he was conversant with the office's docket. *Close the deal.* He looked quickly at the door. "It sure would free up some of the court's time if we can get the Shore case off the docket."

"You have a point. I'll do it," Connor said just as McJames was making his way back into chambers.

McJames looked irritated. Marko could tell he wanted to ask what they had been discussing and if Connor had agreed to something regarding Shore's case, but he didn't get the chance.

"What did you find out?" Connor demanded. Gossip trumped actual work any day.

"It sounds like a suicide," McJames replied carefully.

"A suicide. Who was it?"

"I'm not at liberty to say."

Connor's expression hardened.

McJames looked to the judge helplessly. "The family hasn't been notified yet."

"Well, is it someone I would know?" Connor asked.

McJames' gaze shifted from the judge to Marko. "We all do."

"Really?" Marko asked. He hadn't gotten a good look at the man as he sprinted past him, so this was his chance to insert a note of genuine surprise. "How?"

"Must have been a criminal," Connor concluded. "Was he running from someone? Trying to escape an officer who was trying to arrest him?"

McJames shrugged. "We don't know yet. But Nikki Price found the body."

"Poor woman," Connor said, shaking his head.

"I'm told she is very shaken," McJames reported. "And understandably so."

"That's too bad," Connor said. "She's such a force for good—does so much for this community."

"Don't heap too much sympathy on her. She's coming out of this far better than the jumper. At least she's *alive*," Marko said.

"The jumper *chose* to jump. Nikki didn't choose to find him," Connor countered.

"Allegedly," Marko replied.

This was the Nikki Price effect. People heard her name and assumed the best. He'd never quite understood how Nikki had finagled that persona. He hadn't been close with her for years, but he'd never known her as a truly good person. She did good things, yes, but for the wrong reasons. She wanted people to *think* she was good. It had nothing to do with who she was at the core.

"Regardless, we better wrap this up so I can help assist with the investigation," McJames urged. "It's probably an open-and-shut case, but you never can be too careful."

"Let me know how poor Nikki is doing, will you?" Connor said.

"Sure thing." McJames turned to Marko. "So, are we settled here? Shore is pleading to burglary with a joint probation recommendation. Right?"

"That's the deal," Marko said. He didn't add that the judge had bound himself to the agreement. McJames would find out about that at the hearing.

"I'll cross it off the trial docket," Connor added. Having taken his cue from Marko, he didn't mention Rule 12, either.

"All right, then, I'm out of here." McJames turned and left chambers.

Marko hung back.

"What is it?" Connor asked. Marko was in his space.

"Does it have to be something in particular?"

"You always want something."

"Okay, fine. I want a big case," Marko pleaded. "I'm tired of these property crimes and drug charges. Nobody ever appoints the contract attorneys to the major felonies."

Connor lifted a thick eyebrow.

"You always appoint the public defender," Marko complained.

"The public defender shows up on time. And usually sober."

Okay, he might have deserved that. "Give me another chance, Judge."

"I'll think about it," Connor said. He retrieved his pen, found a stack of papers, and began reading through them. It was a dismissal.

Marko left Connor's chambers, walked through the outer office, and stepped into the third-floor hallway, which was crawling with cops and other first-responders wearing every color of uniform imaginable. Brown deputies, blue police officers, and red emergency medical personnel were doing their thing. Crime scene technicians wearing white bunny suits waited impatiently for clearance to proceed. Plain-clothed special agents with the Division of Criminal Investigations stood to the side, speaking into their omnipresent phones.

Marko made his way carefully around the scene, looking for Allee and Nathaniel. He opened the door to the attorney-client conference room.

They'd left, and it wasn't surprising. Marko was ready to get out of there himself. This many cops and investigators could only lead to trouble.

All this for a suicide? It was overkill, but maybe it was a slow day. Maybe because it had occurred at the courthouse. Maybe something else. *Whatever. Not my problem.*

5

MARKO

Marko wandered down an alleyway, consciously avoiding Main Street, which was lined with ambulances, emergency response vehicles, and police cruisers —some with flashing lights, others parked quietly but conspicuously on the side of the road. He stopped outside the back door to Olde Bulldogs restaurant and bar. It was the target destination for the higher echelon of drunks in Franklin—meaning drinkers still capable of holding a job and, therefore, willing to pay more than five dollars per drink. It wasn't expensive by any stretch of the imagination, but five bucks a pop kept out the riffraff. He paused for a moment, checking the time on his watch, and—because it continued to show 2:09—then his cell phone. It was three-thirty. Mid-afternoon.

I should head home and get some more work done, he told himself. He started to turn away, then stopped. *Then again, the afternoon will be quiet.*

There wouldn't be a lot of filings. The clerk's office had to approve every filing before it became part of the official record. But the clerks were part of the courthouse staff and likely part of the officers' investigation. *If* they had avoided questioning—and that was a big *if*—they had probably been sent home to recuperate from an emotional day. Or simply to get them out of the investigators' way. Regardless, there wasn't a good reason for Marko to rush home.

What the hell? One drink, he thought, heading toward Olde Bulldogs' back door. *Then I'll head out.*

He hurried down the back hallway of the restaurant, past the kitchen and the bathrooms and the hostess stand (which was unoccupied at this early hour), and made his way to the bar before sinking gratefully onto an available stool.

"Marko," the bartender said, nodding in recognition. He placed a cardboard coaster in front of him that read, "Budweiser, King of Beers."

For a formerly American brand that touts its American roots, the slogan is dumb as hell. It should be "President of Beers." Kings and queens were for Europe.

"What'll it be?" the bartender asked.

"Hey, Oliver," Marko said. "I'll have the usual."

"One Old Fashioned, coming right up." Oliver grabbed a short tumbler and a bottle of Kentucky bourbon, pouring as he spoke. "Did you just come from the courthouse?"

"I did."

"What's all the commotion?"

Marko shrugged. "Dunno." Oliver was a good man, but all bartenders were gossips. It came with the territory. Marko had escaped involvement in that courthouse shit-show so far; he was not going to involve himself by flapping his gums.

"Tell you what," Oliver continued as he twisted and dropped a slice of orange into the bourbon. "Nikki came busting in here a little while ago looking for her husband. She was a mess. I've never seen her like that. Hair wild. Mascara running. She's always so put-together—know what I mean?" Oliver placed Marko's drink on the coaster and didn't ask for payment. Marko was there often enough to have a routine; Oliver knew he would pay on his way out. The only question was how many he would have before leaving.

Marko grabbed the drink and took a long pull, then replaced it, eschewing the coaster and enjoying the sound as he set the glass on the scarred wooden bar top. He swallowed and purposely smacked his lips, welcoming the bitter taste followed by the warmth of the liquor burning his throat, then hitting his stomach. He looked around. He hadn't seen her. "Nikki is here?"

Oliver nodded to a high-top table in the corner reserved for the bar's most important customers. Sure enough, there she was, sitting primly next to her husband, the mayor, and the chief of police. *What's she doing in a bar?* She didn't drink—at least she didn't used to.

Nikki caught his gaze and gestured for him to join them.

Marko didn't move. *Maybe I can act like I didn't see her.* Then Benjamin joined in, and the next thing he knew, everyone at the table had stopped talking and turned their attention toward Marko. *No such luck.* He stood.

Oliver had been watching—another skill of good barkeeps. "Let me know what they say," he said. "And I'll pour another."

As Marko approached the table, the four occupants watched him, their eyes studying his every movement. They were silent as he approached. He felt like a young entrepreneur entering the *Shark Tank*—except there would be no money exchanged or support given. It was him and four sharks. Nothing to gain, everything to lose.

"Have a seat," Benjamin encouraged Marko, smiling broadly. He had a thick white mustache reminiscent of the one worn by the Monopoly man, and it quivered as he spoke.

Marko accepted the only empty chair at the table. Clearly, they wanted something from him. He had seen them—minus Nikki—day in and day out for years, seated at this table while he drank alone at the bar. Not once had they called him over. Today, the men had matching longneck beer bottles in front of them, while Nikki sipped on what looked like a Shirley Temple.

"How are you?" Nikki asked, her voice shaky.

"I'm fine." He took a quick pull from his drink.

"I've been better," Nikki said. Her bottom lip quivered. "Did you hear about the tragedy at the courthouse?"

I didn't ask how you were, but sure, I guess I care. "Is that what we are calling it?"

Nikki placed a hand upon her heart. "A poor soul has lost his life, Marko. Of course it is a tragedy."

And that was the problem with people like Nikki. Her words meant nothing. To her, it depended entirely on who this *poor soul* turned out to be. If he was a sex offender or a Jeffrey Dahmer type, she'd drop the "poor soul" bit and replace it with the death being the result of "karma" or "God's will."

"And at his own hand, no less." She sighed and shook her head. "And now, of course, he will never make it into the Kingdom of God. Such a shame."

She didn't seem to expect a response, so Marko remained silent.

When the silence got uncomfortable, Benjamin spoke. "We haven't seen you at church of late, Marko," he observed.

Marko drank half his Old Fashioned in one gulp, then set the glass down on the table. "That's because I haven't been going."

"Why not?" Nikki asked. "Sacred Heart is open to both sinners and saints."

The comment irritated Marko. People like Nikki and Benjamin painted everyone with an either/or brush, but the reality was that most people were somewhere in the middle. "No comment."

"Why not?" Nikki leaned forward, batting her eyelashes.

It was an old trick, but Nikki was far beyond the age where that would work, and even farther past him having so much as a fleeting interest in her. "My mother always said, 'If you can't say something nice, don't say anything at all,'" he replied.

"Your mother came to Mass," she reminded him.

"My mother is dead." Marko downed the remainder of his drink and shoved back from the table, the legs of his chair squealing against the tile flooring below.

Nikki had no right to bring up his mother, a woman who had dedicated her retired life to Sacred Heart Church. She'd been there almost daily—volunteering, attending Mass, and organizing bake sales and carnivals to raise money for one thing or another. But when she'd fallen ill, when the cancer started ravaging her body, Marko was the only one who had been there for her. Everyone else—including Nikki and Benjamin—was conveniently "busy."

Admittedly, the parishioners had dedicated Masses to his mother and collectively prayed for her recovery, but prayers had no impact on the day-to-day challenges of her illness. Prayers didn't pick up and organize her medications. Prayers didn't drive her to the oncologist. Prayers didn't make her dinner and watch as she tried and failed to eat because she was too nauseous.

There was a whole damned congregation, and not one of them could help his mother in her time of need? *Spare me.*

Benjamin's sonorous voice pulled Marko from his thoughts. "The man who killed himself. He worked for us."

"So you'll be looking for a replacement, then, I suppose?"

Benjamin's face colored. Whether it was anger or embarrassment, Marko couldn't tell. But he was fine with it either way; he no longer had any desire to so much as pretend he liked these people.

"Oh, Marko!" Nikki said, tears filling her eyes. "How can you be so heartless?"

Heartless? Has she forgotten what she said moments ago? He'd buried his mother a month ago. One month. He was not over the pain. He was not over the loss. Still, she'd brought it up as an accusation. A "*Your mother would be disappointed*" comment on his failure to attend Mass. He'd had enough of this group, and stood to leave. "I'm sending a few potential employees your way. You won't be out one for long," he announced, then stalked away.

Five minutes around Nikki and Benjamin Price and he was already losing his temper. The church didn't miss Marko and he didn't miss it. Back at the bar, he slid into his usual chair, bellied up where he belonged, and didn't look in that direction again until he was sure every last one of Franklin's movers and shakers had paid their tab and left.

6

ALLEE

Time is constant and linear—except in prison. There, it is stagnant, gathering like the mossy green goop on a remote pond. Allee had been released from Mitchellville nearly a month prior, and she was still adjusting. Days no longer crawled by; instead, they raced along like a getaway car in a bank heist. If it wasn't her life, she would find it almost comical. But it *was* her life, and the change in pace had her feeling wrong-footed, hesitant.

And she was not one to hesitate.

Since her release, the world didn't feel quite like her own anymore. Her continued presence on the outside was conditional, of course. She was on parole and would be for the next two years. Any wrong move and prison would reach out, snatch her, and hold her in its jaws until the parole board saw fit to give her another chance. Or until she discharged her number—meaning another five years of stagnant time.

I am not going back. She would die before she returned. Mitchellville wasn't all that bad as far as prisons went, but it was the loss of control that bothered Allee. She had been caged, but her heart was wild, like those of animals in zoos back when the goal was to display rather than save. She didn't want that for anyone. Not for herself, and not for Nate. And that was why she'd gone to his pretrial conference with him earlier.

She hadn't expected Marko to be late. Years had passed since he'd represented her, but at least back then he'd always been on time. But things and people changed. Everyone except her.

"Where is he?" Nate asked. "He should be here by now. Is it a setup? Is he working for the cops?" His gaze settled on the small window that led to the court attendant's desk and judge's chambers beyond that. "And who is that dude? He keeps looking at me."

"Sit down," Allee said. She had tried to soften her voice, but her manner had always been gruff, and five years in the can hadn't changed that. "You'll give yourself a heart attack."

Nate dropped into the seat next to her, the cushion issuing a soft sigh. She watched him carefully. He couldn't sit still. He shifted his weight, fidgeted, shifted his weight again, and shuffled his feet.

He's high, Allee thought. She wanted to get high. That was the real war, one her prison counselor said she'd always have to fight. *Sobriety is a journey*, her counselor had said, but there was no final destination. She would never be "cured."

I should have brought a book. She looked at the ornate clock on the wall and saw that it was almost two o'clock. She hadn't always been a reader; it was a pastime she'd dabbled with in local jails while doing short stints that had developed into a full-blown hobby in Mitchellville, where she discovered a love of old horror novels. She devoured stories like *Dracula, Carmilla, Frankenstein*, and *The Strange Case of Dr. Jekyll and Mr. Hyde*. There was something vulnerable yet powerful about the monsters of the past. And because they rarely provided intricate backstories, she often found herself wondering who they had been before they became monsters.

Everyone, even monsters, came from somewhere.

At last, the door to the chambers swung open and a woman approached the staircase and stopped at the top. She looked up at the large clock, then began tapping her toe impatiently.

Allee recognized Marko when he finally arrived, huffing and puffing, several seconds later.

Nearly two o'clock. That's got to be some kind of record, Allee thought. If Nate had been five minutes late, the judge would have already signed a warrant, but here Marko was, slogging up the stairs almost an hour—a freaking hour!—past the time ordered by the court, and nothing would happen. Sure, the court attendant was chewing his ass, but it seemed as though that was the extent of his punishment, because after their brief interaction, Marko walked purposefully in their direction—*not* in a rush to help Nate but to escape the court attendant's wrath. When he got within arm's reach, a familiar scent struck Allee's nose. Alcohol. *This dirtbag has been drinking.* And were his pupils dilated? She was surrounded by users. Even Nate's attorney—her former attorney—was using, yet she was the one who had gone to prison for it. The State constantly had its eyes on her through the parole process. She could never use again, but they could. It wasn't fair.

Life's not fair. That's what her counselor used to say. *Get used to it.* Easy for her to say. Allee would never get used to it. The thought would always make her cranky, and that made her argumentative.

Allee watched and listened while Marko spoke to Nate, ignoring her. The shyster apparently didn't even recognize her. Even when she interjected, trying to help, he shut her down. He did not want her to sit in on his meeting with Nate. Too bad. She'd be damned if she was going to let her cousin—a messed-up but decent kid—get shafted like she had been all those years ago. Nate would not survive prison. Women's prison was one thing, but men's prison was an entirely different ballgame.

While she argued with Marko, she saw peripherally a young man—Jaxson something—standing alone in a corner nearby. Maybe the only good thing about living a life with one foot on the outside and the other still in prison was that she was hypervigilant. She saw everyone and everything around her, especially people trying to blend in with the background and hide. Nobody was going to jump out and stab her in the back. Not literally. Not metaphorically.

She didn't know Jaxson well, but they'd run in the same circles before she'd gotten sent off. She was at least five years older than he was, but they'd hooked up a time or two. It wasn't a romance. They'd both been high, and it seemed like a good idea at the time. They had been trying to fill a void with drugs and sex, but it hadn't led to anything. Like everything fueled by drugs, there was no meaning behind it. No thought, no emotion, just action followed by the relief stemming from an absence of thought and emotion.

Allee kept Jaxson within her peripheral vision as she debated with Marko. Suddenly and without warning, Jaxson sprinted toward them, his sneakers issuing small squeaks as they pressed against the marble flooring. Marko and Nate heard Jaxson approaching. Marko raised his briefcase to shield himself. Allee stepped protectively in front of Nate, who curled into a ball. Every man for himself.

For an instant, Jaxson's gaze met hers. His eyes were empty, but she saw no indication that he was actively high. No sway in his step, no dilation or constriction of his pupils. The emptiness in his eyes was the kind that resulted from hard times and bad decisions. He was not the Jaxson she'd once known. Oh, he'd had his demons—like every other addict, they were at the root of his lifestyle—but he was simultaneously full of life. Back then, he had laughed easily and sometimes genuinely. Not today. Every hint of the Jaxson she had known was gone.

He held her gaze but did not slow his pace. He dropped a small piece of plastic—intentionally, she thought—and it slid toward her. She stopped it with her foot like a hockey goalie, then watched in horror as he sprinted not *toward* them but *by* them before jumping onto the railing. He said something she couldn't quite understand, and leaped headfirst. No hesitation; no apparent second thoughts.

Marko and Nate followed Jaxson to the railing and looked down. Allee knew there was no use; Jaxson was gone. Her gaze settled on the small thumb drive at her feet.

Weird, she thought as she bent down and picked it up, quickly tucking it into a pocket. She thought Marko might have seen her do so, but he didn't ask, and she wasn't going to tell. Her days of trusting Marko Bauer were over. Whatever Jaxson had on the thumb drive was meant for her. Maybe he hadn't set out to give it to her, but he chose her in his final moments. And while Allee didn't have much respect for life, she did respect death.

7

ALLEE

Time seemed to stop when Jaxson went over the railing. Then the screaming began—a long, anguished wail. *Someone is going to need to see a counselor.* The sirens followed. The cops and everyone else would be on their way. They'd be occupied with the scene on the first floor for a little while, but soon they would make their way up. They'd find Allee. They'd see that Nate was high. Nate would probably act out and get arrested. They'd bust him, and they'd find something to pin on Allee.

We've got to get out of here, Allee thought.

They were trapped. She could not leave the courthouse without Nate—she was his driver—and Nate could not leave without finishing his pretrial conference.

Marko pulled them into an attorney-client room, suddenly unconcerned about Allee's presence. He apparently had reason to keep his distance from the cops as well—probably due to his dilated pupils and the smell of stale booze squeezing its way out of his pores.

They talked for a few minutes, until Marko left the room with a promise to resolve Nate's pretrial conference.

"What do we do now?" Nate asked after the door swung shut behind Marko. He picked at the skin on his arm, clutching it through two fingers, lifting it and pulling it away from the bone, then letting it drop again.

Allee swatted his hand. "Don't do that."

The courthouse was alive with the sound of sirens, footsteps, and people yelling. It was unsettling, but better than the screaming, at least.

"We need to go," Nate said. He shot out of his chair and started pacing in the small room. His agitation was evident; the source—drugs or shock? —less so.

Allee wasn't sure if leaving was worth the risk. They hadn't technically completed the pretrial, but they'd been there, and the judge's staff knew they'd been there. Could the court system punish Nate for leaving when the conference should have been over an hour ago?

Yes. The answer was always yes. The courts would always find a way to punish people like them.

She made her decision. "Let's just hang tight for a little bit, okay?"

Through the one-way glass in the door, Allee watched as a cop wearing a black protective vest over a blue uniform carefully emerged from the staircase. Gun drawn, he was serious and solemn, brow furrowed and his head on a swivel, eyes searching. Quickly, Allee jumped back, pulling Nate away from the window.

"Is it a cop?" Nate asked. "Allee, I've got some—some stuff."

Allee's gaze swung toward him. "Are you freaking kidding me? In a courthouse? The police and sheriff's departments are attached to this building. What were you thinking?"

"I forgot about it, okay?"

Allee wanted some. She wanted to get wasted and forget all of this. She wanted to forget about today and every day. She wanted just a little buzz. But she also didn't. She needed to help Nate, and he needed her to be sober. He needed to dump the stuff. But maybe they could keep it for a little celebration later. Just once.

But it never was just once, was it?

"Damn it," she decided, peering out the window. The cop was around the corner. "Let's go."

Nate followed her to an elevator near the attorney-client room. It was little known, almost exclusively used by the jailers to bring inmates to the third floor for court. Allee knew of its existence, of course, because she had been one of those inmates on more than one occasion.

"This way." She pulled Nate toward the elevator as the cop made his way around the gilded banisters, toward the spot where Jaxson had jumped. She pressed the down button while keeping her gaze trained on the man in blue. When the elevator dinged, she paused and looked around, waiting for the cop to come rushing in their direction. She shoved Nate inside, and not until the doors had closed and they were on the way to the first floor did she finally start to relax. Her anxiety was quickly replaced by anger.

"What the hell were you thinking?" Allee growled, venting her spleen on Nate.

"I wasn't. I—"

"You seriously brought drugs into the courthouse? When you had a pretrial conference for a felony charge? You've got to have shit for brains." The elevator sounded and the doors opened. Allee took a quick look around. They were at a back entrance to the first floor, a part of the courthouse that was dingy and unkempt. There was no point in polishing the floors, because unlike the public areas, only inmates and jailers saw this part of the courthouse. "Move!"

Nate was still nursing hurt feelings. "I told you I forgot. Why are you busting my balls?"

She guided him out the back door and toward her brown 1976 Ford F150 Ranger. It was the same truck she'd driven in high school. It had seen better years, but she took care of it the best she could. "I'm on parole. I can't be around drugs. You're going to get me sent back. Is that what you want?"

"No," Nate said as he hurried alongside her. He had the decency to at least sound remorseful.

"Get in," she ordered, and hopped into the driver's seat. Before he was fully seated, she started the engine, put the old truck in gear, and pulled out just as more law enforcement arrived.

They drove in silence, alone with their thoughts. At this point, she felt more like a mother to Nate than a cousin. And like a mother, she held some responsibility for how he had turned out. Regrettably, she'd been the first to offer him drugs. At the time, she'd thought he would get it one way or another and he might as well use with a safe person. Addiction inevitably resulted, and now he'd use with anyone, danger be damned, so long as they had the stuff.

The drive was short. Nate still lived with his biological mother in his childhood home. It was only a block from Allee's mother's house, where Allee had been staying since her release from prison. She pulled up outside her aunt's house and put the truck in park, then turned to him. "You need to get into treatment."

Nate snorted. "I'm fine."

"My ass. You almost caught another charge back there—one that would've been so stupid the cops would be laughing about it for years."

"Almost isn't caught."

"Nate, if you ever wonder, 'Am I an addict?', remember the day you took crystal into the courthouse for a meeting with the judge. That'll be Exhibit One. And for the record, your attitude sucks." Everything sucked these days. All she wanted was the freedom that he did, to live life without the ghostly chains of parole clinging to her ankles, but she couldn't. He was taking that freedom for granted. "Do you want to end up like me?"

Nate shrugged. "I don't want to go to prison."

"Then get into treatment. Get sober." She was lecturing again. In treatment, they always said, "Don't lecture." Worse, she was a hypocrite. She was damned sure she wouldn't have gone to treatment if she were in his position. Hell, she had been in his position and didn't go. She was given the chance, and she didn't do it. She thought she could do it herself. "Look, all I'm saying is—"

"I'll think about it," Nate said. He hopped out and swung the door shut.

Allee cringed as her door creaked. "I'm not trying to be a pain in your ass," she said. "You know that, right? I just want to help. I've been there and—"

"I know," Nate said through the open window. The truck did not have power windows or doors. A manual hand crank was the only way to get it back up. "And I'm sorry if I stressed you out."

Allee's anger dissipated somewhat with his apology. She knew full well it wouldn't be his last, of course. His remorse was real, but it was ephemeral. Like all addicts, he meant every word he said right now, right here. But that was the thing about addiction. It was all impulse—desire followed by apology, urge followed by regret. "It's fine," she said.

"Good luck at your meeting," Nate said. He tapped the windowsill and turned to his mother's house.

She had almost forgotten. Allee had a meeting with her parole officer in a few minutes. She'd expected to have time to swing by the house and grab a late lunch, but Marko's tardiness and Jaxson's jump had dashed that hope. She'd have to go hungry. She could not be late to meet her PO. Her freedom depended on it.

After Nate waved to her and disappeared into the house, Allee put her truck in reverse and her foot on the brake, then shifted her weight to look out the back window. An object dug into her hip. Keeping her foot on the brake, she reached in her back pocket and pulled out the thumb drive. She'd completely forgotten about it in the chaos that followed Jaxson's jump. She set it on the dashboard and continued backing out. She turned on the street and gunned the truck, rushing to her PO's office. She was cutting it close on time. If she didn't pick up the pace, she was going to be late. There was risk in speeding, but there was risk in tardiness to parole meetings. Somehow, her life had become one where she was constantly weighing risk versus reward, walking the tightrope of choosing one danger over another. She floored the gas pedal and took a sharp turn.

The thumb drive slid across the dashboard, hit the window, then slid somewhere beneath the passenger seat.

Shit, Allee thought. She'd taken care of her car, but that didn't mean it was clean. It ran, but it was messy. It would take her forever to find it. And she did not have a lot of free time by design. Idle hands led to stray thoughts that inevitably ended in a need to use.

Maybe it's for the best, she told herself. She didn't have the time or the energy to deal with other people's problems. Especially those who were dead and gone. She had to see the person who had control over her freedom. The true ball and chain. Her PO.

8

ALLEE

Pamela Banks was a prim, severe-looking woman who had probably never made a mistake in her miserable but proper life. She was also Allee's parole officer.

"What do the tattoos mean?" she asked.

Allee's gaze drifted around the small, depressing office. No pictures of family or loved ones clung to the walls, no knickknacks littered the desk that was far too large for the space. There was nothing to hint at who Pamela Banks was on the inside. Unsurprising, considering her clientele.

"Do you read?" Allee asked.

"I can't say I have the time."

This was Allee's second meeting with her parole officer. Both times Pamela had smelled strongly of cigarettes. If she had time to smoke, she had time to read. She could even do both at the same time, especially now that audiobooks were everywhere. "Well, there is nothing *but* time on the inside."

"Is that where you started reading? In prison?" Pamela asked. She jotted something on the notepad positioned in front of her. Allee was in one of the two stiff, hardback chairs across from Pamela's desk. Close enough to see something had been written, too far to decipher the words.

"I never said I started reading," Allee said.

"You implied it."

Allee shrugged.

"So..." Pamela gestured with her pen as if to say, *Go on.*

"I'm not sure why that's important."

"You seemed to think it was important enough to ask me if I read. Perhaps you are trying to find common ground with me. A connection."

Allee shrugged again.

"You know what?" Pamela set her pen down. It lay perfectly parallel to her notepad. "If this is going to work, we are going to have to start trusting one another."

If this is going to work referred, of course, to Allee's conditional release from prison and represented a thinly veiled threat—the trap door representing a potentially revoked probation perpetually beneath her feet. She hated the power Pamela and others wielded over her.

"I like classic horror books, okay?" Allee said.

"That wasn't so hard, now was it?" Pamela asked rhetorically. She threaded her fingers together. "So...What about the tattoos?"

"What about them?" She wished Pamela would just come out and say she hated them. That's what she meant.

"They seem sinister."

"Well, they aren't."

"Explain."

Allee displayed her right forearm and indicated the text. "'You are mine, you shall be mine, you and I are one forever.' It's from *Carmilla*." She lifted her left arm, gesturing toward that forearm with her right hand, where the text read, "It is one thing to mortify curiosity, another to conquer it." She said, "That's from *The Strange Case of Dr. Jekyll and Mr. Hyde.*"

Pamela nodded as if in understanding. "Ahh, so the tattoos have to do with your reading," she said. "That's why you asked me if I liked to read when I asked you about the tattoos."

Bingo. Allee sat quietly, waiting for the next barrage of questions.

"So, what do those phrases mean to you?" Pamela asked. "Why tattoo them on your body?"

Allee studied Pamela's office as she prepared a response. Everything was arranged with precision. All straight edges and parallels. "What's your thing with symmetry?"

"This isn't about me," Pamela replied defensively.

"Well, it isn't about my tattoos either. Besides, I thought we were gonna start trusting each other."

They stared at one another for a long moment, until Pamela shifted her gaze under the pretense of changing the subject. "What are your plans for employment?" she asked, setting Allee's interest in literature aside. At least for now.

"I don't know."

"You've got a lot to do, of course. First, you'll need to get a job. Then you'll have to start going to Narcotics Anonymous meetings—"

"Aren't those religious-based?" Allee interrupted.

"Technically, no. NA's literature nowadays refers to spirituality versus religion," Pamela explained, looking up from her notepad. "But even so, would that be a problem?"

"Can the government really force me to go to religious meetings?"

Pamela sat back and crossed her arms. "The government can, will, and, in your case, *has* required you to stay sober. Narcotics Anonymous is an effective, proven way of helping parolees to achieve that goal."

"It's not very *anonymous* if you know I'm going."

"The anonymity has to do with participants not using their membership to gain notoriety," Pamela explained. "But for the record, *nothing* is going to be anonymous or secret while you are on parole." She gave Allee a hard look. "Is that clear?"

Allee nodded.

"Good." Pamela turned back to the list on her notepad. "You'll need to build community relationships. Healthy, positive connections. You can start doing that through NA, but I'd also recommend that you begin volunteering. You'll meet good people, always a plus, and you will keep yourself busy. Idle hands and all that."

"I was planning to stick to myself."

Pamela shrugged. "Well, that's better than running with a dubious crowd, but not preferred. You will need support. Sobriety isn't easy, as I'm sure you've already discovered. We all need a little help. Have you had any temptation since your release?"

Allee didn't know how to answer that question. Nobody had offered her anything, mainly because the old crowd was understandably wary of parolees. She was a marked woman, watched by the government, and the gang didn't want the government anywhere near them. But the desire was there. Her body screamed for it every second of every day. "I haven't used."

"That wasn't my question."

"Best answer I've got."

"Allee, the criminal justice system—" Pamela began, then stopped.

Bites. Justice bites, Allee thought bitterly.

Pamela was staring at Allee. "Do you have something to say?"

"No. Just thinking."

Pamela pursed her lips. "Anyway, the system requires a programmatic, practical approach to your reintroduction to society. Goal number one is to maintain sobriety and get a job. Do you have any leads on employment?"

Allee removed the business card Marko had given her for The Yellow Lark restaurant from her pocket. She gazed down at the cheery yellow bird with *Adam Price, Manager* embossed on its bright feathers. "I have one."

"Where would that be?" Pamela picked up her pen and held it poised over the notepad.

"The Yellow Lark."

"That's a great option," Pamela said, smiling for the first time. "They help lots of probationers and parolees. Ben and Nikki Price are wonderful people. You'll fit right in."

"Why?"

"Why will you fit in or why do they help parolees?"

"Both."

Pamela cleared her throat. "Well, you are a parolee—obviously. And the Price family is a very good family. The adult son manages the restaurant. He's rather..." She paused, biting her lip. "Odd, I guess—but Ben Price is a city councilman, and his wife Nikki, well, she's just a wonderful woman. She is very active in the community."

Allee didn't like the long pause. What did she mean by *odd*? Was he a creeper, or what? "Okay," she said at last. Something was weird, but she didn't have a lot of options. Maybe he was handsy. It wasn't ideal, but she could handle it. She'd had plenty of experience with handsy bosses. And family members. And teachers. And prison guards. She had lots of experience in restaurants, and—most importantly—she was a good cook. She liked it. Cooking was one of the few things she enjoyed outside of getting high.

"If you're working there, you might be able to kill two birds with one stone."

Allee's gaze shifted back down to the cheery little bird. "I don't want to kill any birds."

"It's an expression," Pamela explained. "It means that you will be working *and* building strong connections. The Prices are exactly the type of family you should spend time around—especially Ben and Nikki—and there will be lots of volunteering options, thanks to Nikki. The Yellow Lark is an excellent choice. A perfect place for you to start," she finished brightly.

"Okay," Allee said with more enthusiasm than she felt.

The obsessive positivity surrounding that restaurant and the Prices sent Allee warning signals. If something or someone seemed too good to be true, it usually was. Especially when it pertained to someone like Allee. But she'd give it a chance. After all, she had to keep her PO happy. The alternative was back to the cage, and that was not going to happen.

9

MARKO

If his mother was alive, she would have told him that he shouldn't have driven home. She would have ranted and raved about how he was "throwing his life away." She would have let him know she was praying for him, and advised him that his very soul was in danger.

But she wasn't alive, and endangered or not, Marko's salvation wouldn't become a problem until he died, and he didn't plan to do that anytime soon. Hell, he'd only had four cocktails at Olde Bulldogs. He was fine. Maybe not fine by Iowa law and its .08 standard, but he'd set his cruise control, driven with one eye shut and both hands gripping the wheel tighter than a kid with a new toy, and made it home in one piece. He hadn't hit anything, and nobody hit him. Good enough.

Marko lived in Ostlund, a small town close to an hour south of Franklin. The white, weather-beaten sign posted on the main drag proudly announced, "Ostlund. Established 1868. Population 2,029." It was situated just south of Highway 30, between Boone and Jefferson, two similar rural Iowa towns. The town of Franklin was out of his way. He'd much prefer to focus his practice in Boone, Jefferson, and Ames—all towns along Highway 30—but Franklin was where he was raised and where his mother had lived until recently. Plus, it had the worst crime rate among the little burgs in the area. Accordingly, he had mixed feelings toward the place. On the one hand, it helped him pay the bills; on the other, being in Franklin meant he would encounter people from his past.

Like Nikki Price.

Years ago, when she had been deciding between him or Ben, she had allowed them both to court her. He'd walked into that situation with eyes wide open, so that wasn't the problem. The problem arose when she would insist they go places where she knew or suspected Ben and his friends would be. Invariably, a fight resulted; invariably, Marko was on the losing end. Nikki would coo and ice his black eye and swollen face, but she couldn't hide the sparkle in her eyes. Recalling Nikki's behavior, he now recognized it as cruel rather than kind. She enjoyed watching Ben and Marko fight—and Ben pummeling Marko—as much or more than she enjoyed playing nurse afterward.

He parked his car in front of his house, forcing himself into the present. He made his way into the kitchen, tossed his keys onto the counter, then hurriedly poured himself yet another drink—whiskey on the rocks. He took a long pull and felt the amber liquid work its way into his empty stomach. Not wanting to dull his buzz, he generally eschewed eating anything while drinking. He drank for a purpose. Now, feeling his stomach growl, he turned to the ancient refrigerator.

"What do I have to eat?" Marko asked, swinging both doors open.

His stomach growled again, and he groaned. The refrigerator was empty aside from an expired bottle of ketchup and half a takeout burrito old enough that it was growing fur. When was the last time he had gone to the grocery store? "A liquid dinner it is, then," he said. Besides, he ought to celebrate his safe drive home, right?

He thought about his recently deceased mother while he poured another. She would say he drank too much. She would say he had an "issue," a "problem." He would acknowledge he liked to drink, but he argued he didn't have a "problem." He saw guys and gals with problems all day long. He wasn't like them. For him, it was voluntary. A choice. He could stop whenever he wanted. He just didn't want to stop.

Marko's home was small, two bedrooms, built in the fifties. A ranch-style home with one bathroom, one shower. It needed a makeover, but everything worked fine, and Marko lived alone. He wasn't married and had no children.

A desk took up an entire corner of the tiny living room. This was his home office. He made his way toward it and sank into a rolling blond-leather chair with imperfections and holes in the upholstery that had belonged to his grandfather (who was also an attorney). All the men in Marko's family had been attorneys for as long as the family line went back. All were educated men, but all were notoriously terrible with money, which was why—despite the premature death of his parents—there had been no financial windfall.

He shook the computer's wireless mouse, and waited as the old machine sprang to life, displaying a scenic background of rolling hills and daisies dancing in the wind. It was a stock photo, not a place Marko had ever visited. He opened his browser and navigated to the local court's electronic filing website. He covered his mouth with a fist, belched, then entered his password and clicked on the "Notifications" tab to see what—if any—new appointments had been sent his way. There were only two, each concerning charges for simple possession of drugs. One was for marijuana; the other was for methamphetamine. One came from the court in Jefferson, the town to the west; the other was assigned to him from Boone, the town to the east.

"Damn," he said aloud, and reclined in his seat, discouraged. He'd thought for sure a judge—maybe Connor—would appoint him to something that mattered. He'd take anything. A real burglary with victims. An arson. A sex abuse. *Anything* so long as it was a felony. Nathaniel's case was the very last felony he had open, and that was basically resolved. Once it was over, he'd have nothing but piddly little cases.

"They're punishing me," he said, clicking out of the electronic filing system.

He had gone to court slightly sauced one time—one time!—and the felony appointments had dried up like a mud puddle in the Mojave. Nobody had reported his transgression to the bar, thank God, but Connor had sent him home. Marko had thought at the time that might be the end of it, but Connor had obviously flapped his jaws, because the other judges were no longer appointing him to anything important. Really? One tiny mistake and he had to prove that he could do the work all over again? They knew in their hearts that he could do it. He was better than all the other attorneys, drunk or sober. It was such bullshit.

He downed the rest of his whiskey and meandered back to the kitchen, refilling his glass with ice and grabbing the bottle by its neck. He squeezed it tightly as he carried it back to his desk, where he poured himself another on the rocks before setting the bottle at the corner of his desk, well within reach. Then he went to the social media websites. Scanning them was how he kept his finger on the pulse of the towns and on the comings and goings of his clients.

It was shocking how many of his drug clients had public Facebook pages where they posted evidence of their drug activities. A picture with a meth pipe in the background. Smoke-filled rooms. People passed out with rubber tubes around their arms and hypodermic needles on the floor next to them. They were the dipshits; the real addicts. He'd never done anything that dumb.

Marko's feed revealed a picture from outside the Franklin County court-house. Cop cars with flashing lights and people standing around. It was posted by one of Marko's former clients. He clicked on it. The caption read, "Dude jumped. RIP Jaxson." There were more than one hundred comments. Marko moved to that section, scrolling through names he recognized—people he had represented, was currently representing, or would soon represent again. All these people ran around together.

"What happened?" a woman named Miranda had asked.

Marko knew her. She was in her late twenties, and although she had only recently begun using, there was no drug she called a stranger.

"Can't you read? He jumped," someone had replied.

"Bite me, Nate," Miranda responded.

Marko clicked on the small, circular picture next to Nate's comment. An image populated the screen. Sure as sugar, it was his client—the same Nate he had met earlier. Clearly, Nate wasn't staying out of the drug scene. If he was, he wouldn't be responding to these posts. They would need to have another chat.

Marko clicked back to the previous screen and continued scrolling through the posts, the remainder of which were of a similar nature.

Misspelled words. Arguing. Using "there" when it should have been "they're."

One post did stand out. In one of the earlier comments, the writer wrote, "Goodbye, baby brother. You didn't do this to yourself. I will find out what happened to you."

Marko couldn't say what made the comment jump off the page—no pun intended—beyond the impeccable spelling and grammar, at least. He clicked on the little picture beside the words and a Facebook profile assigned to a woman named Whitney Moore popped up. He didn't recognize her, nor did he know the young man beside her. A young couple, likely in their early thirties, smiled at the camera with perfect teeth, each with a ring-adorned hand on a little boy's shoulder. The photograph was of professional quality, and the little family wore coordinated outfits in soft blue and beige.

"Apparently, the jumper's sister is not part of his crowd," Marko said.

He clicked on her "about" information. Under profession, it said she was a teacher at Franklin Senior High School, 2021-present. She'd been working there only three years. He clicked on her photos and started going through them. There were hundreds, all portraying the same thing. A happy family. One mother, one father, one little boy. A sudden, sharp pang of sadness coursed through him. He drank more whiskey, shook his head, and returned to his feed, scrolling down to see if there were any other posts from clients. He saw nothing. It seemed like everyone was commenting on the one post rather than making their own. Then he came across a link to a news story in the *Franklin Messenger*, posted by none other than Nikki Price. "God rest his soul," she had titled her piece.

Marko rolled his eyes and took a long pull from his drink before clicking on the article. It was about the jumper, Jaxson Michael, but only in a cursory way. The primary focus was on Nikki and her family, how the loss of a dedicated employee was going to affect them emotionally and financially.

"What a bunch of self-centered bullshit," Marko said, closing the window. He grabbed his drink and tilted it back until the ice hit his face. Empty already. He grabbed the bottle and poured himself another.

The Franklin jumper was big news, but it wasn't worth his attention.

There would be no associated criminal charges, no arrest and appointment of counsel.

Another dead end. Nothing seemed to be worth his attention anymore. He had no exciting cases, nothing challenging. He had nothing but booze. He tilted his head back and brought his drink to his lips yet again.

He drank until his vision blurred. He drank until he couldn't remember. He drank until he passed out.

10

ALLEE

"I can't help you," the hostess said. She was young, perhaps nineteen or twenty. She had the enviably bright, tight skin that comes with youth, but her eyes were cold, assessing. The kind of eyes seen on someone who had endured a lifetime—even a brief one—of suffering.

"Don't you mean, 'Can I help you?'" Allee asked. She had come to The Yellow Lark straight from her meeting with Pamela and was still raw. If she hadn't driven directly over, she probably wouldn't have showed up at all. She enjoyed restaurant work and was good at it. That wasn't the problem. The problem was that restaurant kitchens were fueled by booze and drugs —especially the latter. Something she wanted badly but could never have again.

The young hostess ran her eyes up and down Allee's body, pausing pointedly on each prison tattoo. "No," she said. "I meant what I said. I don't want to help *you*."

Who was this girl to judge her? "I want to apply for a job," Allee replied tightly.

"No, you don't." The hostess crossed her arms. "You should leave. Really."

"I don't want to—"

"What's going on?"

A man's voice. The hostess swung around as a man who looked to be in his early twenties rounded the corner and sidled up next to her. As he did so, the hostess stared at him, her mouth slightly ajar and her eyes wide.

"I asked you a question," he said, raising an eyebrow.

"Nothing. Nothing, Mr. Price. Nothing is going on," she stammered. All bravado had evaporated from her tiny frame, revealing a vulnerable, desperate girl beneath the bluster.

Mr. Price? Allee thought. He wasn't a "Mister" anything. The guy was barely an adult. He probably wasn't even old enough to legally drink alcohol.

"Lorna," he began, eyeing her suspiciously. "Were you aggravating a guest?"

"I—"

He clucked his tongue and then turned his attention to Allee. She met his gaze and felt a shiver run down her spine. The hostess's eyes had been hard; Price's, in contrast, were empty. Two black holes of nothingness.

"We hire a lot of...people with unfortunate backgrounds," Price said. "My mother wants to give everyone a leg up. I admire her." He chuckled darkly. "Everyone does. But to be honest, hires like Lorna can lead to...challenges. Sometimes they need a bit more"—he paused to chuckle again—"*guidance*, I guess I would call it. More than I can legally provide. If you know what I mean."

Allee had no idea what Price meant, but she had observed Lorna wince when Price mentioned "guidance." By now, she had literally shrunk into herself, rounding her shoulders and curving her back, trying to make herself small.

"I'm sorry, sir, I—" Lorna began.

Price put up a hand to silence her. "We'll talk later." Turning his attention to Allee, he laughed again. "Now, what can we do for you? Table for one? Or will someone be dining with you?"

"No, I actually...uh...I came to apply for a job," Allee managed to say, ashamed he had her off-kilter.

"Oh, wonderful!" A grin spread across his perfectly symmetrical, hairless cheeks, producing a dimple at the center of each. "It just so happens we recently lost an employee."

Lost. He'd said it nonchalantly, like Jaxson hadn't died but instead gone on vacation. Like he'd won the lottery and quit on the spot without giving two weeks' notice. Like he'd disappeared, leaving the restaurant holding the bag. In a way, she supposed, he had.

Price had been watching her closely with his dead eyes. "Do you have any restaurant experience?"

As he spoke, Lorna stood behind him, glaring daggers at Allee. Allee tried to ignore her. Lorna wasn't the first territorial mean girl to cross Allee's path, and she wouldn't be the last. Mitchellville had been full of her kind— women who were interested only in themselves; women as treacherous as they were beautiful. "I do. Front of the house, back of the house," Allee said, using industry slang. "Mostly in the kitchen, though. I can cook," she added.

"When was your last restaurant job?"

This was the tricky part, when she'd have to admit to her extended stay behind bars, courtesy of the state of Iowa. "About five years ago."

Price raised an eyebrow. "Oh?"

"I left Mitchellville a month ago," Allee said by way of explanation.

Lorna was now shaking her head vigorously. She was well behind him, so he couldn't see her reaction. Nevertheless, it set Allee's blood boiling.

"I see," Price said, uttering another bizarre chuckle. He stuck out his hand. His grip was limp, his hand slimy as she reluctantly took it. "I'm the manager here. Adam Price. You can follow Lorna's lead and call me *Mr. Price*."

It was all Allee could do to keep from rolling her eyes. She'd seen far more life than this kid ever would. Between the three of them, she was the only adult in the room.

"As I mentioned, we just lost someone, so I'd be happy to bring you aboard. What do you say?"

Allee was watching Lorna, who was now waving a hand as if in farewell. Ignoring her, Allee met Adam's soulless gaze. "I say you've got yourself a new cook."

"Great. I'll order you a uniform." He took a step to the side and gestured to Lorna like a game show hostess displaying a prize. As he did so, Lorna's features morphed from a scowl to a pleasant half-smile. "As you can see from Lorna here, our women wear a black skirt with our signature yellow shirt tucked into it. Shoes should be black." His eyes ran unabashedly over Allee's body. "You look to be a medium. Would a medium fit you?"

Allee cringed at the phrase "our women," but she swallowed her pride and answered. "Usually, yeah."

"The cost of the uniforms—I'll order you two—will come out of your paycheck, of course."

"Okay."

"We pay like any other local restaurant—one-fifty per hour and the balance in tips. Our clientele usually tip well—especially if you do a lot of smiling, like Lorna here."

Allee knew that was nonsense. In towns like this, in places like this, waitstaff would be lucky to see ten percent. "Just out of curiosity, how will the clientele see me smiling if I'm working in the kitchen?"

Price's smile didn't reach his eyes. "Tips are shared," he explained. "So you'd better hope that Lorna here"—he gestured to Lorna, whose sneer magically vanished again—"gets her smile on."

"All right."

"Well, then, welcome aboard!" Price said. "You can start tomorrow. Be here at ten o'clock to start preparing for the lunch rush." He paused. "You *can* be here tomorrow, right? I mean, it's not like you have anything better to do."

Allee unclenched her jaw long enough to fake a smile. "I'll be here."

"Wonderful. That's just...perfect."

His final words set Allee's heart pounding. They had been innocuous enough, but there was something sinister in the way he had uttered them. Like she'd left one cage and walked right into another. But surely she was reading way too much into the situation. He was harmless; a dweeb.

She hoped.

11

ALLEE

The employees at The Yellow Lark—even those Allee had known before she went to prison—kept their distance, whether because she was new, a suspected narc, or just marked for observation by probation and parole, she didn't know. *Give it time; they'll warm up*, she had thought. But even after a week had passed, nothing changed.

From what she could tell, staff went methodically about their jobs, heads down and mouths shut. No grab-ass among the waitstaff in the front; no playful banter between the cooks and dishwashers in the back. The employees at the front of the house smiled at customers, for sure, but their smiles faded the moment the customers turned their backs.

Everyone wore the cheery yellow bird, but it was a façade.

Lorna was no longer outwardly rude to Allee, but she remained distant. On her seventh day on the job, Allee passed Lorna in a hallway and lifted a hand in recognition; Lorna mimicked the gesture without enthusiasm. They'd each worked the past seven days, as had most of the other employees, which, in Allee's experience, was odd.

Lorna's blank expression and distant gaze reminded Allee of the tattoo on her left shoulder. Under the cheap cloth of the uniform featuring the cheerful little bird, it read, "Suffer me to go my own dark way." It was from *The Strange Case of Dr. Jekyll and Mr. Hyde*. In Mitchellville, she spent hours reading and ruminating over Dr. Jekyll's desire and ability to divide himself between his good and bad sides. Part of Allee wished she could do the same. Then, at least a portion of her would be free. And good—whatever that meant. She was still trying to figure that out, still attempting to meet societal standards of "good," but feared she'd never fully fit the mold. As a matter of history, Allee had always come up short, had always lived on the edge between jail and freedom.

Previously, she'd viewed prison as the darkest of paths. But between her time behind bars and a week in this place, she had come to understand that, in some ways, the purgatory of conditional parole was worse than the unambiguous hell behind prison walls. Truth be told, most of the employees at The Yellow Lark seemed even more miserable than the women trapped within Mitchellville's gray walls and electric fences.

Allee made her way back to the kitchen, passing a busser who was setting up tables, arranging salt and pepper shakers so each table matched. He was tall and thin with dark circles beneath his eyes, reminding her of a real-life version of Jack Skellington. She'd never caught his name. She'd only met a few of the employees, and they were all at the back of the house. Aside from Lorna, who had been so vehemently opposed to Allee's hiring, nobody at the front had even made eye contact with her, let alone attempted to engage her in conversation.

When she entered the kitchen, her trainer was already waiting for her. He stood just inside the swinging double doors and slightly to the right, his hands folded in front of him, his expression grim, like a mortician ready to take the family to see their loved one's body for the first time. He never spoke unless spoken to.

"Hi, Max," she said brightly.

Max inclined his head in recognition. "Ready to learn?"

"Are you always this to-the-point?" Allee asked with a sigh.

"Well, *are* you?"

"Well, since you didn't ask, I'm doing well this morning, thank you, *Mr.* Max."

Max's calm demeanor belied his discomfort. "It's just Max," he whispered fiercely, then added, "There is only one *mister* around here."

Allee scoffed. "You people act like he owns you."

Max blinked hard, lowered his scruffy eyebrows, and offered her a meaningful stare.

He was creeping her out. "Okay, okay. I'm ready," Allee said at last. "Show me something."

"Good. Follow me," Max instructed. He turned on a heel and strutted down the kitchen line. He moved quickly, but his legs were shorter than Allee's, so she easily kept pace. "Right here"—Max's arm shot out to the left —"is where we prepare the food. This is where you will work." He dropped his arm and continued walking the line. "This"—his arm shot back out— "is where the cooking happens. You do not go into this area." He continued walking. "And this—"

"—is where the food is plated," Allee finished. "Max, I know all this. You've done this every day for the past week. I know where just about everything is located. I'm not stupid."

"Good."

"And I know my job is, 'Don't think, just chop,' but here's a question for you: Where do I go to get extra food if I run out?"

Max turned to face her. "You don't," he said gravely.

"Well, there's gotta be a refrigerator or freezer somewhere. I mean, if one of the cooks needs something, where do I get it?"

"That's none of your business."

"Is it your business?" she ventured.

"No."

"Then whose business is it?" she asked.

"Mr. Price's."

That was weird. She'd never worked at a restaurant where the manager retrieved supplies for the food preparers. "Is that why he's always in the basement? Is that where the freezer is?"

Max looked to his left and right before answering. "Recall you just told me you weren't stupid," he began. "You do not keep track of Mr. Price. He keeps track of you."

Max was afraid. Of what, she wasn't exactly sure. Allee cast a gaze toward the long hallway that led to the basement stairs.

"Don't even think about it," Max advised.

Too late, Allee thought. But she understood the deal. If she crossed the line, especially as a felon, she was looking at a charge of criminal trespass, a no-bond hold for violating parole, and a sad-eyed Pamela sending her back to Mitchellville.

His voice softened. "If you know what's good for you, if you are as intelligent as I think you are, you will heed my advice." He sounded almost fatherly.

Allee nodded. "When do we get paid?" She hadn't seen anyone get a paycheck yet.

"Don't worry about that."

"Oh, I'm not worried. I'm excited." She'd put in seven straight twelve-hour days, from ten o'clock to ten o'clock. Given Iowa's laws on overtime, her paycheck should be massive. At this rate, she'd save up enough to put a down payment on a home in a year.

Ignoring her, Max gestured to the workspace she'd occupied for the last week. "You'd better get to it," he advised. "You don't want Mr. Price catching you with idle hands."

Fighting the urge to roll her eyes, she made her way to her station. Max handed her a knife and stacked vegetables next to her. She sighed heavily and got to work, slicing and dicing.

The work was mind-numbing. Hour after hour she moved her hands, cutting vegetables and fruits, passing them down the line. By the end of the day, her hands were stiff, her legs and back ached, and she was bone-tired and just about to sit down.

Then Adam Price entered the kitchen.

She didn't see him arrive—she was slicing the final two onions of the day—but she immediately felt his presence. It was as if the air in the kitchen was sucked out and replaced by the anxiety emanating from the employees' pores and diffusing into the air.

How does this little pissant wield such power? The Yellow Lark employees were not soft people; they all had criminal records. Most had spent significant time in jail or prison. It was odd that a preppy-looking man—boy, really—like Price could frighten them into submission.

"How is it going, Allee?" Adam inquired. He was well into her bubble, virtually whispering in her ear.

Instinctively, she swung around, raising the knife protectively.

"Whoa!" he said. "Put that down! You don't want me to report to Miss Pamela that you were threatening me with a dangerous weapon, do you?"

Allee obediently lowered the knife. "Sorry," she said. "Instinct. I don't usually let people get that close to me."

"Mr. Price," Adam said, threading his fingers together behind his back and rocking from his heels to his toes.

"What?"

"You mean, 'I don't usually let people get that close to me, *Mr.* Price.'"

Allee didn't respond.

He stared at her expectantly. He didn't blink. Not a twitch of a muscle or the flutter of an eyelash.

"I don't usually let people get that close to me, *Mr.* Price," Allee said at last.

Pleased with himself, he offered her a brief, mirthless smile. "Very good. Very good. I accept your apology, but don't let it happen again. Otherwise, Miss Pamela will be getting a call."

Allee studied him, trying to work out the intention behind his words. He'd mentioned her parole officer twice in a minute. Was it a threat? And why was he still staring at her? "Is there something else you need?" she forced herself to ask.

He raised his eyebrows. "Mr. Price."

She stifled a groan. "Is there something you need, *Mr. Price*?"

"Very good. Very good," he purred. "There's a good girl. I think we'll get along fine, won't we?"

Those eyes. There was nothing behind them. Allee bit back a retort. She wasn't a dog. She might be a parolee, but she was still human.

"Are you preparing to leave soon?" Price asked.

"Yes. I get off at ten." Allee paused, but continued when—as expected—he again raised his eyebrows. "Mr. Price."

"You'll be back tomorrow." It was a statement, not a question.

She felt the others' eyes on her, and her ears were getting warm under her hair. "Umm, sure," Allee replied. "But, well, I've worked seven days straight," she reminded him. "I will need a break sooner or later, Mr. Price. I have things I need to do."

"You'll get a break when I say you get a break."

"It is the law," Allee countered. "You have to follow the law, Mr. Price."

"That's rich, coming from you," Price replied quickly. He paused to ensure he had the others' attention before continuing, another mirthless smile snaking its way across his face. "Allee, I don't think I will be taking *your* advice on what is legal and what is not. You will be back here tomorrow at ten o'clock, and that's final. Or, well, I guess I'll be having a chat with Miss Pamela." He paused to pick at his nails. "And I do know that employment is a requirement of your parole status. Lose this job and it could be right back to the slammer for you. But it's your decision."

And there it was. The reason for the use of Pamela's name. It was a threat, and he seemed fully willing to do it. What had Allee gotten herself into? This attitude, these threats, must have been the reason the staff was so *melancholy*, an unusual word she had read in one of her novels. Adam Price had so much power and control over them because it was unwittingly handed to him by the parole system. He was using their status as criminals to control their lives, their actions, and ...what else? Whatever it was, she was going to find out. "I'll be back tomorrow, Mr. Price," she said at last through gritted teeth.

"There's a good girl."

Allee left her station and marched out the back door before her rage could overcome her self-control. The heavy metal door swung shut behind her, slamming with a loud *bang* that reverberated down the deserted alleyway—or what she'd thought was a deserted alleyway. She was down the stairs and passing the dumpsters when she heard a sound coming from behind the trash cans.

"Who's there?" Allee said, balling her hands into fists. Her guard was already up, her nerves frayed. If this person wanted a fight, they'd picked the wrong girl. Parole be damned.

Allee relaxed when a small, unarmed woman emerged from her hiding spot behind one of the odorous bins. Allee stared at her for a long moment. She recognized her, but she couldn't quite place how or where they'd come into contact. The woman was well-kept—far too clean-cut to have been part of Allee's pre-prison crowd.

"I'm wondering if I can have a moment or two of your time," the woman said.

Her words disarmed Allee. Nobody who wanted to fight spoke like that. "My time?" Allee asked, placing a hand on her chest in a gesture of self-mockery. "I'm not sure why you'd want it."

"I'm Whitney Moore," the smaller woman replied. As Allee—still on guard—watched, the woman approached and presented herself, then extended a hand Allee didn't take. After a long moment, Whitney lowered it to her side. "My brother was Jaxson Michael."

Of course. Now Allee recognized her. She had hooked up with Whitney's brother a couple of times. Once at a house party. They were all wasted —high on meth and coke and whatever else they could find, vaping weed to dull the buzz. His grandmother's funeral was that day, and Jaxson was supposed to be a pallbearer. Whitney had been royally pissed off when she found them. Maybe she didn't remember?

"It's been a while," Whitney continued.

"It has," Allee agreed, the stillness of the night enveloping them for a long moment. "What do you want?"

"I think something is going on in there," Whitney said, pointing to The Yellow Lark's back door. "I'm not sure what, but whatever it is, I think it drove my brother to kill himself."

Allee narrowed her eyes. Price was an ass, and the place seemed to have plenty of problems, but not enough to result in suicide. The guy could have just quit. The poor girl was grasping at straws, looking for something to justify Jaxson's jump. Allee knew plenty of people who had killed themselves, and she also knew that survivors inevitably wasted time trying to figure out why their loved ones had decided to leave them behind.

Perhaps reading Allee's mind, Whitney continued, "I know what you are thinking, but he was doing so well, and—"

When The Yellow Lark's back door swung open, Adam stood in the doorway. "What are *you* doing here?" he shouted. For a moment, Allee thought Adam was talking to her. "I told you to stay away from my employees and stay away from my restaurant!"

As Allee watched, Whitney shrank back.

"Get your ass out of here before I get a restraining order!" the now red-faced Price threatened. "Do you hear me?"

Allee looked back at the spot where Whitney had been standing, but she was gone, having disappeared into the darkness. "I think she's gone," she said. Her voice was as quiet as a whisper compared to Price's. She felt like his words were still echoing down the alleyway.

"Mr. Price," he said pointedly, while casting that familiar wide-eyed, unblinking stare in her direction.

"I think she's gone, Mr. Price," Allee repeated obediently.

"Good. Now get out of here. I'll see you tomorrow," Price said. He turned and slammed the door behind him.

Allee stared at the heavy, rusted metal door, her mind racing. *What is going on here?* She'd worked in restaurants for years. Never once had she seen some of the things that she observed in just a week inside the walls of The Yellow Lark. It wasn't normal, and it was getting worse. Today alone was one of the strangest days she'd experienced in the industry—high or not.

Oh well, she thought, *at least I'm getting paid.*

12

WHITNEY

Whitney balled her hands into tight fists, her nails carving crescent moons into her palms. Everything inside her screamed that she had to know, had to investigate The Yellow Lark. But she couldn't get arrested. She'd lose her job. "Teacher Arrested for Stalking" would be front-page news across the state of Iowa. She'd never find work again.

Her house was only a seven-block walk from the restaurant, but as the sharp spring air whipped against her skin, she wrapped her arms around herself protectively. She should have worn a coat. In her defense, she'd been unable to sleep and had left the house in a hurry. All she could think of was Jaxson and The Yellow Lark, and she'd rushed down here impulsively. It was so unlike her, but she wasn't going to get answers unless she did something.

Suddenly, a tingle ran up her spine. Someone was watching her. She shouldn't be out late at night. Not alone. The streetlamps were abundant downtown on Main Street, but they had grown scarcer with each block traveled. She picked up her pace and was at a trot by the time she neared her small, single-story, cottage-style home.

As expected, the house was dark and quiet when she entered. Her family—the Moore family—was customarily early to bed. Like the house, the family was small—just Whitney, her husband, Leo, and their five-year-old son, Arlo. They kept a strict eight o'clock bedtime, which was why she'd been able to slip out undetected for the fourth time this week. She locked the front door and tiptoed into her bedroom, changed her clothes, and slipped into bed. She was just settling in when the lamp on Leo's side of the bed clicked on.

"Where were you?" he asked suspiciously. He was sitting up, watching her through alert, nondrowsy eyes. He must have been waiting for her.

"I...uh..."

"Are you having an affair?"

"Oh my God, Leo. No! Of course not!" Whitney cried, shaking her head. "I...It's about Jaxson. I am trying to solve—"

"Not *this* again," Leo interrupted, shaking his head and emitting a heavy sigh. "There isn't anything to solve! He killed himself, Whit. You've got to accept that."

"But—"

He looked at her dolefully. "Look, honey. I'm sorry about what happened, too. I liked your brother. But he was an addict and he killed himself, and the sooner you admit that, the sooner you can start to grieve. You've been...obsessed."

She bristled. "I'm not, I—"

"Even Arlo is starting to notice," Leo said, pointing to the floor next to himself.

"He is?" Her love for her brother was one thing, but she couldn't do anything to harm Arlo. He *was* her everything. She crawled across her husband to peer down at the floor beside the bed. Arlo snuck into their room every night, choosing to sleep on the floor instead of alone in his own bed. He was there, breathing the soft, rhythmic breaths of a sleeping child. Seeing him, a defibrillator-like shot of joy rushed to her heart. She had not grown up with a burning desire to become a mother, but when Arlo came into her life, he stole her heart and became her soul. He was special.

"He woke me up and asked where you were," Leo explained. "That's how I knew you were gone."

"I'm sorry," she said, and truly was. "I won't do it again. I didn't realize..." Her voice broke. What had Arlo been thinking when he found his mother gone? He'd been worried enough to wake Leo up.

"Fine. Fine. But you've got to stop," Leo said, his tone insistent. "The Price family has nothing to do with Jaxson's death. He worked there. That's it. Nobody is going to believe it was anything more than that."

At the mention of the Prices, Whitney felt her temper flare, but she held it in check. For Arlo. "Okay. I'll drop it," she lied. She wasn't ready to quit. Maybe she'd acted a little crazy, a little obsessed—but damn it, her brother had just died! Leo owed her more leeway than that. She wouldn't sneak out —for Arlo's sake—but she would not quit looking for answers. Not yet.

Leo turned out the light. "It's for the best," he advised.

"Let's just go to sleep," Whitney replied, pulling the covers up to her shoulders and turning her back to her husband. He didn't understand. Worst of all, he wasn't even trying. He'd never lost a sibling. He'd never lost anyone like that. When she reflected on Jaxson's last days, she felt only remorse. She had known something was wrong, and she'd known it was tied to that restaurant. Yet she hadn't asked, hadn't taken any action. She had failed him. During his funeral, she had vowed to find out what was going on in that restaurant. Jaxson would not have chosen to kill himself. He just wouldn't...unless he had no other choice.

13

MARKO

Marko's head ached. His mouth was dry. He forced his eyelids open.

What time is it?

He was still at his desk. He must have fallen asleep while working. A near-empty bottle of whiskey sat next to him. He looked at his watch. It still read nine minutes after two. He shook the computer's mouse, and the screen sprang to life. The numbers in the lower left corner read 6:30. A bright sun peeked through the cheap vertical blinds that covered the sliding glass door leading to the back deck. It was morning.

The good news was that he hadn't missed any court. The bad news was that his brain had a heartbeat, and his tongue felt like a scout troop spent the night on it. He was hungover—again. *A little hair of the dog, plus two.* He opened his top desk drawer, shook two hydrocodone tablets into his palm, and popped them into his mouth before grabbing the neck of the whiskey bottle and draining the contents. After a couple of minutes, he'd be fine. It was the breakfast of champions.

He stood and made his way to his small bathroom, where he splashed cold water on his face. His headache was already subsiding. A few more shots should cure it entirely. He looked at himself in the mirror and saw a stranger with a puffy face and red eyes. He had to start taking better care of himself.

Tomorrow. I'll worry about that tomorrow, he thought, turning away from the mirror so he wouldn't see the lie in his eyes. He turned the shower on and cranked it all the way to cold. He let it run while he put a few eyedrops in each eye. Then he held his breath and stepped into the frigid water.

Finished, he stepped out, teeth chattering and body shaking. Despite the chill, he felt momentarily refreshed. He donned one of his five identical suits and made his way to the kitchen, where he opened another bottle of whiskey and took two more shots. *I need something in my stomach.* He grabbed a fruit bar he found in a kitchen drawer and shoved it into his mouth, chewing the entire thing while he made coffee. While it brewed, he settled at his desk to see where the day would take him.

Opening the calendar feature, he was somewhat pleased to see he was to spend the day in Stonewall City over in Caldwell County. It was a small town in their district, and a pain to get to. There was no direct route there, which was why the town was dying, but also why few attorneys agreed to take court appointments out there. That gave him a leg up, and he had three hearings on the docket: two pretrials and what should be a simple plea and sentencing hearing.

He looked again at his watch. Still 2:09. *Better get going.* He didn't want to be late and give those bastards one more reason to screw him over. Today was a step toward the new him. Well, not so new; he'd had a couple shots, but they were for recuperative purposes. He would focus on the new version of himself tomorrow.

He stood, went to the kitchen, and poured strong black coffee and a shot into his travel cup. After sticking another fruit bar in his pocket, he grabbed his briefcase and the files that he would need for the day. He was off.

The drive took just over an hour. Arriving early, he pulled into a parking spot, sprayed his mouth with mint breath spray, and jogged up the front steps of the rural courthouse, making it inside by eight-thirty. The plea and sentencing hearing was set for nine o'clock in district court. He always told his clients to appear thirty minutes early so he could meet with them briefly prior to the hearing.

District court was on the second floor of the small but ornate court-house. It was almost shocking that this tiny county had ever had the money to afford marble columns and stained glass, but the Caldwell County court-house was proof that at some point in the rural county's history, the money had been there.

"David," Marko said as he reached the top of the stairs. His client was seated on a bench outside the district courtroom.

David Jones stood. "Mr. Bauer."

"Call me Marko. I've told you that at least a dozen times."

"Right, Marko."

Jones was no longer a young man, somewhere in his late forties or early fifties. Like a lot of addicts, he was at the age where he was still getting in trouble on occasion, but his contacts with law enforcement were lessening in frequency. He still had to fuel his addiction, which led to a burglary or two, but he didn't have the energy to get into fights and commit the other violent crimes he had in the past. Today he was to be sentenced for burglar-izing a couple garages, stealing tools, and selling them on a website that had helped put the twentieth century's dealers in stolen goods—"fences," so-called—out of business.

"Let's talk," Marko said, motioning to the only attorney-client meeting room in the building. He entered the small room, followed by Jones. Marko closed the door behind them, and they sat at the folding table that took up most of the space in the small room. "Today is your plea and sentencing. You are pleading to one count of burglary in the third degree, a class D felony, and the State is going to dismiss the other two counts."

Jones nodded his understanding. He'd been there before.

"That carries up to five years in prison," Marko continued. "We do not have an agreement on sentencing. The State is planning to argue for prison. We can argue for probation."

Jones shook his head. "No probation," he said.

Marko blinked several times. Everyone wanted him to fight for proba-tion. What was up with this guy? "Why not?" he asked, curious.

"I can do a nickel, but I'm not doin' three years of probation on the streets."

"So, you want me to agree to you going to prison?"

"Ask for jail," Jones countered. "Thirty, sixty days—hell, I'll do half a split. Whatever, man. I just don't want to be on a leash."

Marko was moderately hungover, irritable, and unwilling to hide his irritation. This wasn't how the court system worked. "If you go to jail or prison, they'll just parole you out, and you'll have that same leash, plus you'll have done time. It doesn't make sense to ask for time."

Jones was again shaking his head. "Sure it does, Marko. I have to agree to parole. And I won't. I'll do my number before letting them put one of them chains back around my ankles, threatening to yank me back whenever they want. Tellin' me I have to get a job and the only place that will hire me is that damned restaurant over in Franklin. I swear to God that place was created by the devil himself, and if I have to—"

"I got it," Marko interrupted before Jones could get too far into his diatribe. "You want me to argue for jail time? Will do." He looked at his watch, again forgetting that it didn't work, then said, "It's probably time to get in there and get the hearing started."

Marko stood and led the way out of the attorney-client meeting room and into the large district court courtroom. Counsel table was long and stretched the entire length of the bench and witness box. Greta Van Stouten, the Caldwell County Attorney, sat quietly in her spot to the far left of the table. She turned and looked at them as they entered.

"You're on time today," she said brightly, as if Marko's timeliness was a novelty.

Marko bristled. He'd had a handful of late appearances; that was it. "So are you."

"I'm *always* on time."

"It's a pleasure to see you, Greta, you know that?" he replied sarcastically. He needed work, and Caldwell County was one of the few counties still willing to assign him upper-level felony cases—mostly because there were so few attorneys on the court-appointed list. It was good work, but there was a catch. Greta. The woman was insufferable. She thought she was the smartest person in every room, which was impossible unless she found herself the *only* person in the room.

Greta was a good ten years older than Marko, and as out of touch with the law as Caldwell County was with the rest of the state. She did little legal research and simply argued whatever she saw fit, whether the sentence was legal or not. It was annoying, but fortunately for Marko's clients, the local judges *did* know the law and had so far avoided following Greta's frequently asinine recommendations.

"Ready?" Greta asked.

"Yes." Marko made his way up to counsel table and chose a seat on the right, indicating Jones should be seated as well.

"I'll let the judge know." She stood and disappeared into council chambers.

"What's her problem?" Jones asked when she had gone.

"She's just like that."

"Lovely lady."

"Indeed," Marko said.

Greta reentered the courtroom, moving so fast that her long hair lifted behind her—quite a feat, considering Greta's hair was mousy brown with a crimped texture straight out of the '80s. Marko had often wondered if it was a perm or natural. It had to be natural, right? Who would pay to look like that? He almost asked her about it, just to get under her skin, but the judge entered the chamber and they all stood.

It was Connor, the same judge who had been in Franklin a week earlier for Nate's pretrial. The judges in this district rotated, of course, but Marko hadn't realized it was already that time.

"Sit down, sit down," Connor said as he lowered himself onto the bench.

The courtroom was empty aside from Connor, his court reporter, the two attorneys, and Jones. They sat obediently and then looked to Connor expectantly.

"Good morning," Connor said. "It's nice to see everyone here, on time and ready to go."

Marko swallowed a retort. Would he ever catch a break? "I didn't realize you'd be in Stonewall City today, Your Honor."

"I'm not supposed to be," Connor explained. "Judge Ivers had a family emergency," he added doubtfully, "and I drew the short straw."

Judges were an odd breed. Upon taking the bench, they couldn't be seen spending too much time palling around with their old attorney friends, lest they be deemed biased toward one party or the other. That reduced their circle of friends considerably, meaning much of their social time was spent with other judges, whom they didn't seem to like all that much.

"Let's get this show on the road," Connor said. "Ready?" He looked down at his court reporter, who was seated in front of him, her fingers poised over the steno machine.

"Yes," she said.

"We are convened today in State of Iowa versus David Jones, Caldwell County case number FECR014539. Are the parties ready to proceed?"

Greta eagerly answered affirmatively; Marko did the same with markedly less enthusiasm. They then proceeded through the plea hearing without a hitch. Because this was not Jones's first time inside a courtroom, he knew exactly what to say and when. He provided enough information to form a factual basis for the crime but no more; he waived his right to a presentence investigation—a provision otherwise invariably ordered prior to sentencing; waived the mandatory fifteen-day waiting period between plea and sentencing; and finally, waived his right to file a motion in arrest of judgment. With the preliminaries out of the way, they moved directly to the sentencing phase.

"Is there an agreement as to sentencing?" Connor asked Greta.

She stood. "No, Your Honor. The State agreed to dismiss the other two counts of the indictment, but the parties are arguing sentencing."

He nodded his understanding. "Very well. I'll hear from the State first."

"Thank you, Your Honor," Greta said. She paused and shuffled a few papers. "The State's recommendation today is incarceration for five years. As you know, the defendant has a lengthy criminal history." She lifted a sheet of paper and began reading from his criminal history. "He's been convicted of possession of drugs seven times, theft on more occasions than I can count, and this is his third burglary conviction. He has assaults and crimes of dishonesty. He has been to prison twice, on probation more times than anyone cares to consider. There is no place for this man in our community. Therefore, the only option is prison. Thank you." She lowered herself back into her seat.

Well, that was reasonable. At least everything she'd recommended was legal.

"Oh." Greta stood back up. "And I want the court to order this man to stay out of Caldwell County. I don't want him returning upon his release from prison."

I take that back.

Connor blinked in confusion. "Ms. Van Stouten, you know that I can't order something like that. If he goes to prison—and that's a big *if*—I can't lawfully restrict his freedom of movement once he is discharged. That would be unconstitutional—surely you know that?"

Greta sat back down, facial features twisted in frustration.

"And for the defense?" Judge Connor asked, turning his attention to Marko.

Marko stood. "Your Honor, Mr. Jacobs has accepted responsibility for his actions. This was a burglary of a garage. Nobody was home. He didn't harm anyone. He took things that hadn't been used for years. He has an addiction. He'll get a substance abuse evaluation and start treating it. He wants to become a productive member of society. He's ready. So, the defense requests a thirty-day jail sentence."

"That's all? No probation?" Connor asked.

"No probation. A straight thirty days and release him with a clean slate," Marko said, then he sat down.

"The defendant has the right of allocution," Connor noted. "Is there anything you wish to say to me, Mr. Jones?"

Jones stood. "I—I just don't want probation, sir. Send me to prison. Put me in jail. Just no probation. I beg you." Then, without waiting for Connor's reply, he sat back down.

Connor was silent for a few moments, thinking. The courtroom was quiet, so when he started talking again, his voice sounded as though it was booming. "I am not going to follow either of your recommendations," he began.

Marko could feel Jones tense next to him.

"The prisons are full to bursting. I'm not going to add another body for a non-violent crime. That space is needed for the rapists and armed robbers, child abusers and murderers—not someone who digs through crap in an unattached garage and takes things that nobody wants or needs. The owners of the items didn't even realize the items were missing until they saw the online advertisement. So I'm not going to send Mr. Jones to prison."

Greta crossed her arms.

"Nor am I going to agree to a straight jail sentence," he continued. "If substances are the problem—and I don't doubt they are—then there needs to be a consequence should there be a failure to comply with treatment recommendations. That is why I am going to sentence Mr. Jones to five years in prison, suspend the prison sentence, and place Mr. Jones on probation for three years."

"But—" Jones began to stand. Marko grabbed his arm and pulled him back down.

"My decision is final," Connor said. He quickly outlined the terms and conditions of probation, then stood and left the courtroom, his black robe billowing behind him, leaving Marko to deal with his now-distraught client. But to his surprise, there wasn't any dealing to be done, because Jones departed without saying a word. Greta did the same. Everyone was made miserable by the ruling—which meant it was probably both lawful and proper.

In the aftermath, Marko realized his head was starting to ache again. His pretrials weren't until one o'clock, so he had some time to kill. There was a Mexican restaurant nearby with a full bar. It was the only real restaurant or bar in a thirty-mile radius, so Marko decided to head over. A little hair of the dog wouldn't hurt.

14

MARKO

Marko opened his eyes, looked around, and groaned in pain. Light filtered in through the living room windows, assaulting his eyes, piercing his brain. He tried to recall the events of the previous day. He had made it to and through his pretrial hearings—but barely. It had taken every ounce of willpower he had to peel himself away from the bar and return to the Caldwell County courthouse. Margaritas had never tasted quite so good. He'd chewed mints and sprayed breath-freshener to hide the odor of booze so Greta couldn't smell it on him. She didn't; or if she did, she didn't comment on it. A win either way.

His hearings behind him, he had driven home to continue drinking. At least, that was what he thought had happened. There was no one there to tell him any different.

The days were beginning to blend; all ended and began in the same way: booze, fitful sleep, hangover, rinse and repeat. It sucked. His life sucked, and not because of the booze. It was because of the judges and other attorneys. His caseload sucked. He still wasn't getting the cases that he deserved, and he was the best defense attorney they had. Franklin had plenty of cases; there was a shooting, sex assault, or robbery every other day. He'd be more than happy to drive his ass all the way over there for his fair share.

While dressing for the day, he quaffed his usual two hydrocodone. After two three-finger shots of whiskey, he poured coffee and added another shot to his travel mug before grabbing a couple of fruit bars and trudging out to his car.

What the hell is going on? he wondered as he drove the familiar route north. He'd made it to all his hearings in Caldwell the day before. Had someone noticed his intoxication? He doubted it. Connor would have said something, just as he had the last time. So why were the judges still punishing him? They were presuming he couldn't do the job. Without evidence. They were profiling. Not racial, but something. Sure, he enjoyed a drink or two. Sometimes he needed one, to be honest. But drinking had never affected his work aside from causing him to show up a little late. And what was an hour or two here or there? His clients didn't have jobs. They weren't busy. They could wait.

He pulled up outside the Franklin County courthouse and parallel-parked on the east side in a two-hour parking zone. Nate Shore's sentencing hearing was today. It was the only thing he had on his court calendar, and it wouldn't last more than an hour. The court now accepted written guilty pleas for the lowest-level felonies—class D felonies. Nate had already signed a written guilty plea. Preparing the plea, getting a signature, and filing the plea were usually the time-consuming parts. With that done, they should be in and out quickly.

He exited the car, slammed the door, and made his way to the court-house. He'd limited himself to just two more shots after the first couple. He certainly wasn't drunk, but he was comfortably numb, so he needed to be careful and was hyperaware of his balance, which—truthfully—wasn't great. Nate's hearing was set to begin at one o'clock. Marko passed people gathering at the corners of the block, waiting for the light to change so they could cross the street and grab a quick lunch at The Yellow Lark.

Marko rarely ate there. They didn't serve booze.

He entered the courthouse and dashed up the stairs to find Nate and Allee sitting in the very same spot they had been the last time they had met. A sense of déjà vu spread through him as he recalled the man who had run toward them and then jumped to his death. What if he'd rammed Marko instead of jumping, and pushed *him* over the edge? It would have been over for Marko, and he would have barely seen it coming.

"Mr. Bauer," Allee said, rising to her feet. A look of relief crossed her face.

She appreciates me, at least.

"Thank you for being on time," she said tersely. "I'm pleasantly surprised."

Never mind. Marko bristled. He was tired of all the judgment, especially from this tatted-up felon. She was there to bust his balls, just like everyone else. He couldn't help but notice the garish tattoo on her right ankle—one he hadn't seen the last time. "Death be all that we can rightly depend on," it read. *Why do these people always look like this?*

"What *is* that?" he asked, pointing at her ankle. "Why would you tattoo something like that on your body?"

Allee looked down at it and shrugged. "Because it's true?"

"So? Lots of things are true, but people don't tattoo it on their bodies."

"Maybe they should."

Marko shook his head and turned his attention to Nate. "Today is your sentencing hearing, Nathaniel."

"Nate," he reminded Marko.

"Whatever. Have you gotten a job?"

"No."

"Have you obtained a substance abuse evaluation?"

"No."

Marko's gaze shifted to Allee, eyes narrowing.

"Don't look at me." She shrugged. "I tried, but he's a grown man. He says he's tired of the nagging. He's spent plenty of time the past couple of weeks telling me that."

"You haven't done a damned thing I've asked you to do!" Marko barked.

Nathaniel dropped his head, cowed.

"You better keep that sheepish expression throughout the hearing, because it's the only thing that *might* save you."

Nate blew air through his teeth, then shot to his feet, pacing. "Look, I'm sorry, man," he said.

"You will be sorrier if that judge sends you to prison," Marko seethed. "I busted my ass to get you this deal."

Truth be told, it was practically impossible for Connor to send Nate to prison. He'd agreed to bind himself to the probation agreement through Rule 12. Nate didn't know that, of course, and Marko would have told him, but he was tired of clients refusing to listen to his advice. It would do this punk good to sit in the courtroom and sweat.

Even without the Rule 12 agreement in place, Connor was unlikely to send Nate to prison for burglary. Marko and McJames had agreed to a probation sentence, and the case had similar facts and circumstances as the recent Caldwell County case: burglary of an unattached garage; the only items stolen were tools—people should really put tools in a safe—and nobody noticed they were gone until weeks after they'd been taken. The only difference here was that Jones had a lengthy criminal history, while Nate had none. If Jones got probation, Nate was unlikely to end up with a stiffer sentence.

"I said I'm sorry!" Nate blurted.

Marko looked at his watch, and then—remembering it was broken—glanced at the clock hanging on the wall. It was a few minutes before one o'clock. McJames was probably already seated at the prosecution table, his laptop open and his case file carefully arranged in front of himself. "We ought to get in there."

"Okay," Nate agreed.

Marko led the way into the courtroom. There were two entrances, one that came directly from judge's chambers, and a main door that spilled into the back of the gallery used by Marko, Nate, and all but a select few.

Just as Marko had anticipated, McJames was already seated at the prosecution table like a nerdy sophomore in the front row of English class. He didn't turn around when Marko, Nate, and Allee entered. Marko led the way past the partition, motioning for Allee to sit in the gallery. He and Nate took their spots at the defense table, and Allee obediently found a seat in the pews directly behind them.

The hearing proceeded in the same way as Jones's had—except this time McJames and Marko provided a joint recommendation to Connor seeking a suspended five-year prison sentence and probation for three years.

Unexpectedly, McJames stood.

"Your Honor, the victim would like to make a statement."

Under Iowa law, victims of crimes had a right to appear at a sentencing hearing to tell the judge how the defendant's actions had impacted their lives. Victims weren't *supposed* to make sentencing recommendations, but it wasn't unheard of.

Connor looked down at his stack of papers. "The Minutes of Testimony list the owner of the burgled garage as Benjamin Price. Is that who will be making the statement today?"

"Yes," McJames said.

Marko fought the urge to roll his eyes. Price owned unoccupied pieces of property all over the county. This kind of thing was probably always happening to him. That was why property owners had insurance. What could possibly be the impact on Benjamin's life? Nothing; he just wanted to come in here and throw a wrench into things—to sit up there, look down his nose at Marko, and once again show him why Nikki had chosen him all those years ago. It made Marko want to shout, *Dude, get over yourself. I don't want your wife—you probably don't either!*

"Very well," Connor said. "Go get him."

McJames left the courtroom for a moment, then returned with Price. They strode into the courtroom like two executives on their way to a board meeting, exuding an air of confidence and power. Price wore a pair of black slacks and a light blue button-down shirt. He made his way to the witness stand and settled into the seat.

Nate leaned into Marko. "What's happening?"

"It's something we have to let them do," Marko explained. "It'll be over soon." Until now, Nate had been calm, but Marko could sense his anxiety, and he put a hand on the younger man's forearm to stop his fidgeting.

"You are the victim," Connor began, looking to Price. "I won't put you under oath. And just so you know, the defense is not allowed to cross-examine you." When Price nodded his understanding, Connor continued, "Is there something you would like to tell the court?"

Marko held his breath. Judges were human; more than once he'd seen an effective victim impact statement squelch a deal. While Connor had agreed to a Rule 12, that was done in chambers and there was no record of it. In fact, the only two people in the world who knew of that agreement were Connor and Marko. If Connor chose to "forget" the discussion, his word would trump Marko's any day.

Price had been watching Connor; he now turned his attention to Marko. "Yes, Your Honor. I just wanted to say that I have forgiven this young man for his transgressions."

Push me over with a feather, Marko thought. He'd presumed this would be a fire-and-brimstone speech, not one of forgiveness.

"He stole—which is, of course, against both God's law and the law of this land—but there are ways to make reparations for those injustices," he began, turning his attention to Nate. "Get on the right track, get a job, become a productive member of society. Mr. Shore, come apply at The Yellow Lark. My son will give you a job. You've made mistakes, but it isn't too late to turn your life around." He looked again to Connor. "That's all I have, Your Honor."

Gag me, Marko thought.

"Thank you, Mr. Price," Connor said. "You may step down."

Price stepped out of the witness box, made his way past the partition, and took a seat in the gallery behind McJames. The courtroom was completely silent, aside from the click of Price's expensive heels on the marble floors and the groan of the bench as he sat down.

"I'm not going to leave you in suspense, Mr. Shore," Connor began after a short pause. "I'm going to go along with the probation recommendation. I also think it is an excellent plan for you to apply for a job at Mr. Price's restaurant. I can't order that, but I'll remind you it is a specific condition of probation that you find and maintain full-time employment. It sounds like Mr. Price has not only forgiven you, but he has extended you an opportunity." He then reviewed the terms and conditions of Nate's probation in detail.

When the hearing ended, Marko was feeling pretty good about himself. Then he turned around and saw Allee's face. She was downcast. What the hell? He couldn't figure her out. She had wanted probation for her cousin, and that was exactly what he'd gotten. She must be the type of chick who was never happy. That was it. It had nothing to do with the outcome.

It was a win. Nate seemed happy. Allee should be happy. Marko deserved a treat. *I think I'll have a drink to celebrate.*

15

WHITNEY

Sneaking out at night had been a bad idea. Leo was right about that. It was impulsive and probably dangerous. She had Arlo to think about, and her recent behavior made her seem unhinged. She saw that now. Hiding in an alleyway to approach someone after their shift was over was borderline nuts.

A more direct approach might be better. It just so happened the local paper printed court happenings, which was one of the more popular sections. From it, readers could tell what hearings were coming up and who they involved, which was how she found out Nate Shore, Allee's cousin, was going to be sentenced for burglary at one o'clock today.

Which was why she'd taken the afternoon off, claiming stomach flu.

Finding Allee's truck was easy. It was the same one she'd seen her driving years before—a beater with rust running along all the wheel wells. She got to Main Street at 1:15, knowing that if the court was on schedule Allee would be inside, but it was before the hearing would have ended. She parked a few blocks down the street and walked back to Allee's truck, where she crouched and waited.

The few people walking after lunch paid her no attention. Most were homeless or high, the kind of people who minded their own business. The type Jaxson used to hang around.

In the silence, Whitney's thoughts turned to Jaxson. He had been a light in her life. Damaged—flickering, perhaps, at times—but still burning brightly nonetheless. Things had changed when he'd gone to work at that restaurant, and he'd only been there for three months—just three months! That was all, but it had changed him.

Before, he had told her everything: the good, bad, and ugly about his life. He'd made a lot of unwise choices, but he'd always been honest and she had supported him, even in his most troubled times. She wanted him on the right track, but he knew she'd be there for him either way.

But when he started working at that restaurant, he grew more and more sullen with each passing day. He'd been living with Whitney and Leo, sleeping in the basement. After he started work, he'd become a ghost. He worked constantly. Hours nobody should ever work. Sometimes, he wouldn't come home at all for days at a time. They'd argue about it.

Where have you been? Whitney would ask when Jaxson walked through the front door. He'd look like he hadn't slept for days, with deep pools of blackness beneath his bloodshot eyes.

"Working," he had claimed.

Are you using? She had seen no obvious signs—no erratic behavior or missing items pawned for cash. But his hours, the lack of sleep, the bags beneath his eyes...it was suspicious.

"I'm straight, sis. I promise." He sounded sincere.

Then why are you working so much?

"I have to," he'd say with a sigh. Then he'd push past her and go down to the basement. He'd be home long enough to sleep a few hours and take a shower, then he'd go back to the restaurant.

Soon after, she noticed the cuts and burns. Long, angry welts on his arms and cuts on his fingers.

"I got too close to the stove," he had claimed, but he wouldn't meet her gaze. Or, "I slipped with the knife," he'd say, again averting his eyes.

Each day that passed worsened Jaxson's suicide. It didn't make sense. He had his problems, but they were never so severe that he would kill himself. Leo was sure sobriety had caused it. He theorized that Jaxson's hidden demons emerged when he was sober. He believed Jaxson had required a higher level of care that the experts had missed. The system, he opined, had let Jaxson down.

Whitney didn't agree. She saw the restaurant as the problem, and they argued constantly.

"You've got to get over this," Leo had said to her again and again. "You're obsessed."

Maybe he was right. Maybe she was obsessed, but that didn't make her wrong. She couldn't let it go. She owed her brother at least that much. She'd failed to keep him safe in life; now, she could only try to find out what had really happened and why. If it was the last thing she did.

16

ALLEE

Allee stood and watched the judge leave the courtroom. She *should* be happy with Nate's sentence. It wasn't prison and it wasn't significant jail time. On paper, it looked like an ideal outcome. Yet, part of her brain screamed, *No, no, no!* Maybe it was exhaustion; she was strong-willed and had worked in plenty of restaurants, but none had pushed her nearly as hard as The Yellow Lark. Nate wouldn't be able to handle it, she was sure.

Using the door in the back, Marko, Allee, and Nate filed silently from the courtroom. In contrast, McJames and Price exited through the same door that Connor used. For a profession so focused on the appearance of impropriety, she thought, the prosecutor and judge really should be more concerned about the way that looked. It gave off *us vs. them* vibes.

When they reached the hallway, Marko eschewed the usual attorney small talk and glad-handing. Instead, he grew visibly jittery, shifting his weight and moving his briefcase from one hand to the other. "I've got another, uh, hearing to get to," he said. "It's in another county, so I better get going." He glanced down at his watch, and Allee could see the face showed 2:09. It was one-thirty.

He had to get back to something, Allee guessed, and that was probably anywhere he could hold a bottle of booze. The guy had all the signs. It frustrated her not because she judged him for it, but because she, too, was an addict—one required to stay clean or return to prison. On the other hand, he was free to abuse alcohol with no repercussions. Life wasn't fair, and that pissed her off.

"What goes around comes around," Allee's prison counselor used to tell her. "People get what's coming to them," Pamela would say. But when? When would someone like Marko suffer the same types of consequences as she and Nate were dealing with? The answer was never. Never. Because the people around him would save him from it, prop him up, help him survive. He had a life raft and a rescue ship ready and waiting while she and Nate were destined to flounder, alone, just to keep their heads above water.

"Go," Allee said. "We're fine."

Marko scurried away while she and Nate watched in silence. When the top of Marko's head disappeared down the stairs, she turned to Nate. "You'll need to sign up for probation within the next forty-eight hours," she advised. "You should call over there today, just to get it over with." It was something that Marko should be telling his client, but he obviously wasn't going to do that, so Allee would do it for him. She may not know the law, but she knew what a defendant ought to be doing.

"Okay." Nate looked down at his shoes and shuffled his feet.

"You're going to have to stay sober. You can come to NA meetings with me."

Like much of rural America, Franklin was a small town with a lot of drug addicts, which was both good and bad. Good, because there were plenty of Narcotics Anonymous meetings throughout the day comprised of people willing to help; bad because temptation was everywhere, with plenty of people willing to help a person go wrong.

"I'm not going to those dumb meetings."

"You need to. Come on, Nate—"

She stopped talking when she felt someone approach.

"Hello, Allee. Nathaniel." Ben Price was sporting a broad smile. "You are on your way over to the restaurant, no doubt." It was not a question.

"It's my day off, Mr. Price," Allee said. She had much less difficulty calling Ben Price *mister*. He was a full-grown man and a member of city council.

"One of the kitchen employees had an incident," Price said solemnly. "He's back in jail."

"Oh," Allee said.

"I guess it's to be expected when we employ troubled souls," he said with a sigh. He quickly turned on the charm. "No good deed and all that."

Allee didn't know how to respond. It *was* something he should expect. If he wanted to employ folks who were on probation and parole, he should expect them to get into trouble now and again. Especially if he worked them so hard they didn't have the energy to stand. When people were exhausted, methamphetamine started sounding like a pretty good solution.

"We need extra bodies in the restaurant," he continued. "That's why it's so fortuitous that you will both be working for us."

Fortuitous. It felt more like a trap. Allee's mind drifted to the tattoo on her left hip, which read, "When a falsehood can look so like the truth, who can assure themselves of certain happiness?" It was a phrase from Mary Shelley's *Frankenstein*.

Frankenstein's monster was the one that the whole world wanted dead and gone. Just like her. "I am off today," Allee said. *It's my only day off.* "I can bring Nate with me when I come in tomorrow." She was trying to buy time, but she didn't have any currency.

She did not want Nate working at The Yellow Lark. While it was true that he was an addict and—as of today—a felon, and therefore not a desirable job candidate, there had to be other options. There had to be someone, *anyone*, other than the Price family who would hire him. Allee was bone-tired after only a week and a half, and she hadn't seen a paycheck yet. Nate couldn't work that hard. Few people could.

Ben studied Allee's face. "You're a team player, I can see that," he said. "The team needs you. I need you to work today. Can you do that? Can you be a team player?" He was talking to her like she was a child, which irritated the hell out of her, but his tone was marginally better than that of his son, who treated her like a dog.

"I suppose I can," she said with a sigh. "I'll drop Nate off at his house, go by my place and get my uniform, and then I'll be there. It will probably take me an hour or so."

"That's wonderful! You work today and bring Nate tomorrow." He actually pumped a fist in the air with a sudden burst of excitement. "Thank you, thank you, Allee! I can't wait to tell your parole officer what a hard worker you are."

"Thank you, sir," Allee said. She felt warmth on her cheeks as a wave of satisfaction spread through her. Nate tugged at her sleeve and motioned to the door. Allee waved goodbye to her boss's boss and headed down the stairs toward her car.

"I don't want to work there," Nate said the moment they stepped outside. "I didn't know it was *that* guy's restaurant. I shouldn't *have* to work there."

Allee's prison counselor had a saying: "You reap what you sow." She almost replied to Nate using that very phrase, but bit it off because it wasn't helpful, as it was one of those adages that only applied in the negative sense. Good acts went unnoticed and unappreciated and never turned into anything, whereas bad decisions inevitably resulted in a scythe to dreams and the only thing reaped was a bite in the ass.

She ignored Nate's complaining all the way to her truck. She manually unlocked her door and was about to get in and pull the lock on Nate's door —there was nothing automatic about her truck—when Whitney Moore emerged from behind the truck.

"Jesus!" Allee said, jumping back.

"Sorry," Whitney said. "I didn't mean to scare you."

"I saw you," Nate said with a shrug.

Allee glared at him. "You could have warned me!"

Whitney ignored the family spat. "I need to talk to you," she said to Allee.

"One second."

Allee hopped into the truck, unlocked Nate's door, then told him to get inside. The conversation wouldn't be long. She made her way to the back of the truck, crouching to meet Whitney eye-to-eye so Ben wouldn't see them if he came their way. "What do you want?" she asked. "I've gotten called into work."

"I've been gathering information about the restaurant."

"And?"

"I think working there had something to do with my brother's suicide."

Allee raised an eyebrow. "You do?" It seemed like a stretch. Sure, working at the restaurant sucked, she thought, but for people like her, most of life sucked. Jaxson had quit jobs before; no reason he wouldn't have walked off this job rather than off himself.

Whitney nodded vigorously. "I'm going to get to the bottom of it. That's why I'm trying to talk to employees. But you saw Adam's reaction to me last night," she said. "He doesn't want me anywhere near their business, which makes me even more suspicious."

That much was true. Adam had lost it on Whitney the night before. If he wasn't doing anything wrong, what did he care if Whitney spoke with his employees? On the other hand, this was the second time Allee had seen Whitney creeping around in just two days—maybe *she* was the weird one.

Whitney stared at Allee earnestly. "I think my brother had proof. He mentioned the restaurant and he said he had proof saved somewhere shortly before he died. I didn't think anything of it at the time. I didn't know what he wanted to prove. I still don't." She shrugged. "But I need to find out. I looked at his laptop and there's nothing on there. I searched his entire room and found nothing. You knew my brother. Did he say anything to you? Anything at all?"

The thumb drive, Allee thought. That could be the proof. But she'd lost it. She couldn't tell Whitney that she had it and then lost it in her garbage-filled truck.

As they'd spoken, they had unconsciously straightened. She looked around and saw Ben standing on the corner, staring at her. She turned to Whitney and flashed a wide smile. "Don't panic, but we've got eyes on, and he doesn't seem happy to see us talking."

Whitney's gaze followed Allee's. When her eyes settled on Ben, she crouched back down, eyes wide, like a deer spying a hunter. *That's exactly what I told you not to do*. It was too late for hiding. "Listen, I don't know anything that could help you—I don't. But if I remember or see something, I'll get ahold of you."

"You don't have my number."

"Are you on Facebook?" Allee asked. When Whitney nodded, she continued, "I'll send you a message."

"Okay," Whitney replied, sounding more resigned than satisfied.

Allee clambered into her truck, shoved it in gear, and left the area. She was tempted to floor it but remembered her parole status. Every cell in her body screamed for her to run, but she couldn't, of course. Quitting a job without having another already lined up was a violation of her probation. The best she could do was to find somewhere else for Nate—and later, herself—to work. Between Ben and Adam Price on one side, and Whitney and her dead brother Jaxson on the other, she was smack-dab in the middle of whatever was going on at The Yellow Lark. If she didn't figure something out, it was only a matter of time before Nate joined her, stuck in the middle.

But there was one light at the end of the tunnel. The thumb drive. Whitney had called it "proof." Proof of what? Maybe she didn't want to know, but if she didn't look for and find it, she'd never know whether she wanted to know—did that make sense? She looked to Nate in the passenger seat. She'd bring him home and take a few moments to search for it. There wouldn't be much time, though. Thanks to Ben, she had to pick up another shift today.

The Yellow Lark was waiting.

17

MARKO

Allee knew—he could see it in her eyes. Takes one to know one. He'd seen the same look in the eyes of others—that mix of pity, disgust, and curiosity. As he descended the stairs, he could almost feel her glare on his back. Screw her. Who was she, of all people, to judge him? That was a good result —the best the kid could expect. He was going to have a celebratory drink. Everybody did that.

Between leaving Allee behind and the thought of a stiff drink, the tightness in his chest eased more each floor until he finally reached the ground floor and pushed open the double front doors. He stopped momentarily, breathing in the fresh air of freedom. Allee was a freaking felon. A parolee. She was not even his client anymore. He represented Nate, not her. He should've held his ground and kept her out of it. She could take her opinions and her stupid, creepy tattoos and shove them—

His thoughts were interrupted when he saw a disheveled man standing at the corner of the block, staring across the street toward The Yellow Lark. *David Jones*. The client who was sentenced a few days ago in Caldwell County. He hadn't wanted probation, but he'd gotten it.

Marko watched as Jones muttered to himself, mouth moving but no one near him. He could have stopped, had a chat, tried to understand what was bothering David so much, but the guy's case was over. He couldn't bill the time, so what was in it for Marko? *Nothing.* He'd be left talking to a man who was looking more and more mentally unhinged by the minute. *No thanks*, Marko thought, spinning on his heel and darting down the back alleyway. There were two ways into Olde Bulldogs.

The restaurant was nearly empty. He'd caught it between the lunch and dinner rush, which was perfect. Oliver would have time to keep the drinks coming.

"What'll it be?" he said when Marko pulled out a stool and bellied up to the bar.

"The usual."

"Old Fashioned coming right up." Oliver grabbed a glass and placed a few ice cubes at the bottom before pouring a mixture of whiskey and simple syrup into it. He topped it with bitters and a maraschino cherry, then slid it over to Marko.

"Thanks," Marko said, taking a long pull. "I was thirsty."

"You usually are," Oliver observed.

"It's quiet around here," Marko said, ignoring Oliver and looking around the empty restaurant.

Oliver shrugged and wiped nonexistent stains off the bar top. "This is how it is during the day. The Yellow Lark has siphoned off a pretty good share of our lunch and late-lunch clientele."

"Really?"

"It's quicker, cheaper, and more relaxed." Oliver shrugged. "I guess that's what people want in the middle of the day during the workweek. But on the weekends"—a satisfied smile spread across his thin lips—"we get 'em all back. They don't serve booze. Brunch isn't brunch without liquor."

Nothing is anything without liquor, Marko thought as he looked down at his half-empty cocktail. He picked it up and downed the remainder.

"Another?" Oliver asked.

Marko thought of all the things that needed to be done on his pending cases. They were piddly possession-type charges, but he still needed to read through the case reports, watch body camera video, and respond to emails. "Not today, Oliver," he said, thereby proving that he could walk away sober. He removed a ten-dollar bill from his pocket and placed it on the counter. "I'd better get home. Keep the change."

It took every ounce of willpower he had to walk away. He left through the front door because it was closer to where he'd parked. With each step he was proving himself. He could walk away. An alcoholic—a real, honest-to-goodness drunk—couldn't.

To his surprise, Jones was still standing at the corner, still staring at The Yellow Lark, still muttering to himself. While Marko watched and tried to decide whether to check on his former client, Allee and Nate drove by in an old truck.

As with any small town, Franklin's Main Street could be busy during parts of the day. It was home to the courthouse, the largest bank in town, an apartment complex, and both Olde Bulldogs and The Yellow Lark. As Marko watched, cars rushed by, their harried drivers talking on the phone, hurrying to accomplish midday errands and get back to work before the end of their afternoon break. Marko's attention was drawn to a yellow, late-model Mustang roaring down the street, windows down, stereo blaring. As the car passed him, time seemed to slow. A rapper's voice emanated from the car's stereo, reverberating off the buildings.

When the car was almost to the corner, Jones stopped mumbling and stepped in front of it. The Mustang hit Jones, the force of the collision tossing him in the air like a ragdoll, his limp body smashing the car's windshield and then rolling over the roof before falling to the pavement. The driver following the Mustang tried to stop, but not quickly enough, and he too ran over Jones's broken and already still body.

Tires squealed. Passersby screamed. Traffic in both directions came to a screeching halt. The driver of the Mustang jumped out of his car, panic etched into his features.

"He jumped out in front of me. You saw it, didn't you?" he asked, his eyes locked onto Marko's.

Marko shook his head. "I didn't see anything," he lied, then hurried away and got into his own car, leaving the scene before he could get caught up in questioning. Still, Marko wondered. *Why would he do that?* Something was going on in Franklin, but he'd never know what because he sure as hell wasn't going to ask around to find out. He was not going to get involved. Whatever was going on in Franklin was not his problem.

He parked in his driveway and opened the front door of his residence.

He set his laptop bag and his files next to his computer and went straight for the whiskey in the kitchen. The drink at Olde Bulldogs had gotten his juices flowing, and there was only one way to block the image of Jones being struck by the Mustang. Had he looked at Marko? Did he make eye contact with him? Hell, he couldn't remember—and he didn't want to. All he wanted was to numb himself; three shots later, he was well on his way.

18

ALLEE

"Damn it! Where is it?" Allee asked herself, frustration coloring her cheeks.

She was parked in her mother's driveway. She'd dropped Nate off and then gone straight home to get her uniform and to take a few minutes to search for the thumb drive. Whitney had called it "proof." That word meant something to Allee. As a felon, she was someone who had *proof* presented in court against her. Maybe this time it could be used for good.

She started in the front passenger area, where she thought it had landed when it flew off her dashboard. She opened the door and stood there, staring at the floor. She really needed to clean the truck. The floor was covered in fast-food bags, discarded clothing, empty pop cans, and snack wrappers. It was disgusting.

"Well, it's not going to find itself," she muttered.

She grabbed a garbage bag from inside her mother's garage and brought it back to the car. The work was slow-going. She picked up four pop cans and shook them—a thumb drive was small enough to slip inside, right?—before tossing them. She picked up a discarded fast-food bag and shook it as well. Something rattled around inside.

Could it be?

Was she going to get lucky? She'd never been lucky, not once in her life. She opened the bag and found a french fry, hard and dry. Not luck. Just a disgusting, ancient piece of fried potato. It looked exactly like it had when she bought it, but she couldn't recall when that was. A week ago? A month? Before she'd gone to prison? It didn't matter, although it said something about what restaurants were using to preserve foods.

She tossed the fast-food bag and continued. There were pieces of paper, crumpled. These were all from before she'd been sent to Mitchellville. She uncrumpled one and read the address of a place she'd met her old dealer. Thinking of him—and his drug supply—sent her heart into a momentary flutter; she broke into a sweat. She wanted some dope. Why was she stuck doing all this while others around her could use? She still had her dealer's number.

She could call, meet him at this same place...

No. She crumpled the paper and tossed it. *First thought wrong*—wasn't that how her counselor had phrased it? An addict's first thought is always wrong. She took a step back and slammed the door shut. Doing this alone was a bad idea. She had no idea what was in there. What if there was dope somewhere? What would she do if she found it? She wanted to say she'd throw it away, but her reaction to an address where she had previously met her dealer had just about given her a flashback. She hadn't been sober long enough. There hadn't been enough time or treatment. She didn't have the tools to stay straight. She needed help in her search. But who could help?

Not Nate, for damned sure. He was a mess. She didn't trust anyone else.

Whitney? No, she answered herself quickly. Whitney was a teacher, someone who always followed the law. She'd called the cops on Jaxson plenty of times when he was alive. There was no telling what Whitney would do if she found a teener of crystal. That was all she needed, to get jammed up when she was trying to help Whitney with *her* problem.

No, if she was going to do this, she had to do it herself. And she didn't have the strength. At least not yet. It was another failure in a long line of failures for Allee. But there wasn't time to dwell on it. She needed to get to her shift at The Yellow Lark.

19

ALLEE

Allee trudged out The Yellow Lark's back door, barely able to lift her feet. She'd been looking forward to a day off, but Benjamin Price had put an end to that after Nate's hearing. She'd been tired then, but she was well past that now. She'd been on plenty of meth highs and had suffered the crashes that followed, sometimes requiring a half-gallon of vodka and a full twenty-four hours of sleep to recover. But this level of exhaustion was far worse. After a meth trip, she'd have a physical shutdown. This was mental, emotional, *and* physical fatigue. It was everything pulling her down at once.

I can't do it, she thought. She could not handle one more day of work. She needed the morning off. Luckily, she had a meeting with her parole officer, Pamela, the next day at eleven o'clock. *Mr.* Price had to give her time off for that. She told him she wouldn't be in until one o'clock. He'd accepted it, but he wasn't happy about it.

It was dark, the air chilly. Spring was unpredictable in northern Iowa; some days were cold as winter while others gave a peek into the future months. Tonight, she wasn't dressed properly. The weather hadn't mattered for a long time. For five years, she'd been in prison with little outdoor time, and now she was shut inside another type of prison, with even less time outdoors. She made her way to her truck, unlocked the door, and got inside. Then her phone started pinging as the messages poured in. *Ping.*

Pause. *Ping.* They came in rapid-fire. She started the engine, then grabbed her phone and reviewed her messages while giving the old truck a few minutes to warm up.

She clicked on the first message and had to fight the urge to groan. *Whitney Moore.* She was starting to understand the Prices' reaction to her. It was exactly why she hadn't told Whitney about the thumb drive and another good reason not to allow her to help with the search for it. The woman was clearly unstable. But still, she read the message, which contained a link to an article on the *Franklin Messenger* website. Allee clicked on the link. The article was titled, "Man Walks into Traffic," and was dated earlier that day. "A Caldwell County man, David Jones, was killed earlier today on Main Street in front of the Wyandotte County Courthouse."

She gasped. She'd been at the courthouse and left to drive Nate home after his sentencing hearing and their encounter with Ben Price. She had returned to The Yellow Lark after that, but had entered through the back door, as always. She'd noticed in passing that Main was blocked off, with multiple cop cars on scene, but she was too tired and too busy to think much of it. It could have been a drug bust; it could have been heightened security for the courthouse. Regardless, it had nothing to do with her, so she went on with her business.

The story continued: "Witnesses say the man had been standing on the street corner facing The Yellow Lark—a popular Franklin lunch spot—for close to an hour before appearing to intentionally step into the street in front of an oncoming car."

She opened another window and searched for the name "David Jones." Unsurprisingly, there were thousands of returns, but only one David Jones had a home listed in Stonewell City, which was in Caldwell County. She clicked on the link and gasped again. She'd seen him immediately prior to his death! He'd been loitering outside the courthouse, muttering something about "false freedom," when she and Nate had left the building. She'd assumed he was under the influence of something. She turned back to the article.

"Jones was recently convicted of burglary in the third degree, for which he received a five-year suspended sentence in the Caldwell County District

Court. His attorney of record, Marko Bauer, could not be reached for comment."

"I bet Marko couldn't be reached. He was probably passed out somewhere," Allee muttered to herself. She returned to the app and typed, "What's your point?" The article was interesting, sure, but it wasn't her business, and Whitney and Allee weren't friends. Whitney wanted something.

The response came immediately. "It's suspicious, right?"

Allee understood what Whitney was implying, but she wanted to make her write it, to see how ridiculous it looked in black and white. "I don't follow."

"Two suicides, both within a stone's throw from each other. I checked. That David Jones guy used to work for The Yellow Lark while he was on probation for his last crime. I mean, come on. Isn't it suspicious?"

Allee sighed. Whitney wasn't going to let this go.

"Do you ever consider minding your own business?" she typed.

"No. Not when it comes to my family, and neither do you, I hear."

"You'd never survive in prison."

"I don't plan on finding out," Whitney sent back quickly. "Hold on. Someone's at the door."

Allee sighed irritably. She didn't have the time or energy for this. It was late and she needed to get home. She put her truck in gear and headed the few blocks to her residence. She parked at the end of the driveway. The house was dark, her mother already long asleep. She let herself in with a key and made her way to the basement, where she'd been living since her release from prison. She was a 40-year-old woman still living in her mother's house. *What a joke.*

It wasn't until she'd changed, washed her face, brushed her teeth, and gotten into bed that she realized Whitney had never returned to the message thread. Had something happened to her? Allee thought of the tattoo on her right ankle. "Death be all that we can rightly depend on." It was from *Dracula*. The words written in 1897 were still as true today as they had been then.

Death was coming for everyone. The only question was, when?

20

WHITNEY

You'd never survive in prison, Allee sent.

Whitney stared at those words, allowing the horrible thought of incarceration to sink into her brain. It was true. She wouldn't. She never even thought about it before—ever. She was a law-abiding citizen. A high-school teacher. Sure, she did some poking around outside The Yellow Lark, but she didn't trespass, and she wasn't looking to do anyone wrong. She was good.

"I don't plan to go," she sent, then there was a bang on the door. It was loud, insistent, demanding. "Hold on. Someone's at the door." She sent the message and another knock followed.

"Who is here at this hour?" Leo said, coming out of the bedroom, rubbing his eyes.

She was in the living room sitting on the couch they'd purchased at a second-hand store, her laptop balanced on her knees. "I don't know."

He narrowed his eyes. "It's not someone who has to do with your... investigation, is it?"

"You told me to drop it, so I did," Whitney lied. The lie slid off her tongue easier than she had expected. She'd never kept secrets from Leo. Their relationship was built on trust. An open book. *Not anymore.* That restaurant took her brother and was now separating her from her husband. What more would it take?

Three more loud bangs at their door, then a deep male voice shouted, "Police!"

Whitney's gaze met Leo's. Their eyes widened. His communicated an unspoken question. She shook her head. She hadn't done anything.

"Daddy, what is that?" Arlo had wandered into the small living room and was rubbing his eyes. A stuffed dog he had named "RuffRuff" was curled in the crook of one arm.

"Police! Open up, or we'll break the door down!" The voice was even louder, more insistent. Time was short.

Arlo whimpered and rushed to Whitney's side. "Mommy!"

She shut her laptop and set it aside, opened her arms, and invited him to crawl onto her lap. He did, instinctively curling his tiny body into a ball.

"Answer it!" she said to Leo.

"Coming!" Leo shouted, hoping to preclude the door being kicked in.

Arlo shivered in Whitney's arms. He was in kindergarten, a big kid overnight. He'd stopped hugging his mom, turning away to give her back hugs instead of the true arms-slung- around-her, clinging-like-he'd-never-let-go hugs of his younger years. But he clung to her now, his small fists gripping her shirt.

Leo looked back at Whitney, his hand lingering on the doorknob. She gave him a small nod. He returned it. Solidarity. They were in this together. They'd been arguing often, but the reasons for those fights seemed meaningless in the moment. He pulled the door open. A beat of silence was followed by a sudden burst of noise and movement. Blinking red and blue lights penetrated the room.

"Is Whitney Moore here?" a middle-aged man in uniform asked. He had pockmarks across his cheeks, scars from adolescent acne.

"Of course," Leo replied, flustered in a way that Whitney had never seen him. He was usually so calm, so collected in the face of a crisis. "What do you want with her?"

"We have a warrant for her arrest."

Arlo gripped Whitney's shirt tighter. He didn't understand the words, but he was responding to the officer's tone and volume.

"Where is she? We know she's home," the officer said.

Whitney stared at him. It didn't seem real. Any of it. She was right there, sitting on the couch. Couldn't he see her? How had he not seen her?

"Where the hell else would she be?" Leo asked, his tone darkening. He was getting angry.

"You tell me."

"What's the warrant for?"

"Conspiracy to commit murder."

What? Whitney thought. *Murder?*

Leo laughed, a dark chuckle that held no mirth. "My ass. You think Whitney—the English teacher, mother, and all-around good girl—has conspired to commit murder? No," he continued, shaking his head. "You've got the wrong person."

"Maybe you don't know her as well as you think." The officer was leaning into Leo, his nose inches away from her husband's.

"Maybe you have shit for brains." Leo replied, not backing down. "I know her better than anyone, and I'm not going to put up with you insulting her, our marriage or—"

They were seconds from a physical altercation, and Whitney knew who would win. It wouldn't be Leo. She might be going to jail, but Leo couldn't. Where would Arlo go? She needed to defuse the situation before their little boy was left alone, taken into foster care or, God forbid, a shelter somewhere. "I'm right here," she said. Her voice came out high-pitched, but it didn't waver, and sounded far stronger than she felt.

Men in uniform darted past Leo, approaching her.

"Whitney Moore, you're under arrest for conspiracy to commit murder," the acne-scarred officer said.

"You have the right to remain silent," a younger officer began reading from a card. "Anything you say or do can be held against you in the court of law." He continued speaking in a drone-like tone.

Whitney ignored him, focusing instead on the fear in Arlo's eyes.

"*No!*" Arlo shouted, throwing his arms around her neck and pressing his little body into hers.

Tears filled Whitney's eyes. She hugged Arlo tightly.

"Let go of the child," Scarface ordered.

Anger flared in Whitney's chest. This was her child, her family. Didn't she have a right to say goodbye?

"I said to release the child, or I'll have to forcefully remove him."

Arlo swung around, twisting his body so he was sitting in his mother's lap. Tears rolled down his cheeks, mixing with the snot streaming from his nose. He ran an arm along his face, wiping it onto his sleeve. "You're supposed to be good. But you're bad."

Scarface ignored him. "I won't ask again."

She pulled Arlo into a brief, tight hug. "I love you," she whispered into his ear. "Always and forever. I'll be back real soon. Okay?"

Arlo nodded.

Whitney placed him on the couch beside her. Leo was suddenly right there, pulling him into his embrace. Whitney hugged her husband with little Arlo in the center, his small body shaking with sobs.

"Let's go. Family time is over," Scarface said.

"What the hell is wrong with you?" Leo asked. "Have a heart. Let her say goodbye to her family."

A smirk twitched the corner of the officer's mouth. "When you find out who she tried to kill, you'll understand why this 'family time' bullshit she is trying to pull isn't tugging on anyone's heartstrings."

What is he talking about? The thought shot through Whitney's mind. Someone yanked Whitney's arms from behind, clicking cold metal around her wrists. She was pulled back away from the only family she had left in this world, and marched out of her home, leaving Leo to console their inconsolable son.

She'd thought she was broken when Jaxson jumped off that ledge. She'd felt her soul had been destroyed with the loss of her baby brother. But she was wrong. Whatever was about to happen to her was already proving that bad things could always get worse.

Jaxson wasn't the only person she could lose.

21

MARKO

He could swear his head was going to explode. His stomach felt like there was a lizard crawling around in it. His brain throbbed, pulsing inside his skull. His body ached like he had played a football game last night. He'd never been hung over like this! Christ, what did he do? He took some shots after seeing that guy get run over—but come on! He'd made it to bed, at least. He needed to get a shower. Shit, he was still dressed! What time was it?

He kicked off his shoes and stripped down, headed for the shower. The cold water didn't help, so he cranked it up. Still nothing. He could fix this. There was only one solution. He got out of the shower and trudged into the kitchen, still dripping wet.

Three shots this time. He poured one after the other and downed the whiskey in less than a minute. The tingling in his throat spread through his body, instantly numbing the headache and giving him a boost of energy. He changed into the cleanest work clothes he could find in the hamper: a pair of no-iron slacks, a slightly wrinkled button-down shirt, and the same tie he'd worn yesterday. He was examining himself in the bathroom mirror when his phone buzzed, indicating incoming email.

Who was emailing him this early in the morning? He received emails for all electronic filings in his court cases, but those would not start coming through until the clerk's office was open at eight o'clock in the morning. It was barely seven o'clock. He took two pills with a glass of water and then retrieved his phone from his nightstand.

The battery was almost dead—he'd forgotten to charge it. *Damn. I gotta get my shit together.* He opened the email application and clicked on the top message. It was from Connor. "Check your case queue."

Marko felt his heart race, and he continued reading. "I appointed you to a major felony last night. You're welcome. And don't screw this up."

"Appointed me?" Marko said, his heart picking up speed. "To what?"

He entered the kitchen, retrieved two hydrocodone pills, and washed them down with another shot of whiskey before going to his computer and opening the electronic filing system. *There it is! An appointment for Moore, Whitney, Wyandotte County Case Number FECR120957. Right here in town. That's a good sign. I'm back, baby!* He clicked on the case number and opened the file. There were only two filings: a criminal complaint and an initial appearance order. He first clicked on the initial appearance order, issued by Judge Connor at eleven o'clock last night. The order named Marko as Whitney's attorney, set bond at $25,000 cash only, and set a preliminary hearing in ten days.

"What is the charge?" Marko wondered aloud. Twenty-five thousand wasn't an exorbitant amount, but it was cash only. Few people in Franklin— the bluest of blue-collar towns—had an extra twenty-five grand just sitting around. Judge Connor wanted the Moore woman in custody. He turned to the complaint. *Conspiracy to commit murder.* He scrolled down to the affidavit signed by the officer. "The said Whitney Moore conspired with LP, a minor, to murder her husband." It wasn't terribly descriptive, but he'd get what he needed later.

He flipped on the news and turned it to a Des Moines station, planning to half listen when the reporter said, "I'm standing here in front of Franklin Senior High where Whitney Moore, the teacher charged with hiring a student to kill her husband, previously worked."

Marko froze. *A teacher.* His new case instantly became more appealing. Teacher cases were always major news, especially when their alleged crime involved a student. Finally, a case that was worth his talents. He needed to go see her, and quick. He shoved his laptop into its case, grabbed a few pens and a notebook, then headed out the door, grabbing his keys and his suit jacket off the living room chair on his way out.

He was blocks from the jail when he saw the flashing red and blue lights. He'd been in a hurry. He must have been speeding. He cupped a hand in front of his mouth and tried to smell his breath. How many shots had he taken? Four? Five? And the pain pills. Could he pass a breath test? Why today of all days? *Aw, shit.*

22

MARKO

"License and registration." The officer was a stern-faced young man, maybe twenty-five years old.

Don't panic, Marko told himself. *Move slowly, don't talk directly in the officer's direction, do not get angry or emotional.* Marko fished his license out of his wallet and leaned over to his glove box, popped it open, and removed his vehicle registration. He handed them both to the officer while facing straight ahead the entire time. "Sit tight. I'll be right back," the officer said, tapping the window frame with Marko's license.

Should I eat a breath mint? Marko wondered as he watched the officer's retreating form in the rearview mirror. *No.* It would just make him more suspicious. And he *was* suspicious.

Marko had experienced plenty of close calls in the past, but sensed he was in real trouble this time. Luckily, the officer didn't seem to recognize him. He was probably too young. Ten years ago, Marko had quite the winning streak. He'd won so many suppression hearings and trials that any law enforcement officer would have been as happy as a five-year-old on Christmas morning to pull him over in this condition.

An eternity passed while Marko watched the officer in the rearview mirror. He was on the phone for a few minutes, and then he just sat there. This was just one more reason why so many people hated cops. Was he intentionally wasting Marko's time? He had a client to get to—for once, an important client! A case that could make his career, and here he was sitting blocks away from the jail—and his client—while this young cop fiddle-farted around!

When a second cop car pulled in beside the first, Marko swallowed hard. A call for backup was never good. Both cops got out of their vehicles and approached him side by side. The new arrival was not young, and was well known to Marko. The older officer leaned into Marko's window.

"Well, well, well, what do we have here?" he asked with a smirk.

"Dennis Shaffer." Marko nodded his head in a way that he hoped conveyed a level of respect he did not have for this clown.

"*Officer* Shaffer to you," the older cop replied. "Looks like the tables have turned." Shaffer chewed hard on a piece of gum, working his jaw vigorously, but there was no smell to it. It wasn't a fresh piece, so Marko wouldn't be able to argue it interfered with Shaffer's sense of smell.

"I don't know what you mean, Officer Shaffer."

"You don't remember accusing me of planting evidence? I'm hurt," Shaffer replied, feigning sorrow. Then his voice hardened. "But *I* remember it. And *I* remember the internal investigation, the unpaid leave, and the public humiliation. And it all ended in them clearing my name."

Marko shrugged. "Well then, no harm, no foul."

"See, there's where you're wrong," Shaffer snapped, his gum gnashing in Marko's ear. "It took years for me to rebuild my reputation. A false accusation like that, well, there were plenty of people who wanted to believe it."

"You know I had to do what I believed was in the best interest of my client," Marko replied levelly. "I was doing my job. I know you understand that."

"Get out of the car," Shaffer ordered as he stepped away from Marko's vehicle.

"Oh, come on," Marko said. His heartbeat picked up, thudding inside his chest.

"I've got to do what I've got to do," Shaffer said, lifting one shoulder and letting it fall. "I know you understand that. Now get out of the car."

"I can't believe this." Marko pulled the handle and shouldered the door open.

"How much have you had to drink to—" Shaffer stopped short and looked at his watch, then whistled. "Hitting it hard pretty early, aren't we, Marko? It's not even eight a.m. yet."

Marko knew better than to respond.

"You still buzzing from last night? Or was this a hop and pop?"

Again, Marko knew better than to respond.

Shaffer studied him before making his decision. "I'm going to need you to do field sobriety testing."

"I'm going to deny your request," Marko said. "You don't begin to have reasonable suspicion."

Shaffer crossed his arms. "You're refusing all testing."

"I am."

"You know I'm going to have to arrest you."

"You were going to arrest me whether I consented to testing or not."

"Suit yourself." Shaffer pulled a pair of handcuffs off his belt. "Turn around."

Marko followed instructions. Everything in his body told him to fight back, to resist, but he forced himself to remain outwardly calm. Nothing would change the fact that he was going to jail. To do anything other than calmly follow instructions would only create fodder for the prosecutor to claim that he'd been uncooperative, emotional, and therefore likely intoxicated. All they had right now was that Marko smelled like alcohol. Hardly anything coming from a rookie cop and a cop with an obvious grudge against him who had a well-deserved reputation for falsifying evidence.

Marko quietly allowed Shaffer to lead him to the second cop car. As he trudged along, an old truck passed, slowing so the driver could rubberneck. He met the driver's gaze, intending it as a challenge, but the fight left him like air from a balloon when he realized it was Allee. She shook her head disapprovingly, then sped up, leaving Marko alone to deal with his legal problems and his conscience.

23

ALLEE

"I don't want to work here," Nate whined as Allee parked behind The Yellow Lark.

Allee sighed. *Join the club*, she thought. "We've been over this. You burglarized the owner's garage. He wants you to work here. He's influential. You don't have any real choice."

"I don't *have* to."

"You're right," Allee agreed. "You don't. You can go do the prison time you earned, instead."

"I wouldn't have to work in prison," he grumbled.

"You wouldn't *have* to work, but trust me: you'd want to. It's the only way to get any freedom of movement on the inside." She suspected that was intentional, and it *did* make sense. "You want freedom, you work for it," as Allee's prison counselor had always said.

Nate groaned.

Allee shut the engine off and sighed. "You've got to grow up. You're not a kid anymore." He looked like one to her, with that peach fuzz growing on his chin and the acne covering his forehead, but he wasn't. "There are real consequences to violating probation."

"Fine." He got out of the truck and slammed the door. "But I don't like it."

She didn't either. "Go. Now. I'll join you after I see my PO." She started the engine and pulled out of the parking lot. This was as far as she could take him. She could not force him through those doors. She could not make him work hard. All she could do was hope. She circled the building, driving down the alleyway that brought her back to Main Street.

She saw the flashing lights. *Not another suicide*, she thought.

She was directly across from the courthouse, and her pulse slowed as she began to understand. Two cop cars were parked on the side of Main. It was probably a drunk driver; maybe a drug bust. The person had a nice car. Range Rovers were sweet. Maybe it was a doctor or lawyer or their spouse? It was good to see one of those rich bastards get what was coming to them. She lingered, idling at the corner, her blinker flashing. She watched as a middle-aged officer exited a white Ford Explorer with *Franklin Police Department* etched on the side. He approached the Range Rover, his back straight and his head high. He wore a smile that seemed almost maniacal given the panic the driver probably felt.

As she watched, the officer knocked on the window. The window rolled down. A short conversation ensued, then the officer pulled the door handle and Marko Bauer exited the vehicle and was handcuffed after a short exchange.

He was probably drunk. Served him right. It wasn't her business. She needed to get to her PO's office. She turned onto Main Street and drove past Marko, their eyes meeting for one fleeting moment before she was past him. Was it panic or desperation? As she continued driving, she glanced in the rearview mirror. The officer was walking Marko back to his patrol vehicle. She caught one last glimpse of their expressions before turning the corner. The officer was gleeful; Marko looked broken.

Why did he drink? He was successful, obviously had at least a little money. He was a lawyer, and not bad-looking. It was the first time she'd ever wondered this about Marko. Everyone had a reason for their addictions. Sometimes it was just luck of the draw, a family gene prone to addiction, but most ran deeper than that. Something had happened to cause his need to escape.

Her own reasons were born from both genetics and trauma.

"You burned the chicken, you dumb bitch!" she remembered her father shouting at her mother.

It wasn't always chicken, but it was always *you dumb bitch!* That would start the argument. Allee's mom wasn't one to back down; they had that in common, but Allee had always wondered if they'd been different—if she and her mother had been more submissive, meeker—would they have suffered so much physical violence?

"Your father doesn't mean it," Allee's mother would say afterward, when they were both sitting in the bathroom, applying makeup to cover their bruises.

Over the years, Allee became an expert in applying makeup, watching one online tutorial after another, learning that if done correctly, makeup could completely alter a person's appearance. It could hide perceived flaws; it could hide injuries. It could also make injuries that weren't there seem as though they were.

The beatings were the worst when he'd been drinking, which was every day. By the time Allee was sixteen, she couldn't bear it anymore. She ran away, lived on the streets, got caught in the drug-using, couch-surfing crowd. The people she'd met in her time working in restaurant kitchens. They didn't care she was a kid. She didn't act like one.

Meth was exchanged for sex, and sex was exchanged for rent. Her paychecks went into a bank account jointly owned by her and her father—sixteen-year-olds couldn't have their own accounts—and her father made sure to drain it as often as possible. Her couch-surfing lifestyle lasted a year. Then the old man died of liver failure, and she returned home.

At seventeen, she was shooting meth every day. Despite that, she was what people called a "functional addict." She maintained her job and was even promoted to working the grill. That was when she'd discovered her love of preparing food and the idea that one excellent meal could be almost as good as the best high.

She shook her head, dispelling thoughts of her past. Memories triggered her and drove a desire to use. It didn't matter how much time she'd spent in prison; she still wanted meth. Her body still needed it. But for now, she fought the desire, and instead of turning down a road that she knew would take her to familiar playgrounds and playmates, she continued to a small, boxy building and parked outside. The sign out front read, "Second Judicial District, Department of Correctional Services."

It was time to meet with her parole officer.

24

MARKO

So, this is jail.

Marko had been inside plenty of jails, but this was his first time on the other side of the bars. As a defense attorney, he'd always wondered what was so bad about it. They had TV, they were fed, and they didn't have to work. It seemed almost like vacation to him, but they didn't seem to see it that way. His in-custody clients were the absolute worst. They called and left messages and wrote long letters, and they had others call and leave messages and write letters demanding their release. Like he could do something about it! He'd never quite understood the urgency.

Now he did.

He was trapped. He could hardly breathe! If he didn't get out of there, he was going to go nuts! People weren't made to be in cages.

He shouldn't be in jail. He'd refused the breath test. That was the last and final nail in his pretrial release coffin, of course, but he didn't have a choice. He wouldn't pass it, so taking it would only result in providing evidence against himself. So far, the State had nothing aside from Shaffer's word, and that would be easy to thwart in trial. The guy had said the quiet part aloud during their encounter: he was pissed that Marko had once alleged he'd planted evidence. That would be captured on his body camera, right? He'd be even angrier this time, when Marko called him a crooked cop looking for revenge in open court.

He'd lose his license for a year. There was no consequence to refusing to perform field sobriety tests, but that wasn't the case with refusing a breath test at the station. It was a law called the "implied consent" law, and it said all drivers on Iowa roads consent to taking the breath test when asked. If the officer had cause to invoke implied consent, drivers had to take the test or lose their license for a year.

It was better to live a year without a driver's license than put his law license at risk. They wouldn't get a conviction, but he was going to have to find another way to get around. How the hell was he going to do that?

The driving suspension wasn't immediate. He had seven days to figure it out. If he didn't, he might have to withdraw from all his cases, pissing off the judges and losing all his credibility—or what was left of it. And Connor, especially, was going to be pissed. But honestly, the new appointment was the reason Marko was in this mess. He was hurrying to see his client, just as Connor would have expected!

Now he was sitting on his ass in the same jail, waiting to see a magistrate and bounce. How embarrassing. He would know the magistrate. He knew them all. They'd see that he was arrested for driving drunk in the morning. A time of the day when it was too late to be a hangover from the day before, but too early for end-of-the-day drinking. The rumors would be rampant. By the end of the day, he'd be a raging alcoholic. But he wasn't an alcoholic; he had control of his drinking—he'd shown that yesterday when he had walked out of Olde Bulldogs after just one.

It was the hangovers that he couldn't control.

A jailer walked by. He was a middle-aged man with a round belly and a large, bulbous red nose. *Tell me that guy doesn't drink.* Marko stood and motioned to him.

The jailer saw him and stopped. "What?"

This jailer had brought clients in and out of meeting rooms for years for Marko, but Marko had never learned his name. Jailers had always seemed like movie extras to him: nameless faces that served a purpose, but not an important one. He regretted that now.

"Can I post bond?" Marko asked.

"I don't know," the jailer said, crossing his beefy, heavily-tattooed forearms. "Can you?"

"Of course. I've got the money in an account. I just need to transfer it."

"Okay." A smile twitched in the corner of the jailer's mouth.

"I just need someone to help me do that," Marko explained. When the jailer didn't respond, he continued, "Can I get access to a computer? Just for a few minutes. That's all." *This guy is a complete asshole,* he thought. *Remain calm.*

The jailer showed a line of yellow, crooked teeth. "You think we have the money to get computers for inmates?"

Marko shrugged.

The jailer sobered, his features darkening. "Well, we don't, so you'll just have to wait—just like the commoners." He spun heavily on the heel of his boot and was gone.

Marko had heard the message loud and clear: he was just like everyone else. There would be no special treatment. He would have to wait his turn. He didn't like it, but he had no choice. He had nobody on the outside to help him. He had no siblings. His parents were both dead. His office was a revolving door of clients with whom he had never developed much of a personal relationship. The past few years had been lonely, but now he was truly alone.

25

ALLEE

Pamela threaded her fingers together and placed them on the desk in front of her. "So, why did you want to see me this morning?"

Allee had told Adam Price that she had to meet with her parole officer. He'd assumed it was the required monthly meeting and she hadn't corrected that assumption. This meeting was by her request, not Pamela's.

"I want to quit my job."

Pamela pursed her lips. "Do you have another job lined up?"

Allee shook her head. "Not yet."

"Then you can't quit your current job." When Allee predictably glared at her, she got defensive. "Don't give me that look, Allee, this is how the system works. You need money to live, and you must work for money."

Allee groaned. "But I hate working there. Everyone does."

"It's hard work, isn't it?"

"Yeah. And they've yet to pay me."

Pamela's eyes narrowed. "I'm sure it's a clerical error. You've been working there for more than two weeks, right?"

"Yes."

"Bring it up with management."

"Right. And upset Adam Price? No freakin' way."

"Allee." Pamela's voice dropped a few octaves. "You're being dramatic, but you've got to take this on. This is real-world stuff. You can't just avoid it. That's the addict in you talking, telling you that you can simply ignore a situation and make it go away."

No. The addiction is telling me a hit of crank will solve the problem. At least for now.

"Talk to your supervisor. It will be fine."

It would not "be fine." Pamela didn't know Price. He was creepy in the way he stared, wide-eyed, as he breathed through his mouth. Allee hadn't seen a single employee seek him out to ask a question. There was a reason for that. Neither typical restaurant employees nor felons were easy to control. The fact that control had come so easily to Price said something, and whatever it was, wasn't good. "So, you're telling me I can quit my job if I find a new one?"

"And if I approve it."

Allee had an idea. "Would working for an attorney count as a job?"

"Yes." Pamela said the word slowly, suspiciously. "But I don't think any attorneys will hire you without experience."

Allee recalled the crestfallen look on Marko's face as the officer cuffed him and ushered him into the back of the police cruiser. He had to be smart enough not to take the field tests and to decline the breath test. Assuming he did all that, he was gonna need help, just like any other drunk. They all did. "I can think of one," she said, shoving out of her chair and rising to her feet.

"Keep in touch, Allee," Pamela ordered.

"I will," Allee promised, closing the door behind her.

26

MARKO

Lying on the threadbare mattress in his cell, half asleep and half alert, Marko decided jail—like airports and automobiles—was just another form of sleep purgatory. His eyes opened at the sound of loud banging, and he turned his head to see what was happening.

The large-nosed jailer was outside his cell, banging on the bars. "Wake up! Someone is here to see you," he shouted.

Marko sprang to his feet. "The magistrate?"

"Nope. That's going to be a while," the jailer said. "Sheriff says they gotta bring one in from another district, seeing that you are so important and all."

"Who, then?"

"Beats me. It's a broad—big, hard-looking bimbo. Probably one of your clients, or maybe a girlfriend—although she don't seem your type. I can tell her to get lost if you don't want to talk."

"Don't," Marko said quickly. He made his way to his cell door and waited. "I'll talk to her." He had no idea who it was, but anything was better than lying on that bunk, watching his life pass by, waiting for some fat-ass magistrate to mosey on over to Franklin to see him.

"Follow me." The jailer unlocked the door and pushed it open. "Spread 'em," he said, motioning to Marko's legs. Marko complied, and the jailer placed shackles on his wrists and ankles, binding them.

Such bullshit. There was nowhere for him to go. "Are these really necessary?"

The jailer shrugged. "Probably not, but it's policy. You're a lawyer, you know all about policy. We gotta treat everyone the same. You know—equality and all that happy horseshit."

Once he had Marko shackled, he led him down a long, winding hallway. The leg restraints were meant to prevent running, of course, but they were also intended to send a message.

Mission accomplished, Marko thought. The restraints made walking difficult, especially with the wrist restraints making his body heavier in the front. The result was more of a shuffle than a walk. He was too old for this. The jailer led him into a small meeting room with a table separated by a plastic partition. Allee sat in a chair on the other side. She looked bored when they entered, her legs crossed, elbow on thigh, chin in hand. She straightened when the door swung open and Marko shuffled forward, dropping into the chair across from her.

"Thirty minutes," the jailer said to Allee before departing.

"What are you doing here?" Marko asked.

"I should be asking you the same thing, but I already know the answer. I was on my way to work. The Yellow Lark."

"Not often former clients follow my suggestions."

"Not often I visit lawyers in jail."

"Are you here to gloat?" Marko asked. He was too tired and dehydrated to listen to her shit. His head was starting to hurt. He needed a drink.

"No. I'm here to help."

She was going to help *him*? Somehow, he didn't think so. "How? Are you going to bond me out?"

Allee laughed without mirth. "Hell, no. I don't have any money. I've been working at that restaurant like you suggested. Been there two and a half weeks and still haven't been paid."

"That's weird."

"I think it's a scam."

"Doubt it. The Prices run the place."

"Their son Adam—he makes us call him *Mr.* Price—is the one who manages it. Maybe they don't know."

Doubtful. Failing to pay employees—if reported—could get the Department of Employment snooping through your books, which was never a good thing. "Well, yeah, but Nikki is kind of a religious fanatic. She'd never let someone steal from the poor."

"Most of us are criminals," Allee scoffed. "I think we're in a different category in their eyes."

"I don't know..." He no longer attended Mass, but he remembered the teachings of Catholicism. He had simply sat there and listened, but Nikki was a believer. "Maybe she doesn't know. I mean, she's the elected county recorder. She's got to be checking the books," he explained. "If she's not, that would be pretty dumb."

Allee shrugged. "People *are* dumb."

Nikki was a lot of things—arrogant and self-centered, to name a few—but she wasn't dumb. "You said you are here to help me?"

"I want to help you *and* help me."

How was a convicted felon going to help the best attorney in this part of the state when she couldn't even get him out of jail? He had to hear this. "I'm listening."

"You've got money, right?" Allee said.

"I have some, yeah. But I can't access it because I don't have a computer."

"I can help you with the transfer of funds to post bond."

She was out of her mind. He was not going to give her—a convicted felon and addict, even one who seemed to be in recovery—access to his bank accounts. She must think he had shit for brains. "At this point, I've waited long enough. I might as well see the magistrate."

"You're going to need a driver."

A driver would certainly make things easier. "How do you know that?"

"You were arrested for OWI," she said. "I have to believe you were smart enough to refuse the breath test. You're gonna lose your license. You're hosed."

She was smart, he'd give her that. Well, streetwise. "How do you know that?" Franklin was a small town, but there hadn't been time for the news to spread. Nor had there been time for *The Messenger*, the local newspaper, to cover it.

She looked at him with disgust. "Marko, you were driving. You are always drinking. Simple." When he didn't seem to understand, she explained. "As much as you drink, you run into a cop—doesn't matter why—you're toast. I may not have a college education, but I'm not a dumbass."

Had his drinking been that obvious? Whatever. Who cared what this bimbo thought. "All right. Don't get so huffy. What are you proposing?" he asked, having a pretty good idea.

She paused for a long moment, then said, "I already told you. You will need a driver." Her words were slow, deliberate, controlled. "You're a contract attorney, meaning you've got cases all over. Without a license, you're screwed. I want to be your driver."

He sat back. "You want to work for me?"

"Yes."

"Why?"

"We've already been over this. The Yellow Lark is—"

"Right, right." Marko started to wave a hand dismissively, but the wrist restraints stopped him. "They aren't paying you." It was probably a simple accounting error. He had been thinking about using one of those cab services, but this might just work, and it would probably be much cheaper. "How much?"

"Fifteen dollars an hour."

He whistled. "I don't have that kind of money, and that's got to be way, way more than they're paying you over at The Yellow Lark."

She crossed her arms. "Beggars can't be choosers."

He had options. Not great ones, but options all the same. "What makes you think I'm desperate enough to beg?"

Allee sat quietly, her gaze traveling over his prison jumpsuit, settling on the chains around his wrists.

"Fine," he said with a sigh. "Ten bucks an hour. You will be clean and sober, and you will be available between seven o'clock and five o'clock Monday through Friday. I only pay for your time when I use it."

"Fourteen, but you pay me thirty-five a week."

That was almost five hundred a week! She was insane. "Twelve an hour —but I'll give you forty hours."

"I can do the math," she said quickly. "No. You pay fourteen per hour and pay me for thirty-five and I'll consider eating any overtime—I need outta The Yellow Lark."

She must have done just fine in Mitchellville. She had probably talked all the cons out of their cigarettes and candy bars. "Fine."

"Then I'm hired."

"Yes," Marko said.

"I'll need something in writing from you to my PO."

"You'll get it."

"When do I start?"

"Soon as I get out of here."

Allee jotted her cell phone number on a piece of paper and slid it over to him. "Call me when you get out. You can buy us something to eat and me a tank of gas."

"Wait!" Marko said. "Where are you going?"

Allee smiled for the first time. "I've got a job to quit."

"I need something else," Marko said.

"Anything, boss."

It sounded strange coming from her. He didn't know if he could get used to it.

"What do you need?" Allee said.

"I need you to talk to another inmate," he said. "I was on my way to see her when Officer Douchebag picked me up."

Allee lowered herself back into her seat. She was listening.

"I just need you to tell her that you work for me, and I will come visit her soon. Tell her that I'm—" He cleared his throat and looked down at his chains. "Tell her I'm tied up right now." It was corny, but true. "Tell her I'll be in to see her later today. Now, go."

"You haven't told me who the client is."

"Oh, right. Her name is Whitney. Whitney something."

Allee sat stock-still, staring at him.

What's that all about? Marko wondered.

27

ALLEE

"Whitney," Allee said. "Whitney Moore?"

"That's her," Marko replied. "Do you know her?"

"I don't *know* her, but I've seen her around," Allee said. "I knew her brother. He's the one who jumped off the balcony."

"Really?" He cocked his head to the side. "You didn't seem all that broken up about it at the time."

"I try not to get too rattled about anything. I'm broken enough." If he'd been where she'd been, he'd understand.

"I get it."

No, he didn't. "What is Whitney in for? Harassment? Trespass?" She assumed it was something involving The Yellow Lark. Price had threatened law enforcement involvement, and Whitney hadn't stopped trying to contact Allee. It was probably the same with other employees.

"Conspiracy to commit murder."

"Excuse me?" Allee normally tried to hide her emotions, including shock. She held her cards close and wore a poker face. It was a habit learned in prison, the only way to survive in a hostile environment. But this news had her breaking that habit. She needed to get herself together. "She doesn't seem like a killer, is all." She shrugged with practiced nonchalance.

Marko smiled wanly. "One thing I've learned in this business is that everyone can kill, given the right circumstances. Especially spouses. Marriage can bring out the crazy in anyone. Just one of the reasons I've never married."

"Sure," Allee agreed. "But this feels, I don't know...wrong. Who did she conspire with?"

"With whom did she conspire?"

Was he seriously giving her a grammar lesson while he was behind bars? "Yeah. That."

"And *allegedly*."

"Right. With whom did she *allegedly* conspire?"

"A student."

"A student," Allee repeated. "That means she wanted a kid to kill her husband." Her tone was deadpan, disbelieving. Whitney, with access to the most desperate addicts through her brother's connections, had apparently chosen to approach a kid with the task instead. That didn't feel right. Unless there was sex involved.

"It's not that unusual a fact pattern," Marko said, almost defensively. "Pam Smart did it. It isn't unheard of."

"She was having an affair with a child," Allee replied, shaking her head. "Let me rephrase that: she was sexually assaulting a child."

"Maybe Whitney Moore was, too."

"No way. I've talked with her. I don't see it. And Smart had other problems."

"Maybe Whitney Moore does, too."

"What? Like she's unhinged or something?"

"Everyone is a little crazy."

Allee thought back to Whitney's recent behavior. Hiding behind trash cans at The Yellow Lark. Crouching down beside Allee's truck, waiting for her to leave Nate's sentencing hearing. It was not normal behavior. Maybe Jaxson's death had dislodged something in her brain. "Who is the kid?" Allee asked. "The one she *allegedly* hired to kill her husband?"

"I don't know. All I've seen so far is the criminal complaint. Because it is a public record, kids' names can't be listed and are redacted. All it gave me were the kid's initials—LP—and the age: seventeen."

Allee stood and pressed a little silver button on the wall. "All right. I'll go talk to her."

There was a crackling sound and then a voice came through the intercom. "Are you done?"

"Yes," Allee said. "But I'm going to need to see another client."

"Client?"

Allee's eyes met Marko's. They could hear the disbelief in the jailer's tone. "Yes...client," Allee said when Marko nodded his approval. "I'm working for Marko Bauer. I'm his—" She paused, clearing her throat. They hadn't agreed on a job title. "Driver" wouldn't get her in to see Whitney. "Investigator."

"Bauer, is that true?" the jailer asked.

Marko's eyes flitted to Allee's, then to the speaker on the wall. "Yes," he said, louder than necessary. "Client is Whitney Moore."

"All right. I'll be back to get Bauer and return with Moore," the jailer said. Moments later, he appeared on Marko's side of the partition. "Hiring people from jail, are we now?"

"Something like that," Marko said.

"I got good news, Bauer. The magistrate is ready to see you," the jailer said. "I'm going to put you in a different meeting room with a different jailer. The initial appearance is going to be remote on account that you're so special and nobody here will see you."

"Call me when you are out," Allee reminded Marko as the jailer led him away. He turned back and nodded assent.

He would call; she knew it. Marko was just like every other man she'd known in her life. He didn't want anything to do with her until he needed her. And Marko needed her. What he didn't know was that she needed him, too. She did not want to work for Price anymore. Working for Marko couldn't be worse, could it?

She scrolled through Facebook while waiting for the jailer to return with Whitney. Clicking on her new client's account, she quickly scanned the photographs. There were lots of pictures of Whitney and her husband smiling at the camera. At the beach. At a park. Dressed for a wedding. By all accounts, their marriage appeared solid.

Social media was a liar's medium, of course. The whole deal was to tell a story—usually a fabricated one—showing the world what the account holder wanted the world to see. Allee knew that seeing the truth about people required some digging, some reading between the lines, and a nose for bullshit. Declaration of love posts, for example. They meant the marriage or relationship was failing. If not, why say anything? If the marriage was good, it didn't need a public declaration. She'd never been married, or really even in love, but if she was, she'd damned sure keep those emotions private.

Allee didn't find any of those sorts of posts, but that didn't mean Whitney and her husband *weren't* struggling; it just meant they weren't compelled to convince others that they were happy. She scrolled to the bottom of the most recent picture of the couple, looking to see if Whitney's husband was tagged. He wasn't. That meant one of three things: she'd *never* tagged him, he wasn't on Facebook, or he'd removed the tag, severing his ties to her. Considering the charges against Whitney, the last option was not unlikely.

If they weren't having troubles before, they certainly would be now.

At the sound of the door at the other end of the partition swinging open, Allee fumbled to close the app and pocket her phone. This was her first task as Marko's employee. She wasn't about to screw it up. She needed to show her value from the get-go.

28

ALLEE

Whitney entered the meeting room a shell of the woman Allee had known briefly years ago, back before Allee had gone to prison. Her eyes were red-rimmed, with purple bags clinging to them. The green threadbare jail jumpsuit hung from her frame. The overhead lights cast shadows beneath her high, sharp cheekbones, giving her a ghoulish appearance.

She shuffled inside, her legs and arms chained just like Marko's had been. The chains were the same size, Allee could only assume, but on Whitney's gaunt frame they looked so much bigger, seemed so much heavier. It hadn't been all that long since Allee was sitting in the same seat, looking out from the other side of the glass, wondering if she'd ever see freedom again, but this woman looked pathetic.

Allee was reminded of the tattoo scrawled across her back, inked by her last prison roommate: "Girls are caterpillars when they live in the world, to be butterflies when the summer comes; but in the meantime we are grubs and larvae." It was another quote from *Carmilla*. She and Whitney had few similarities, but right now they were women living in a dark world, and like grubs digging around in the dirt, with each passing day, it seemed less and less likely that their summer would ever come; that they would ever find their wings.

"Thirty minutes," the jailer said, returning Allee to the business at hand. He eyed her suspiciously, like he still couldn't believe she was working for Marko. Which was fair. Allee had entered the jail with that plan in mind, but even she could hardly believe she'd pulled it off.

Allee nodded. The jailer left.

Whitney flinched when the large steel door slammed closed behind the jailer. "I'll never get used to that," she said as she lowered herself onto the stool. "What are you doing here?" she asked without preamble.

"Hello to you, too."

"I'm sorry." Whitney lifted a hand to brush a strand of curly brown hair away from her face, the chains rattling. "This place is getting under my skin." She looked around, her gaze settling on the camera mounted in the corner of the room. "Thanks for coming."

"It's not a social call."

"I didn't think so." She paused, pursing her thin lips. "So, why are you here?"

"I'm working for your attorney."

Whitney's eyes widened in surprise, but the expression disappeared as quickly as it had come. "I thought you were working at The Yellow Lark."

"I was—technically, I still am—but I'm going to quit once I leave here."

"That's good."

"Your attorney asked me to stop by." Allee spoke before Whitney could start questioning her about the restaurant. She didn't want to get side-tracked, and she didn't have time for Whitney's fixations. They only had thirty minutes.

"Why? Who is my attorney?"

"Marko Bauer."

"Is he any good?"

Allee lifted one shoulder and let it drop. "He has been in the past."

"But he isn't anymore?"

Again, Allee shrugged. "He's represented me before. I ended up in prison."

Whitney's eyes widened.

"I can't blame it all on him. I didn't do myself any favors. I was addicted to drugs, and I wouldn't listen to him. That was a mistake—one I suspect you won't be making."

"I don't do drugs."

"I know that. If you were a user, I would know you much better." Allee didn't say it, but *like I knew your brother* hung between them, filling the silence with his ghost. "Anyway," Allee continued, "Marko wanted me to tell you that he's tied up, but he'll be here as soon as possible."

"Can he get me out?"

"Doubtful." Allee was no lawyer, but she'd seen the inside of plenty of cells and spoken with enough attorneys to understand the law well enough to know that any bond set would be too high for Whitney to post.

"Have you heard from my husband?"

"No, but he doesn't know we're representing you," Allee explained. And even if he did, she doubted he'd call them. "He's probably in shock right now, what with your being accused of hiring someone to kill him."

Whitney shook her head. "I can't believe this! How? How did this happen?" The words sounded genuine. Attorneys rarely counseled defendants to take the stand because there was too much risk, but if she spoke like that to a jury, they might believe her.

"I will talk to your husband, but first, I need to know who 'LP' is. Do you have a student with those initials?" Allee was no lawyer, but she knew Marko wouldn't learn the kid's identity until the prosecutor filed the Trial Information and the attached Minutes of Testimony. The Trial Information, a formal charging document, would include the formal charges, allegations, and case number. It was public record, so it too would contain only initials. But the Minutes were not public record, would not be redacted, and would contain the full name and address of every victim and every known witness against Whitney, including information for the co-conspirator juvenile. The State would have up to fifteen days to file it, but Allee didn't want to wait that long to start her investigation.

"There's probably several kids with those initials. Let me think." Whitney was silent for a long moment, eyes closed, then they popped open. "There's Lucy Peterson."

Allee pulled her phone out and typed the name into the "notes" tab. She'd have to remember to bring a notepad when she returned. Typing on her phone was slow-going, and she quickly tired of squinting down at the tiny screen.

"Does Lucy have a problem with you?"

Whitney shrugged. "Not sure. She's a good student, but she's one of those kids who expects straight A's. She works hard, but I grade on a curve. All the kids know that there are only a few kids who get that top grade. Last semester, Lucy wasn't one of them."

"Okay." Allee typed *bitter over grades* next to Lucy's name. "Anyone else?"

"Um, there's Leon Pena."

"Why doesn't he like you?"

"He's the opposite of Lucy. He hates school, doesn't want to be there. We do everything we can to keep him from dropping out."

Allee could relate. She wished someone would've worked for her like that. She had to ask. "Is Jose Pena his father?"

"Yeah."

Allee nodded. She knew Jose well from back in the day. He was a drug dealer—a good one, one of the higher-ups who always found a way to skirt the law. He was known as an enforcer on the streets. Any bill unpaid led to a meeting with Jose's two pit bulls, Tzar and Tyrant, and the potential for a meeting with his nine-millimeter automatic. With a father like that, Leon didn't have much of a chance.

Allee typed in the kid's name and put *drugs* next to it. "Anyone else?"

"There's Luke Price." Allee cringed. It couldn't be a coincidence. "His parents are—"

"Benjamin and Nikki Price," Allee finished. "What's Luke's issue?" She hoped Whitney would just answer the question and spare her the shit about The Yellow Lark. They didn't have the time and Allee didn't have the interest.

Whitney shrugged. "Obviously, you know I have problems with his brother and his parents."

"Clearly."

"Luke's a jock. He keeps his head down in class. He doesn't earn straight A's; he's mostly a B student, but there's nothing wrong with that."

Nothing wrong with it. Allee's mother would have done a dance if Allee had brought one B home in high school. "All right." She typed Luke's name into her phone and wrote *Yellow Lark* next to it. "Any other LP names?"

"Not that I can recall right now. I'll keep thinking." Whitney's eyes shifted around the room. "I've got plenty of time to do that now."

Allee nodded and stood. She'd achieved her goal in telling Whitney that Marko was coming soon, and she'd gathered some information. It was time to get out of there before they got sidetracked focusing on Jaxson. She stood.

"Where are you going?" Whitney asked.

"I'm going to get working on this." Allee pointed to her phone screen. "Like I said, Marko will be here soon."

"Okay," Whitney said, but she wore the look of a deer with a truck hurtling toward it.

Allee pressed the silver button.

"You done?" The jailer's voice came through the intercom.

"Yes."

"I'll be there to get her in a minute."

Allee turned back to Whitney. "Hang in there. It'll be all right."

Then she turned and walked out. Her door was not locked. She was not a prisoner. As she made her way down the long hallway that would lead to the free world outside, she wondered if there was any truth to her words. Would Whitney be "all right"? Was anyone stuck in the system ever all right?

29

MARKO

"Marko Bauer, I presume." The magistrate was a thin woman with a reedy voice. She had a blonde pixie haircut, a hawklike nose, and beady eyes set deep on either side of that beak.

She was pleasant, the type who was probably a damned student body president, first in her class, and all that shit. Marko wiped his sweaty palms on his jail jumpsuit and took a deep breath to calm himself. He was in a small room in front of a computer screen, the jailer hovering a few feet away, and the magistrate—who didn't bother to introduce herself—was on a computer somewhere. Good thing he was appearing by video; with a nose like that, she could probably smell fear. "Yes, Your Honor."

"You've been charged with operating while intoxicated, a serious misdemeanor."

Marko nodded.

"You're a lawyer, right?"

"Yes."

"Then you know your rights. Will you waive an advisal, or do you need me to read them to you?"

"I'll waive."

"You also know the penalties for operating while intoxicated, right?"

"Yes."

"If convicted, you'll face up to a year in jail with a mandatory minimum of two days in jail and a fine of one thousand, two hundred and fifty dollars. You will be required to obtain a substance abuse evaluation and follow through with all recommended treatment." She looked up and leaned closer to the camera. "I don't know you, but I'm going to go out on a limb and say that judging by the time of day and your apparent fall from grace, you probably need treatment, Mr. Bauer."

Marko fought the urge to roll his eyes. Who the hell did she think she was? Her job was to judge actions, not people. He'd never had an OWI before. That was proof he had a handle on it. "Yes, Your Honor."

"You have no criminal history, I take it."

"No."

"I'll release you on your own recognizance."

"Thank you, Your Honor." Marko issued a sigh of relief. It meant he wouldn't have to meet with a pretrial release officer, which would have been a pain in the ass, and he didn't have to post a bond.

"See to it that you stay out of trouble. I'll set the preliminary hearing in a month or so. I presume the prosecutor will file the Trial Information before then."

Marko nodded. The screen went black, and he turned to the jailer. *Let's do this.*

It took an hour for the jailers to out-process him. When he was finally free, he walked out the side door used for releasing inmates, then around the building and through the front door to the desk.

"Did you forget something?" the woman at the reception counter asked.

"No. I'm here to see a client."

"Who?"

"Whitney Moore."

The woman narrowed her eyes, like she thought he was up to something.

"Trust me." He lifted his hands in surrender. "I don't want to go back in there either, but I need to see my client."

"Fine," the woman said, pressing a button on her radio and mumbling something into it. She turned her attention back to Marko. "The jailer will be here in a few minutes."

A few minutes stretched into ten by the time the same jailer with the large nose appeared, opening the heavy steel door to the jail. "Not tired of me yet?"

Oh, Marko was tired of him, all right. Sick of him, in fact. But the jailer and Marko both knew Marko wouldn't say what he thought—agitating jailers was a great way to earn long waits to see future clients. The power of the drone bureaucrat.

While Marco remained stoic, the jailer led him to the attorney-client room in silence. Marko sat down on the side of the partition opposite where he had been an hour or so earlier, and the jailer disappeared again before returning with Whitney.

Unlike most female teachers Marko had known, Whitney Moore did not radiate warmth. She was in her thirties, well-groomed, with long, dark hair, and bright, light skin. She was pretty enough, but there was a hard edge to her.

"You're my attorney?"

"Yes. I'm Marko Bauer."

"I met your investigator."

So, they were skipping the niceties and getting straight to business. "You met my driver."

"Why would you send a driver to talk to me?"

It was a good question. But now was not the time. "Never mind." Marko waved a dismissive hand, thankful he was free from the weight of the chains. He didn't wear them long, but he would never wear them again.

"I don't understand. Is she a driver or is she an investigator?"

"She's both, I guess," he said with a sigh. "I just hired her today. We've got some kinks to work out with her employment."

"I see."

No, you don't. But he wasn't going to tell her the full story. No way.

"I didn't do this," Whitney said, unprompted.

"I see," Marko said.

"No, you don't. Someone is framing me."

If he had a dollar for every time he'd heard that phrase, it would pay for the first few weeks of Allee's salary. "Your husband?"

Whitney bit her lip. "I don't think so."

"Is he having an affair?" Framing his wife for conspiracy to commit murder wasn't the traditional way to get rid of a wife; that usually involved divorce or murder on the husband's end, but, if true, it would be creative. He'd get all the money, child custody, and she'd be sitting in jail rather than the other way around.

"I don't know." Whitney looked down at her hands, fingers intertwined and resting in her lap. "I don't think so."

"Have you ever suspected him of cheating?"

Whitney shrugged. "Not really, but who knows? People have affairs every day."

It was an odd answer. "Were *you* having an affair?"

Whitney scoffed. "No. I don't have the energy for that. I'm a schoolteacher and a mother. When I'm not working, I'm with Arlo."

Her voice broke on what Marko assumed was her son's name. He watched her closely, searching for a tell. He saw none. Her emotion seemed genuine, but he didn't know her well enough to decide. Marko produced a notepad and wrote *Stepping out?* Then he looked up. "I'll look into it." Maybe that was something Allee could do. When he was a young attorney, he was fine with tracking down witnesses and interviewing them. He didn't want to do that anymore.

"Okay."

"In the meantime, you'll need to sit tight."

"I won't get out?"

"No."

"But I didn't do this! And what about Arlo?"

"Jails and prisons are full of people who say they didn't do it," Marko replied, ignoring the question about her son. Considering the present allegations, social services would not allow her to see him unsupervised even if she were out. Life was not going back to the way it was for Whitney. Not ever. But now was not the time to bring that to her attention.

"But I really didn't do it."

Marko shrugged. "Welcome to the criminal justice system."

Whitney shook her head slowly. "You can't ask for a bond hearing?"

"Sure, I can ask, but that doesn't mean the court will lower your bond," he said. "You've been accused of hiring someone to murder your husband. No judge wants to let you out so you can complete the task."

She leaned forward in her chair. "I. Didn't. Do. It."

"I hear you, okay? But someone wearing a black robe found probable cause to issue the warrant for your arrest. That means, in their opinion, there is enough evidence somewhere to believe that a crime was probably committed, and that you probably committed it. I can't change the law."

"Fine. Whatever." She shifted her weight in the plastic chair.

"You'll have a preliminary hearing soon. Since you are in jail, it has to take place within ten days of your arrest. It's a probable cause hearing."

"I thought you said a judge already found probable cause."

"From the complaint, they did, but now the prosecutor will have to bring a witness in to testify under oath and subject them to cross-examination. This is a hearing just to ensure you aren't being held on some nebulous or specious charge."

"But I am."

She sure was stubborn. "I—"

"Just one witness?"

"That's all they need. The rules of evidence don't apply in preliminary hearings."

"I don't know what that means."

"It means that one witness can testify to everything. All hearsay comes in as long as the evidence is relevant."

"That doesn't sound fair."

Judges weren't in the fair and unfair business. They were in the lawful and unlawful business. Marko shrugged again. "Life's not fair."

Whitney lifted her arms, displaying the chains. "Tell me about it."

There was a long silence, then Marko tapped his pen against his notepad. She had no idea he had been in that exact seat an hour earlier. "I'm going to get working on this," he promised. He stood. He had a raging headache and he'd spent far too much time inside this jail.

"When will you be back?" Whitney asked.

"I'll probably send Allee back if I have further questions." The more he thought about it, the more he thought this whole Allee thing was going to work out well. "I'll see you at the preliminary hearing." He turned and left the meeting room, then the jail. He never wanted to see the inside of that place again.

And now that he had Allee, maybe he wouldn't have to.

30

ALLEE

There was something special about that first, warm ray of sunshine touching her skin and the first intoxicating breath of fresh air inhaled after stepping outside a jail or prison. Allee hadn't been the one imprisoned this time, but she'd been inside for almost two hours, and that was close enough. Seeing Whitney—and, to a lesser extent, Marko—behind bars was a sobering reminder.

Freedom was fleeting. She couldn't go back. She had to watch her step, toe the line, do things right or she was going to find herself looking to Marko Bauer—who had his own problems—for help.

As she walked to her truck, she removed her cell phone from her back pocket. It was new, purchased by her mother after Allee's release from prison. There were only three numbers pre-selected and programmed, and they belonged to her mother, her probation officer, and Nate. Everyone else was in her past and could only lead her astray. She clicked on Pamela's name and the call symbol. The phone rang twice.

"Probation, parole; second judicial district; this is Pamela."

"Hi, Pamela. It's Allee."

"Oh, Allee. I didn't expect to hear back from you so soon. Did you forget something?" Allee could hear and almost feel the trepidation in Pamela's voice. She was expecting bad news. A new arrest, drug use. It came with the job, Allee guessed.

"Remember how we talked about me possibly switching jobs?" Allee asked brightly.

"Yes."

"I would like to do that."

"I explained earlier that you must have a new position before you can quit the old one. You can't possibly have gotten a job that quickly."

"I did."

"Where do you want to work?"

"For Marko Bauer. I'm going to be his investigator and his driver," Allee said. The silence at the other end was lengthy. "Hello?"

"Marko drinks," Pamela finally said.

"So does everyone who isn't in recovery or on bond, probation, or parole. I don't."

"I'm not sure that he can create the best environment for your recovery," Pamela hedged.

Allee had expected this. "I understand why you would think that, but booze was never my thing. Hangovers, nightmares, and all that shit. I don't like it."

"I don't know..."

"I can't keep working at The Yellow Lark," Allee said. "I can't. There is a much higher risk of relapse if I stay there." She waited. "Please." She wasn't above begging.

There was a beat of silence. She was thinking. The lack of a no meant probably. "As long as you agree to start going to NA meetings," Pamela said at last.

"Done."

"Don't make me regret this," Pamela said.

"I won't. I promise." It would be Allee with regrets if things went sideways, of course. She was the one who had to deal with the consequences.

"All right," Pamela said. "Go talk to your boss at The Yellow Lark."

"Thank you," Allee said. She ended the call before Pamela could change her mind.

She almost floated to her truck, the weight of the world seemingly off her shoulders. She unlocked it and hopped inside, humming as she made the short drive over to The Yellow Lark. Nate was in the kitchen on the prep line. He looked at her when she walked in, his eyes drooping with exhaustion and accusation, as in, "What have you done to me?" She almost apologized, almost took responsibility for his circumstances even though she knew none of it was her fault, but Adam Price's entry into the kitchen interrupted them.

"Oh, good, Allee. You're here. I need you to—"

"No."

"No?" Price repeated, his tone hardening.

"Whatever it is you want me to do, I won't. I quit."

"You can't quit."

Allee lifted an eyebrow and crossed her arms. "Why not?"

"It's a parole violation."

"No. Quitting without permission is a parole violation," she corrected him. "I happen to have permission."

"No, you don't."

"Yes, I do."

"Nobody ever finds a different job. No one will hire any of you."

Allee shook her head. "Well, I found the only person who will." She turned her back and started walking to the door.

"You have to give me two weeks' notice."

"That isn't in my parole contract."

"But you *have* to," he whined petulantly.

"You can mail me my paycheck," she said over her shoulder.

"You won't be getting one."

Allee stopped and half-turned back. "I've worked more than two hundred hours," she said. "I *will* get a paycheck."

Adam Price shrugged his skinny shoulders. "What are you going to do about it?" He paused, a sneer forming on his lips. "Take me to court?"

Allee shook her head. He was trying to get a rise out of her, cause her to do something that would jeopardize her freedom. Her reaction would have been different five years ago, before she'd been locked up. She probably would have grabbed the nearest knife and held it to his throat, but she wasn't that person anymore, no matter how much this sniveling little weasel deserved it. She couldn't allow herself to slip back into that person.

Staying any longer was tempting the devil within. She'd held her temper, but just barely. She gave Nate a pitying look, then walked out the back door. She hated to leave him there, but their situations were different. The Prices were his victims; she was theirs.

As she stepped outside the restaurant, she felt the same as she had leaving the jail earlier that day. *Free.* She would never return to that restaurant, not even as a customer. She walked across the street and turned to look at the restaurant. Her eyes traveled to the cheery yellow canary on the sign beside the restaurant name. The bird on the sign wore the same maniacal expression as did the embroidered ones on the uniforms. It seemed to return her stare, and she had the sense that, like jail, the fear of this restaurant still had a hold on her, and that at any moment it could bring everything she'd been working toward to a screeching halt. She shook her head and continued walking to her truck. It was nonsense. A restaurant wasn't at all like a jail. She was being dramatic.

Or was she?

31

ALLEE

The Yellow Lark was literally in her past now, shrinking in the rearview mirror as she drove toward the south side of town. The houses changed with each block she passed, growing smaller, more dilapidated, with ever-smaller yards that increasingly featured old, discarded furniture and tall weeds. A heavy sense of need settled in Allee's chest, constricting her airway. These were familiar playgrounds, and she was on her way to speak with an old playmate. Although she was looking for information rather than a fix this time, her body didn't seem to know the difference. She knew exactly what Pamela would tell her if she knew where Allee was going, who she planned to see. "You are playing with fire," she would advise. "You will get burned."

Jose Pena's house was a small, ranch-style home with an attached garage and a yard wild with weeds that looked exactly as it had five years ago. While his home was better maintained than those around it, it could never be described as "well-maintained." Rather, it simply meant the place wasn't crumbling like the neighboring houses and was in less danger of being condemned by the city. She parked and felt her heart rate triple and her hands grow slick with sweat. It would be so easy to slip back into her old ways.

Maybe he's not home, Allee thought.

She got out of the truck and was nearing the front door when it swung open. *No such luck.* She recognized Jose's hard, dark eyes staring at her, and saw the familiar tattoos on his heavily muscled arms, which were crossed as he watched her. Apparently deciding she posed no threat, he dropped his arms to his sides, a smile slowly forming on his caramel-colored face. "If it isn't one of my best customers, back from her business trip," Jose said. "Or were you vacationing?"

"Vacationing," Allee replied sourly. "In Mitchellville. A real garden spot."

"Well, you're back. That's what's important. I'm glad to see you."

"It's not what you think," Allee said, fighting the urge to return his smile. Jose could be cruel. He could be her downfall even now, but he'd always been kind to her. He sold drugs, yes, but he treated all his paying customers with respect. Those who didn't pay, on the other hand, needed to keep counting their fingers and toes to ensure they were all still there.

"What can I get for you?" he asked.

"I'm clean," Allee said. When he narrowed his eyes, she quickly added, "I'm also not a snitch, if that's what you're thinking."

He stared at her for a long, tense moment, his brow furrowed and his frown deepening. Then it all disappeared, his face smoothing back out. "I don't suppose you are. You haven't been out long enough to get into that kind of mess." He believed her easily, but that was not because he trusted easily. To be working with the cops, she'd have to have new charges. That was the only way the cops would have anything to offer in return for her agreeing to put her life in danger. Snitching was dangerous work. Jose checked the arrest records daily. Her name hadn't been on it, so he had quickly concluded she was on her own.

"Then why are you here?"

"I was hoping to speak with your son, Leon."

Jose's eyebrows lifted. "Why?"

"I'm working for Marko Bauer—you know the guy?"

A look of surprise flitted across Jose's face. "He's represented some of my people a time or two. He's also been a customer a time or two," he added with a smile.

"Well, he's representing Whitney Moore," Allee explained. "She's that teacher accused of hiring a hitman to kill her husband."

Jose scoffed. "Hitman. She hired a hit *boy*, and that *boy* was always working for the cops," he said. "You wanna come inside?" He held the door open.

"What do you mean? Who is the kid?"

"I'll let my boy tell you. Come on in."

Allee did not want to enter the residence. It would only heighten her desire to use, but she also knew that Jose and Leon were unlikely to talk to her out in the open. People in their world—what used to be Allee's world—were careful about their business. They were used to others stabbing them in the back, trading knowledge for freedom with the cops. Fortunately, Allee had never coughed anyone up, which was the only reason Jose hadn't slammed the door in her face.

The house was cluttered, the same as always. The furnishings were cheap except for a giant flat-screen television and its accompanying sound system mounted on the living room wall. A card table with four metal folding chairs positioned around it served as a kitchen table. The cabinets were outdated. Oddly, all the appliances looked new and expensive. Allee had difficulty imagining Jose at a stove or washing dishes.

Jose motioned for Allee to sit at the table. Then he turned and called down the hallway, "*Leon! Get out here!*"

A moment later, a sleepy-eyed teenager came trudging down the hall-way. "What is it, Pops?" he asked.

"Someone is here to talk to you." Jose's gaze shifted to Allee. The kid followed suit. He looked like a skinnier, taller version of his father. His eyes were softer, of course. Time would fix that.

"What about?" Leon asked.

"Whitney Moore."

"Mrs. Moore? She's in jail. That's what I heard."

"She is," Allee said. "I'm here to talk to you about that."

"Are you a cop or something? I don't talk to cops." His gaze rested briefly on his father, who proudly nodded his approval.

Allee pulled a chair away from the table and sat in it. "I'm Allee. I work for her attorney, Marko Bauer."

"Is it okay, Dad?" When Jose nodded, Leon shrugged. "What do you want to know?" He sat in the chair across from her while Jose leaned against the counter, arms crossed, watching, assessing.

"Anything," Allee said. "I just met her in jail and the criminal complaint doesn't say much. Just that she hired a kid with the initials LP to kill her husband."

Leon scoffed. "And you thought it was me?"

"No. Whitney mentioned several current students with those initials. She says she's innocent. I know your father and I know you go to school where she teaches. I figured you'd be the right place to start if I wanted to get to the truth."

Leon shrugged. "There isn't a lot to tell. I had nothing to do with it."

"You've heard something, I'm sure. Kids talk. You may not know anything firsthand, but surely you've heard rumors about who this LP is that is mentioned in the complaint."

"Yeah. I know." He sat back, crossed his arms. She thought he wasn't going to answer, but then he continued. "Luke Price. That's the LP."

Price. Was she ever going to get away from that family? "What can you tell me about him?"

Leon shrugged. "Not much. We don't hang out. He's a jock; wears leather jackets and goes to football parties. I provide the fun for the parties, but I don't go."

"Why not?" Allee asked.

"Because those kids are dumbasses and sooner or later they are going to get busted," Leon explained. "The less they know about their supplier, the better."

It made good sense in his business. He undoubtedly learned it from his father. Jose had always worked in the shadows, collecting his money, avoiding any socializing with his customers and making no claims to glory or riches. It was smart. The quiet ones were far less likely to become police targets, and Jose's criminal record was clean. "What else can you tell me about him?"

"He's a pussy," Leon said quickly. "No way that kid was going to kill Mrs. Moore's husband. I don't know what she was thinking. She should have come looking for someone like me."

Allee was surprised, given Jose's influence. "Surely you wouldn't have done it?"

"Of course not." Leon snorted. "But I could have led her in the right direction, not to a jock who wanted to play bad boy."

A kid who made his papa proud. "Why do you think Mrs. Moore chose a kid like Luke Price?"

Leon shrugged. "She's a flirt. She's always smiling too much at kids like Luke."

"Has she ever had a relationship with any of the kids?" Allee asked. "I mean, anything you've heard about."

Leon shrugged again. "The jocks talk, man, but most of it is lies. They're always talking about getting with one chick or another. It's mostly trumped-up bullshit."

Some things never changed. "I see. And are the allegations about Mrs. Moore 'trumped-up bullshit?'"

"I dunno. Not my business."

"Okay. Thanks," Allee said, standing. "I think that's all the questions I have for now. Thanks for talking with me."

Leon tried to appear nonchalant, but he was clearly relieved that the conversation was over and that his father hadn't gotten involved. People in their world didn't like questions, not even those posed by a defense team. That hadn't changed either.

Jose walked her to the door. "Let me know when you're ready to taste some of my new product. You've been away for a long time. You're missing out on some good stuff."

Allee swallowed hard. She wanted to taste it now—and right now—but she couldn't. She'd be drug tested and find herself housed right next to Whitney in the local jail, awaiting her parole violation hearing. "I'm on parole. I can't. You know that."

"Parole only lasts so long. Hit me up when you're free," Jose said with a knowing smile. Then his face changed. "But between now and then, stay away from Leon unless you clear it with me first."

Allee left Jose's house feeling a mixture of relief and regret. Would her desire to use ever stop? Was this a fight that would continue for the rest of her life? She didn't think she could maintain it. She had barely resisted. *Barely*. How was she going to make it through the next few years without violating her parole?

32

MARKO

"I have a few drinks here and there just like everybody else, but that doesn't mean I'm an alcoholic," Marko stressed. He was talking with a substance abuse counselor as part of a court-ordered evaluation and was hating every second of it. It was bullshit.

The counselor, a pinched-face woman named Linda, leaned forward. She was somewhere north of thirty and south of forty, but there were premature grooves around her lips from years of smoking cigarettes. "What do you mean by 'a few drinks?'"

"I mean one or two…you know, sometimes more." Sometimes enough to make even her look attractive.

"Ever black out?"

Of course he had. Who hadn't? "Well, yeah. I suppose."

"What did you mean by 'here and there?'"

"I mean I have a social drink sometimes." She was parsing what he said like a law clerk examining an appellate court opinion.

"What about yesterday?"

"What about yesterday?" Marko repeated, sitting back and crossing his arms. If she was going to ask how much he had to drink and when, she was in for a rude awakening. He had no idea. It had been a bad day. It happened to everyone.

"You were stopped in the morning. I believe the reports said eight or so on a weekday. Were you *social* drinking at that time?"

It was just a little hair of the dog. He'd overdone it the night before, and he'd overcompensated. That was it. "I'm not discussing a pending criminal matter."

As directed, he'd proceeded straight from the jail to Community Resources, the place in Franklin that provided substance abuse evaluations for the court and treatment if it was recommended. He'd walked to his car, still parked on Main, to find a bright red parking ticket attached to his windshield wiper and flapping in the wind.

He'd snatched the ticket, gotten in his car, and pounded the steering wheel in frustration. He still had a driver's license for another six days. The suspension would start seven days after his refusal to take the breath test and would be in place for a calendar year. He had to get all the court-ordered shit behind him while he could still drive. Now he knew better. He should have waited; this bitch was getting on his nerves.

"Do you want a drink now?" Linda asked, bringing Marko back to the present.

"You mean, like, *right* now?"

"Yes." Linda leaned even further forward, her head bobbing up and down like a bobblehead giveaway on family night at the ballpark.

"You're annoying me, so yeah, I could go for a drink right now."

She sat back, appearing satisfied. "So it's not just social drinking. You drink when stressed."

There was no question posed, so he wasn't going to answer.

"You have no answer?"

"You never asked a question."

She smiled as if to humor him. "I forget I'm interviewing a lawyer. I probably should be more precise with my questions."

She should.

"So...Do you find yourself drinking more when you are stressed, or when your emotions are high?"

"Doesn't everyone?"

"No." She shuffled a stack of papers in her lap. "You have a very stressful job, Mr. Bauer—no one could deny that. As a result, you experience stress daily. Would you say you drink every day?"

"I drink when I feel like it. Like I said, it isn't a problem."

"Yet you're here." She gestured around the room. It was a small office with cheap, dusty knickknacks covering every available surface. Lots of turtles.

He'd made a mistake. He was trying to get his ass to the jail to talk to the first decent client he'd been assigned in forever. If he hadn't been speeding, he would have made it. "Obviously."

"Here's my problem, Mr. Bauer," she began.

He didn't want to hear her problem, but he remained silent. The quicker she said what she thought he needed to hear, the sooner he could leave.

"You are a lawyer," she continued, writing as she spoke. "You've been working in the criminal justice system for a long time. You know how this works. My evaluation is based on self-reporting and a urinalysis test. You've been out of jail less than twenty-four hours; you knew your UA would be positive for trace amounts of alcohol. The rest is self-reporting, which requires honesty." She looked up at him to emphasize what she was going to say next. "Let me be blunt. I don't think you've been honest with yourself, and you certainly haven't been honest with me."

He could give a rat's wet shit what she thought. "Your point?" Marko asked.

"My point is that I'm going to recommend extended outpatient treatment."

She had to be kidding. He hadn't lost his job, or a relationship. He had no prior criminal record. "What? I don't meet the criteria. I haven't lost—"

"That's my exact point," Linda said, leaning back in her chair. "You *know* the criteria. Therefore, you can—and I believe you have—taken steps to minimize your scores on my evaluation. You are being deceptive; in effect, you're using this evaluation to fuel your addiction, and I won't allow it."

"I don't believe this," Marko said, shaking his head. "I don't have time for treatment sessions."

Linda's stony expression did not soften. "You had time to drink."

Marko shook his head and stood. "That was before and after work," he said. "I mean, *after* work." Christ, he couldn't believe he said that. "You're going to ruin my life!"

"You have a decision to make, Mr. Bauer. I know what's going in my report."

There were plenty of people who got away with a lot of shit while out on bond, or even on probation or parole. But judges got really pissed when people missed treatment. This was going to be a pain in his ass. "Fine," he said at last. "When is my first session?"

"Tomorrow at nine o'clock."

Marko stood quickly, making his way toward the door, his mind reeling. How could he get himself out of this mess? He didn't want to go to treatment. He wanted everyone to leave him alone. He wanted a drink.

"I'll see you tomorrow," Linda added.

Marko waved a hand over his shoulder, but he did not look back. He continued down the stairs and out the front door of the building. He really had no time for this. He needed to focus on Whitney's case. It was his big break, his chance for larger, more important cases, and people were already screwing him over.

33

ALLEE

Allee pounded vigorously on Marko's front door, her knuckles cracking against the cheap wood.

She had called him on her way from Pena's house. Marko was supposed to have called her when he got out of jail, which of course he hadn't, so she had tried him. There was no answer on her first two tries. He finally picked up on the third try, sounding off. At first, she couldn't identify what was different about him. His words were tight, clipped, like he was barely holding them together. Perhaps he was tired, she'd thought. He wasn't used to jail, after all. But as the conversation continued, his enunciation failed, and words began to merge. By the time he gave her his address, she'd barely been able to understand him.

It took her an hour to get to his house. An hour! That was information he'd failed to include when he'd said he needed a driver. He didn't live in Franklin. He lived in a Podunk town straight south of Franklin. It wasn't a lie, but it was an omission. She'd assumed, incorrectly, that since he practiced in Franklin, he must be a local attorney. She had no way of checking his home address—attorneys' home addresses remained private on request —but he should've told her. He'd had every opportunity to inform her, to tell her she could walk away, but he hadn't. She probably wouldn't have walked away—she hated working at The Yellow Lark that much—but still.

She had seethed the entire drive, alternately gripping the steering wheel tightly and flexing her hands. He was drunk already. She could hear it through the phone. He was drunk and she needed him to be sober. Only a few hours had passed since his release from jail and he was already letting her down.

"Marko!" She hammered the door again. "Open up!" Was he passed out? Was he okay? It would be just her luck to quit a job only to find out that her new employer had died of a freak alcohol-related accident.

"I know you're in there!" She glanced over her shoulder. If a neighbor heard her, they'd probably call the cops.

Marko's house was small, quaint. The houses around it were the same: single-story ranches built to house middle-class families. Fortunately, he didn't live in one of those expensive neighborhoods where the inhabitants were rich and bored, wasting their time gossiping and spying on neighbors. "Neighborhood watch" was just another way to say "neighborhood nosiness."

"Open up!" Allee kicked the door, and it rattled within its frame. That did it; she soon heard a shuffling sound inside, but she didn't let up. Instead, she began to bang with her fists in rapid succession, one after the other. She didn't want him to pass out again before he opened the door.

Finally, the deadbolt clicked, and the door opened a crack. She thrust out a hand, shoving it the rest of the way, pushing against Marko's weight and forcing her way inside. The house was almost dark, with two bare bulbs illuminating the living room, which was furnished with only a ratty faux leather couch and a faded plaid chair.

"Jesus! It smells like a skid-row bar on Monday morning in here!" she said, scrunching her nose. The air was dense with a heavy scent of stale beer and something sour that she hoped was rotting food, not vomit. She would drive Marko around. She would help investigate his cases. She was not his nurse. That was where she drew the line.

"Well hello to you, too." Marko stumbled backward, unsteady on his feet.

"You're drunk!" Allee said, eyeing him. "I knew it. You left jail and got drunk."

"I left my substance abuse evo—er, evanlue—"

"Evaluation."

"That's it," he said. She heard, *Thatch chit.* "And then I had a drink or two," he continued, holding up two fingers. "They want me to do treatment. Me. Can you believe that?"

She stared at him. He was wasted at four in the afternoon on the evening of his arrest for drunk driving. Yeah, she could believe it. "So you left there to come here and drink yourself into a stupor?"

"You don' unnerstan," Marko said. "I'm saying goo—goodbye to it."

He was making excuses, giving himself permission to do what he knew he shouldn't. It was a telltale sign of addiction; Allee had learned that through her years of treatment inside the walls of Mitchellville Prison. She understood him because she'd been there. She was still there, albeit a little further on the other side.

An hour earlier she was at Jose's place, thinking shit like, "One time can't hurt," and "Pamela won't catch me if it's just once." But it never was just once. The dragon was always waiting, and "once" was an excuse that would lead to another excuse, like, "This is my last time," and "Never again," and "Relapse is part of recovery," and so forth and so on until she was back in the can.

"Sit down," Allee said, pointing at the couch.

Surprisingly, he didn't argue, but trudged toward it and flopped onto his side. "I'm sorry," he mumbled.

It was the first time she'd ever heard him apologize.

"I just..." His voice trailed off.

Allee went around the room, unlatching and throwing open windows, welcoming the light breeze and the accompanying feel and smell of soft, clean air as it forced its way through the stuffy house.

That's better, she thought. She turned to Marko, who was already asleep and gently snoring on the couch. She quickly scanned the room, her gaze settling on a blanket piled on the floor in a corner. She grabbed it, smelled it, and—finding it only moderately foul—tossed it over her new boss and stared at him.

What was she going to do with him? He had to get his shit together. She needed this job. She was depending on him now. There was only one thing to do: she had to cut him off. As a recovering addict, she was well-versed in the behaviors of addiction. Hers was drugs, but alcohol wasn't that different. It, too, was a mood-altering substance.

First, she needed to find the booze. All of it.

She started with the kitchen. The refrigerator was empty, aside from a bottle of ketchup that had expired six months earlier and a twenty-four pack of cheap beer. She tossed the ketchup in the trash and got to work cracking open each beer and pouring it down the kitchen sink. The liquid seemed to protest, gurgling and gasping and fizzing as it seeped out of sight. She opened the window above the sink to dispel the yeasty smell of the beer.

She then turned to the cabinets. They, too, were empty of food aside from a box of dried noodles that upon closer inspection turned out to be empty. She threw the box in the trash. The last cabinet she checked was packed with booze—probably hundreds of dollars' worth of a discount brand, meaning that he'd been driving the ninety minutes to Des Moines to get the warehouse sizes.

Once every bottle and can had been poured down the drain, the empties lined up along the counter like captured soldiers facing an enemy firing squad, she turned her attention to the other rooms. She found one half-empty bottle of bourbon behind the television in the living room and multiple smaller bottles of vodka shoved between cracks in the chair cushions. She searched the couch cushions around Marko—who was still out cold—for more.

She continued searching the entire house, collecting every tiny, single-serve, so-called "airplane" bottle hidden around the residence like a participant in an alcoholic's Easter Egg hunt, but in lieu of a wicker basket, she used a plastic bag she'd found under the sink to collect her trophies. After dumping each down the drain, she loaded the dozens of empty bottles and cans into the trash bag and slung it over her shoulder like the sobriety Santa, took it out to her truck, and tossed it into the bed.

Returning to the house, she searched his pants pockets until she found his keys and put them in her own pocket. She didn't need him driving drunk to get more booze. She found a pad of bright yellow sticky notes and a pen, and scrawled, "Call me when you finally wake up," then printed her name below that. She walked over to him, pried open one of his closed fists, and placed the note inside it. When she released his hand, his fist closed around it and dropped back onto the couch.

With all that done, she left. They had work to do, but Marko wasn't in any condition to do any of it. Tomorrow would be better. It had to be.

34

ALLEE

On the long drive back to Franklin, Allee considered what to do next. She could go home, where her mom would spend the rest of the afternoon and evening nagging Allee about why she wasn't at work.

Whitney's address was listed on the criminal complaint in a section dedicated to the defendant's address, date of birth, and other personal information. Allee knew exactly where to look, of course, because she'd spent plenty of years staring at her own complaints, her own ever-changing addresses and phone numbers. She was pleased to see Whitney lived only blocks from her mother in Franklin.

When she was at last back in Franklin, she drove straight to Whitney's address. From the street she saw a small, one-story ranch house similar to Marko's, and likely built in the same time period, but in contrast to Marko's, it exhibited an obvious effort to add character. Bushes lined the front of the house; window boxes were filled with budding flowers. Painted shutters clung to the windows, giving the appearance of thick, false lashes around eyes.

She parked on the street, checked the address one last time, then approached the front door, moving in long, hurried steps—fearing that any delay might result in a loss of nerve. She had no idea how to do this. She didn't like to answer questions; who was she to be pushing this man for information? Holding her breath, she pressed the doorbell and stepped back. She heard movement, then a voice from inside the house.

"Who is it?" a man called. He was just on the other side of the door, no doubt looking through the peephole.

"My name is Allee Smith, I—"

"You're not a reporter, are you? If you're a reporter, I don't want to talk with you."

"No, I'm—"

"You don't look like a reporter."

Allee glanced down at her ripped jeans and prison tattoos. She didn't look like someone who would work for a law office either. Not that Marko had much of an "office." He was a one-man failing operation, a body broken and bloodied, slowly bleeding out. *That's why I'm here,* she reminded herself. She needed to staunch the bleeding.

"What do you want?"

"I work for Whitney's attorney, Marko Bauer. I was hoping you might have a few moments to speak with me about Whitney's case."

After a brief pause, the lock clicked and the door swung open to reveal a man standing before her. He was in his early to mid-forties, she'd guess, medium height, medium build. He had kind eyes with crinkles around the corners and thick, dark hair with flecks of silver.

"Are you Mr. Moore?"

"Yes."

"I'm Allee Smith. I work for Marko Bauer."

"Yeah, you said that." His body blocked the doorframe. He'd opened the door, but he wasn't ready to let her inside.

"I met with your wife this morning."

"Yeah?"

"She's...okay." Allee didn't want to lie to him. She needed to build a rapport, and that required a foundation. She didn't want that foundation to be lies. "She's doing as well as can be expected."

He nodded, then stepped aside, motioning into their home. "Come on in."

Allee thanked him and stepped across the threshold. The house was likely a replica of all the other homes on the street, built in the cookie-cutter housing boom where builders threw up one after another, each identical to the next. But Whitney had found a way to make the home her own, quaint and inviting. The living room had a matching couch and loveseat, each with a handsewn quilt slung over its back. A coffee table sat snugly in the middle with a Joel Sartore photography book featuring shots he'd taken of animals living in the world's zoos and wildlife sanctuaries.

"Let's sit in the kitchen," Moore said.

Allee followed him toward the back of the house.

In the kitchen, he motioned for her to have a seat. "Would you like some coffee?"

It was benign and harmless to others, but for her coffee was still a stimulant. Maybe someday she could drink it, but not yet. She was still too fresh out of prison, too easily sidetracked. Start with coffee and she'd end up mainlining by the weekend. Allee shook her head. "No, thank you."

"Call me Leo."

"Okay. No, thank you, Leo."

The silence was brief but heavy, with Allee gathering the nerve to continue while he stared at her without blinking. She'd never done a job like this, never interviewed people before.

"Just so you know," Leo began, apparently weary of the silence, "I don't think my wife did what they are saying she did."

That's a good start. It was her suspicion, otherwise he'd never had allowed her into the home, but the confirmation was bolstering. "Can you tell me why you feel that way?"

He sighed and ran a hand through his dark hair. "Because...Oh, hell, I don't know," he admitted at last. "We don't have a perfect marriage—nobody does—but we are happy enough."

She'd never been married. All her relationships were hookups—stimulant-fueled chaos—but his manner and the words seemed honest enough.

"She teaches at the high school," he continued. "Kids aren't the same as they used to be. They've always been cruel, but these kids, they're different. They think the world owes them something. They think they deserve straight A's without putting in the elbow grease. Whitney makes them work hard and they resent that."

"You think one of the kids—I'm told it was Lucas Price—made a false accusation as revenge for a bad grade?" Allee wasn't much of an academic when she was young, but she suspected that was a bit of a stretch. Kids didn't care that much, did they?

"Don't get me wrong." He put up his hands, palms facing out. "I'm not saying the kids are bad. I just, well, they're under a lot of pressure. Everyone wants to get into their college of choice—if they are college-bound, that is —and their parents insist they are the best of the best. They are given everything and don't have to lift a finger for it. They don't work anymore to pay for their vehicles; their parents buy them. They don't volunteer out of the goodness of their hearts; they do it to put it on their resume. Those kinds of things, well, they add up. These kids don't know the difference between right and wrong anymore. They just do, want, and ask questions later."

"I see," Allee said, but she didn't really understand any of it. She had no frame of reference. She hadn't spent time around kids that age since she was one of them, and that was a long time ago. Back when they all had jobs, they all pulled their weight. But working in a restaurant had led to Allee using for the first time. There were downsides to working at a young age, but she kept that thought to herself. "Marko wants to get a start on the defense, just so we can stay ahead of the curve." Assuming he ever sobered up.

"I'd talk to the kids—maybe the principal and other teachers. I know some of it, but so much happens over at that school. Teachers receive veiled threats from parents. Kids make off-color jokes that morph through the gossip chain into false facts."

"Okay. I'll do that," she said.

A small boy wandered into the kitchen, rubbing his eyes and yawning. He stopped and stared, startled when he saw Allee at the table.

"Hi there," Allee said, forcing a smile. She didn't know how to talk to kids.

"Who are you?" The boy moved to Leo's side, pressing his small body against his father.

"I work for your mom."

"My mom? Where is she?"

Allee's gaze shifted to Leo. She didn't know how he'd explained Whitney's absence to their son. She didn't want to say anything to mess that up.

"Still gone, son," Leo said.

Tears sprang to the child's eyes. It was time for her to go. She stood. "I better get going." That was all the questions she had for now, anyway. She started making her way toward the door, Leo following close behind. He wanted her out of there.

She reached for the doorknob, but then had a thought. She turned. "I do have one last question."

"What's that?" Leo suddenly seemed tired, as if he'd aged ten years in ten minutes.

"Do you have a life-insurance policy? One where Whitney is the beneficiary?"

Leo nodded. "I do, but it isn't much. I think the coverage is twenty-five grand—something like that. Nothing to kill me over."

Allee nodded, thanked him, and continued out the door. A small policy wouldn't be a solid motive for murder, but she wondered why so small when they had a kid together? Did he keep it small because he suspected Whitney was capable of killing him?

35

MARKO

Marko forced his eyes open despite a crusty seal of sleep. He didn't recognize his surroundings. At least, not at first. He'd fallen asleep plenty of times while sitting at his desk, but never on the couch. It was old and uncomfortable with a spring that forced its way between his shoulder blades.

What the hell? His eyes popped open, wide, wild. He rolled onto his side. Once again, his head was pounding, but this time his stomach soured and sloshed. His head was smoking, but he'd be okay...but Christ, his stomach! He knew he needed to get up and to the bathroom before he could add cleaning up a mess to his growing list of ailments. He was too old for this. He was drinking like a college kid and just needed to stop. As he leaned over the toilet, he decided that he needed a drink to get through this hangover, then he'd take a couple of days off.

When he finished, he wiped his mouth with the back of a hand and flushed the toilet, then noticed a bright yellow, crinkled paper stuck to his pants. He smoothed it and read:

Call me when you finally wake up.

--Allee

Finally? What time was it? He'd call her when he got around to it—she worked for him, not the other way around. He needed to nurse his wounds first. Luckily, he kept a small bottle of his buddy Jack Daniels below the bathroom sink. He crawled over to the vanity and wrenched the door open. He blinked. It took him a moment to register what he was seeing. Or rather not seeing.

Where is it? he wondered, his mind frantic.

It had been there yesterday; he saw it when he was brushing his teeth in the morning. Did he drink it? *Maybe.* He stood on shaky legs and made his way to the kitchen, opening the lid to the trash can. It was empty.

That's weird. The bottle couldn't have disappeared into thin air. Maybe he'd misplaced it.

Oh well, there was more. It was a mystery, but one for later. He trudged over to his bar cabinet, pulling it open. He could almost taste the whiskey on his tongue, feel it burning down his throat, replacing the searing pain in his head with a pleasant fuzziness.

Empty. He gaped, his mouth wide. How could that be? It was full to bursting the night before. A fist of panic pressed into his chest.

Don't worry, he told himself. There was more. He made his way around his small home, searching in every small crack, every tiny cranny where he'd hidden bottles of booze. Gone. Gone. Gone. They were all gone! His heart thrashed, the panic growing and blossoming into something larger, something that filled the room and threatened to consume him.

"Think," he said aloud. "What happened to it all? How could that many bottles disappear overnight?"

Allee.

He grabbed his phone, opened his call log, and pressed on the most recent call. It was still only a number; he hadn't saved her in his contacts yet. Now, maybe he never would. The phone rang twice.

"So, you're up," she said. "I bet your head hurts like a bitch."

"You're fired!"

"You can't fire me. You fire me and you'll be pedaling forever."

Marko gritted his teeth. "Where's my booze?"

"In a sewer somewhere. Christ, with all you had, probably every rat from here to Franklin is wasted."

Who the hell did she think she was? "What? You dumped all my booze?"

"Yup. Right down the drain. I did take the cans and bottles to recycling. Even felons care about the planet."

"I want the money," Marko growled. Iowa paid five cents for every bottle returned at redemption. It wouldn't add up to much, but he wanted every cent back. He'd have to restock. It would cost hundreds of dollars and a trip to the box store ninety minutes away. "And gas money."

"No." Allee's voice was flat. "I'm keeping it as advance payment for work I've done. And before you ask, I'm keeping your keys, too."

"You're...*what?*" He only had a few more days left to drive. He needed more booze, and for that he needed his keys.

"You hired me to drive, so I'm keeping the keys."

"That's theft!" he sputtered.

"Probably more like unauthorized use of an automobile—I have no intention of keeping your car. Besides, really? What are you going to do? Tell the cops that your employee took your keys so that you couldn't drive drunk again even though you aren't supposed to be drinking right now? Because that's what got you into your little criminal mess to start." She gave him a moment to respond, then sighed. "I didn't think so."

"Why are you doing this?"

"Because I need you, Marko. Whitney needs you. And while what you do with your own life would usually be your problem, right now we need your help. Got it?"

Whitney. He'd completely forgotten about her. He hadn't even filed a motion for mandatory discovery in her case yet. He needed to get her case on track.

"While you've been passed out, I've been working," Allee said. "So if you're over your little tantrum, I'll head back over there and fill you in on what I've learned."

Marko lowered himself into his living room chair, his legs suddenly weak. "Okay."

"And by the way, thanks for telling me you live out in the middle of nowhere," Allee said.

"You didn't ask," Marko said with a shrug.

"You should have told me."

"Would it have mattered?"

"Honesty always does."

Marko fell silent. She was right. When she showed up with her proposition to drive him, he'd known the distance would throw a wrench in things, and that was precisely why he hadn't mentioned it. But she'd wanted the job as much as he'd needed her to do it. His mother would have told him to apologize, but hey, they'd both gotten what they wanted, what they needed. It wasn't like his dishonesty had changed anything.

When it was clear he wasn't going to respond, she sighed. "Drink a lot of water. I'll be there in an hour."

He sat back, staring at the ceiling for a long moment. He didn't want water. Fish crapped in water. He made his way to the tiny bathroom and faced himself in the mirror. A felon recently released from prison had better control over her life than he did. He had to pull himself together because Whitney and all his other clients were depending on him. More importantly, his future depended on it.

Water was a start, but he wondered if she'd dumped the hydrocodone.

36

ALLEE

"Why do you do it?" Allee was seated on the floor in what was supposed to be the dining area, with Marko sitting nearby, cross-legged. "Why do you drink so much?"

Marko shrugged. "I guess I don't know what you mean, but I've always liked to have a couple of beers or whatever."

"Okay, I understand a couple, but you're drinking like a high school kid's first time out. What's up with that?"

"I don't know. I guess everyone else slowed or stopped drinking altogether, and I never did. Somewhere along the line it changed from a fun, social thing to an escape."

Allee opened a bag she'd brought from her mother's house, withdrew a plastic container, and handed it to him. "Here," she said. "Breakfast."

He popped it open to find a sausage and egg omelet. "Where did you get this?"

"Does it matter?" She shrugged. "You need the grease." While he cut a small piece with a plastic fork, she continued. "I made it. I got the ingredients from my mom's kitchen—and before you go accusing me of thieving, I'll pay her back once I get my paycheck from The Yellow Lark."

"You haven't been paid yet?" Marko asked. He tentatively placed a forkful of omelet in his mouth, savored it briefly, and then groaned aloud.

Allee wasn't surprised. She was an excellent cook. She'd been a bit worried that she'd lost her ability while in prison, but it turned out that cooking was like riding a bike. A bit wobbly after so many years out of practice, but it was a skill that never quite disappeared.

"Where did you learn to cook like this?"

"I've worked in a lot of kitchens. And I think maybe I'm a bit of a natural."

"I'll say."

It was the first time Marko Bauer had ever complimented her. She didn't expect to get so much pleasure from it, but her cheeks reddened. She knew she shouldn't get too excited about it. He was a drunk, and liable to turn on her any second. She watched as he attacked the food like the starving man he was. Alcoholics never ate right—it ruined the buzz. Judging by the contents of his refrigerator, he'd been on a liquid diet for a while. He lived in Ostlund, where all-night, anytime fast food was not an option.

He took a few more bites. "Why?"

"What? Cook?"

"No. The drugs."

Allee sighed. It was a story she'd always had a hard time telling, but her prison counselor had helped her through it. She needed more counseling—it would be necessary for the rest of her life—but she didn't have insurance or the funds to pay for it yet, so she left that on her mental *goals* list with the hope that she could move it over to *accomplishments* within a few months. "My father just disappeared one day, walked out on us when I was only thirteen. That's when I started working at restaurants. That's also when I started getting invited to the parties thrown by the other employees," she began.

"My mom was stuck in her grief and didn't keep close tabs on me, so I started showing up. I was young, dumb. I had no idea how much alcohol I could consume. One night, I drank too much. One of the men, a guy in his thirties, well, he—" She swallowed hard. It was always hard to say. The words that followed applied to other people, not her. It was a phrase she'd never wanted to attribute to herself. But after countless hours with her prison therapist, she'd learned to use the words. She was a victim, and accepting that yielded strength. "He raped me."

As always, the words triggered visions of that night. It came back to her in flashes. Truthfully—and thanks to the booze—that was all she had. Maybe she should be thankful for that, but she wasn't. His large hands on her, holding her down, ripping at her clothes. A scream twisting up her throat, cut short by an elbow on her neck, a hand over her mouth. She shook her head, dispelling the thought. "I never drank again after that. But I still needed an escape, so..." She shrugged. "Meth."

"But weren't you exchanging sex for meth?"

It wasn't a novel idea, and he wasn't applying it to her alone. So many women traded sex for drugs. They were addicted, they needed it. When the money wasn't there, Allee's body always was. "Yeah, I did. But I justified that, at least to myself, as a choice. I was choosing to trade sex for drugs. What happened to me when I was thirteen, I had no choice in that. Anyway, eventually the stuff got bigger than me. It always does. There are no long-term recreational meth users."

Marko nodded and took another bite of omelet. They were silent for a long moment, then she removed a small bottle from her purse and tossed it toward him. He didn't lower his food or relinquish his fork to catch it, so it hit him in the chest and fell into his lap.

"It's ibuprofen," she said. "Now that you've eaten something, you can take some."

"Why do I have to eat before I take it?"

"I don't know. It's bad for your stomach not to. That's what the prison doctors used to say."

"Huh." Marko opened the bottle and shook two pills into his hand. He stared at them for a long moment, then tossed them into his mouth, swallowing them dry.

They fell silent again, each alone with their thoughts, choosing not to share. Allee's were dark, shifting back to the days when she was young, vulnerable, attacked.

Marko broke the silence. "What's happening with Whitney?" he said. "You said you had information."

Allee told him about her meetings with Leon and Jose Pena and with Whitney's husband Leo, thankful to be on less emotional footing.

"Wow!" Marko said, leaning back so his back was pressed against the wall. "You've been busy."

"Yeah, well, I didn't have anything else to do."

Marko nodded.

"So, what now?" Allee wasn't a real investigator. She'd started her investigation where she thought it made the most sense, but she didn't know how to proceed.

"Whitney's preliminary hearing is tomorrow," he replied. "That'll give us some more information."

"Okay..." Allee's voice trailed off. Was this all the help he would need for today? Her job needed to be full time.

"Damn it. I missed treatment."

"Not good."

"No shit. I'm going to take a shower and get dressed," Marko said, pushing himself off the floor. "I've got hearings in Brine County this afternoon. Do you know where that is?"

"Yeah. Brine." There was a casino in Brine. Allee wasn't much for gambling, but Nate loved the roulette tables. She'd driven him there a couple times since her release.

"Good."

He stood and walked toward the bathroom. Allee watched him and wondered if they'd broken through something fundamental today. Her conversation with him about liquor and meth had been the most honest discussion she'd had since her release from prison. If he had enough for her to do, this might work out.

37

MARKO

"I didn't do it," Whitney said for what had to be the hundredth time. It was becoming her mantra: "I didn't do it. That's the truth. I didn't do it."

Like the truth mattered. "That's fine," Marko replied half-heartedly... again.

They were in the courtroom, seated at the defense table and awaiting the magistrate who would preside over today's preliminary hearing. Allee and Leo were in the front row of the gallery behind them. Predictably, McJames had taken this case on and sat at the table to their right. With McJames was a police officer—the same young officer who had stopped Marko a few days earlier—in full uniform. The two were chatting quietly, their voices low and casual, occasionally sharing a laugh.

Whitney leaned into Marko, her long curly hair shadowing half of her face. "I didn't do it," she repeated.

"I heard you," Marko said through clenched teeth.

He was completely sober for the first time in months. He'd had a steady dose of liquor in his system for as long as he could remember. His only break was when he had mononucleosis back in January, and he honestly didn't know which was worse, the illness or the lack of booze. He hated sobriety. He sweated more than usual; everything and everyone irritated him; he had no patience for life. Right now, all he wanted was a drink. Just one. Just enough to take the edge off.

"All rise," a bailiff shouted from the back of the courtroom.

Marko stood and motioned for Whitney to do the same. She struggled under the weight and awkwardness of the chains. He wrapped a hand around her bicep and hauled her up just as Magistrate Leigh Lane entered the courtroom.

While Whitney was charged with a felony that would ultimately end up in district court, all cases began in magistrate court, colloquially known as traffic court. Cases remained in traffic court until the prosecutor filed a Trial Information and a judge on the district court bench accepted it, or until there was a preliminary hearing. If the magistrate found probable cause, it was bound over to district court for further proceedings.

Lane—snidely referred to as "Double-XL" by courthouse wags—made her way ponderously to the bench. She was an enormous woman with thick eyebrows and small, piercing brown eyes. "Have a seat," she said once she was situated.

There was a long pause as she booted up the courtroom computer. A cough erupted from somewhere in the gallery. There were whispers and the creak of benches. Marko didn't have to look behind himself to know the courtroom was filled with onlookers. The case was a sensational one, with all the elements of a newsworthy story: a young, attractive femme fatale teacher; a student from a God-fearing family; a plot to commit a deed that would condemn his soul to an eternity in hell. In the Midwest's Bible belt, this was more than enough to draw a crowd.

"First things first," Lane said. "There has been a motion for expanded media coverage made by a number of media outlets filing jointly, including a request for a live video feed. Does either party object?" Her gaze swung first to McJames.

"No, Your Honor," he said.

She turned to Marko.

Marko stood before Lane had shifted her gaze. "Your Honor," he began, "the defense does object. My client has a right to a fair trial and this kind of media coverage before the trial negatively affects her ability to receive one.

Potential jurors will be exposed to salacious, false details before jury selection even begins."

Marko knew it was a losing battle. Iowa judges were politicians who stood for retention, and there was nothing a politician loved more than a camera watching them doing something. But he had to try. Lane was silent for a moment, her features arranged in a thoughtful expression. "I'm going to grant the motion," she said without explanation after a long, tense pause.

"But—"

"These hearings are public," Lane interrupted, cutting him off. "The public has a right to know what goes on."

Marko opened his mouth to respond, but she spoke before he could.

"If you disagree with my position, depending on what happens today, it will either become a moot point or you can take it up with the higher court," Lane ruled, leaving no room for negotiation.

She was alluding to today's hearing, at the conclusion of which one of two things could happen. Most likely, after hearing the evidence, she would find probable cause and bind Whitney's case over to district court to schedule hearings in preparation for trial there. Alternatively, she could find there was no probable cause and dismiss Whitney's case, which sounded good but wasn't necessarily a win, as dismissals were "without prejudice"—meaning the prosecutor could turn around and refile the charges.

Having made her decision, she looked to counsel. "Is the State ready to proceed with the preliminary hearing?"

"Yes, Your Honor," McJames said.

"Call your witness."

"The State calls Officer Bryant," McJames said.

The young officer seated at the prosecution table stood and made his way to the bench. He remained standing while Lane administered an oath. "He's your witness," she said.

"Thank you," McJames said.

"Who is that cop?" Whitney whispered. "I don't recognize him. Does he even know anything about the case?"

"It doesn't matter," Marko advised under his breath. "He's just there as a placeholder. McJames doesn't want to subject his primary officers to cross-examination this early in the case, so they've called the witness they are least likely to call at trial."

He'd been over this with her. The Rules of Evidence did not apply in preliminary hearings, meaning hearsay was admissible. This officer could testify to all information known to any officer within the police force.

"I don't like it," Whitney said.

Marko shrugged. He didn't know what to tell her. It didn't matter whether she liked it or not.

Whitney leaned back in her chair, her urge to fight apparently replaced with defeatism. If she'd ever thought the system was fair, she would quickly recalibrate her opinion. To the layperson, it seemed absurd, but Marko knew better. This was just the beginning of what would be a war comprised of a series of battles between attorneys. Whitney hadn't figured it out yet, but while she might be the subject of the battle, the eventual goal had little to do with her. It was about winning, and neither Marko nor McJames was willing to lose. Whitney was caught in the crossfire.

38

ALLEE

"Officer Bryant, how do you know Whitney Moore?" McJames began.

"She was my high-school English teacher, sir."

Allee started in her chair, caught off guard. She had expected the prosecutor to jump right into the facts so he could bring the preliminary hearing to a close quickly. That's what every prosecutor had done with Allee's cases and those of her old friends and acquaintances. Prosecutors hated preliminary hearings and tried to avoid them—at least that was what she'd thought.

"When did you graduate?"

"In 2010."

"Did you have a relationship with Mrs. Moore?"

Bryant was taken aback. "What do you mean?"

"Did you like her?"

"She was one of my favorite teachers," Bryant said. "She was *all* the boys' favorite teacher."

"Why?"

Bryant shifted his weight. His eyes met Whitney's briefly, then he returned his gaze to McJames. "Because she paid us extra attention."

Allee waited while McJames stood stock-still, milking a long, pregnant silence. He was dramatizing the story, making the case for the cameras. He wanted to sensationalize the story. Marko needed to object! McJames wanted his voice and image on every news station, showing him fighting for the "good guy." He was using Whitney's case as a tool for his own social status and higher political office. Anyone could see that! It made her want to puke.

"Explain that, please," McJames encouraged at last. "How did she give you extra attention?"

"Well, I remember she'd give us extra credit if we gave her copies of our senior pictures. She hung them up all around the room. She would always talk to us by getting up real close," he added, holding his hands a foot apart. "She'd...flirt."

McJames smiled slyly. "I see. Now, how did the boys feel about her?"

"Generally?" Bryant asked.

"Sure."

"Well...I mean...look at her."

All eyes—including Allee's—shifted to Whitney. Already a diminutive woman, she appeared to be making herself smaller, rounding her shoulders, trying to shrink into herself.

"And?"

"Almost all of us were in love with her," Bryant said. "We'd do anything for her."

"Anything," McJames echoed. He looked around the room until he was convinced he had everyone's attention. "So, tell me, did an investigation open involving Mrs. Moore recently?"

"Yes, sir. It was Friday, April twelfth. The communication center received a call from a concerned mother. She requested that an officer respond immediately."

"Who returned that call?"

"I did."

"Who was the concerned mother?"

"Nikki Price."

She'd known it was coming, but to hear the name aloud made Allee feel queasy again. *The Prices.* She couldn't get away from them. Maybe nobody could.

"What did she report?"

"She said that her son was in a relationship with a teacher," Bryant said.

McJames waited for the murmuring to die down before continuing. "What did you do at that point?"

"Well, I'm a new officer. That's why they have me returning calls, and because this sounded like something important, I asked Mrs. Price to come down to the station and to bring her son."

McJames nodded in evident approval. "Did they come to the police station?"

"Yes, sir. They arrived within ten minutes. By then, I'd talked to the chief, and he'd assigned it to Officer Shaffer."

"What happened next?"

"Officer Shaffer met with Mrs. Price and her son, Lucas. I think he goes by Luke."

"How old is Luke?"

"Seventeen."

"Is he still in school?"

"Yes. He attends Franklin Senior High."

"Who is his English teacher?"

"My understanding is that until her arrest, it was Whitney Moore over there." Bryant nodded in Whitney's direction.

"Were you in the meeting between Officer Shaffer and the Prices?"

"No."

Allee's hackles rose. This was all hearsay, but Marko had already told her he couldn't object, that hearsay wasn't a valid objection in preliminary hearings. Part of Allee hadn't believed him. Part of her questioned whether the booze had fried his brain. But she'd looked it up when she returned home and found that Marko was right. Rules of evidence didn't apply in preliminary hearings. It still felt unfair, but nobody cared what a female, middle-aged, recovering addict thought was fair.

"Was the interview recorded?"

"Not that first one," Bryant said.

Why not? What were they trying to hide? They were in a room capable of recording, so why not record the conversation? All the cops had to do was hit a button, yet they'd chosen not to. There was a reason for it. Strategy behind it. Were they doctoring someone's testimony?

"Okay. What was the nature of that first conversation between Officer Shaffer, Luke Price, and Mrs. Price?"

"Well, my understanding is that Luke was saying that he got involved in something that he shouldn't have gotten involved in. I thought it would be high school drinking, partying, the usual stuff like that, but according to Officer Shaffer, the conversation went sideways quickly."

"Explain that," McJames directed. "How did it go sideways?"

"What I was told was Luke said he was having sex with his teacher."

The mood in the magistrate courtroom seemed to intensify with his utterance of the word *sex*. McJames had the full attention of the gallery. The spectators were riveted by his questions and Bryant's responses, poised and ready to lap up the juiciness of it, like a swarm of mosquitos wetting their beaks through a victim's skin.

Only Allee—and maybe Marko, if he was still awake—were listening critically, looking for holes and inconsistencies in Bryant's story.

McJames had a hand to his mouth as if in thought. "A teacher...would that be Mrs. Moore?"

"Yes," Bryant replied. "From what I read, he said it had been going on for a while, and he needed to come clean."

"Is the Mrs. Moore that Luke was talking about the same Mrs. Moore who is sitting here in the courtroom today?"

"Well, yes."

"Can you describe what she is wearing and where she is seated?" This was done to ensure the State had arrested the correct defendant.

"She's at the defense table next to Mr. Bauer. She's wearing orange jail coveralls."

"Did Luke tell Officer Schaffer anything else?"

"Yes. He said that the day before reporting it—"

"Would that have been April eleventh?"

"Yes." Bryant paused and swallowed hard. "The kid—I mean Luke—said that Mrs. Moore had asked him to kill her husband. He said that she claimed she wanted them to be together, but she needed him to kill her husband first."

This was all wrong, Allee thought. Whitney was not an idiot. No way she was screwing the kid—and even if she was, she'd have to have shit for brains to ask a seventeen-year-old to kill Leo. What would that get her? Twenty-five thousand and a relationship with a teenager? And what about Arlo? That was real emotion she had observed. No way she would kill Arlo's daddy. And even if she could get past all that, why Luke? You're gonna kill someone, you find a kid from a bad family. Someone was lying. She could feel it. It was not Bryant—he was saying all the right stuff—but it was between the lines. Cracks that could open into canyons. But why would Luke lie? What was in it for him?

39

MARKO

"He's lying," Whitney hissed desperately in Marko's ear. She was so close that he could feel the heat from her mouth, the moisture of her breath.

He waved her away, not looking to her, even peripherally. She could have her indignation—he expected it—but he needed to focus on the testimony. He kept his eyes riveted on Bryant, searching for weak spots in his story.

"Did you hear me?"

He waved her off again. How many times did he have to tell his clients that the truth never mattered? *The truth will set you free,* so many of them claimed. That was bullshit. The truth was a work of fiction. It lived as a story, as a thought in a person's mind, intangible as a patch of fog. It hung around, but attempts to grasp it would only lead to empty hands.

"Did the defendant explain to *young* Luke how she wanted her husband killed?" McJames asked, emphasizing the victim's age.

"Yes. According to the report, Luke said that Whitney told him that her husband got off work early on Fridays, around noon," Bryant explained. "The kids at senior high have an open lunch period. She'd asked him to go to her house and kill him."

How? Marko wondered. It was one thing to suggest murder, but quite another to introduce a full plan. Predictably, McJames didn't follow up. He didn't have to. All he needed was a claim there was a conspiracy. He had that now, albeit a loose one based entirely on hearsay. And that was fine with Marko. It was one more hole in the case. If Luke Price's testimony was the bulk of the State's evidence, they were going to be in trouble at trial.

"Did young Luke record his conversation with the defendant?" McJames asked.

"Yes," Bryant said.

As the direct examination wore on, the outrage emanating from Whitney diminished. She sat back in her chair, the fight in her ebbing like a gas burner switched from high to low.

"May I approach?" McJames asked, waving an object to the magistrate to show his purpose.

"Go ahead," Lane responded. Earlier in the hearing, she'd worn a bored, almost disinterested expression. That had changed. Now she—along with everyone else in the small courtroom—was eager to see and hear more.

McJames strode to the witness stand and handed a disk to Bryant. "This disk has previously been marked as State's exhibit one. Have you had an opportunity to review it?"

"Yes."

"What is it?"

"It's a copy of the recording Luke and Nikki Price gave to Officer Shaffer during the interview."

"What is on the recording?"

"It's a conversation between Luke Price and Whitney Moore."

"The defendant?"

"Yes."

"Who made this recording?"

"Luke said he did. He said he always has his phone with him, and when Whitney started asking him to kill her husband, he decided to record her."

Marko doubted *that* was the reason for the recording. His guess was the kid had been bragging about his hookups with the hot teacher and he'd been challenged by one of his football buddies. The recording would have been his proof to play for all the boys in the locker room.

"Is this a clear and accurate depiction of the recording as you remember it?" McJames asked.

"Yes."

"Your Honor." McJames turned back to the magistrate. "I'd offer State's exhibit one into evidence."

Lane's gaze swung to Marko. "Any objection?"

"No objection," Marko said. He would like to object. He would have liked to have had some warning, too. Would have been nice if Whitney had given him a heads-up. This evidence, if it contained what the prosecutor claimed it did, would sink Whitney's defense. But the proper foundation had been laid, and this was the purpose of preliminary hearings: to determine probable cause. It didn't matter if the defense felt blindsided. It wasn't meant to be a fair fight. The prosecutor had come in with full knowledge, and all Marko had was a barebones complaint.

McJames smiled in the general direction of Lane. "May I publish?"

"Yes," she replied.

McJames returned to his table, produced a pair of speakers from his laptop bag, and connected them to his laptop computer. He pressed play. There was a tense pause, then voices emanated from the speakers.

"I don't understand." It was a young man's voice. Luke Price, no doubt.

"It's simple." The voice without a doubt belonged to Whitney.

Next to Marko, Whitney froze, seemingly in shock at hearing her own voice.

"Kill him."

"How?"

Luke's voice was louder, Whitney's more distant, consistent with Luke holding the recording device.

"Leave at lunch," she said. "Go to my house. He'll be there. It's Friday."

There was a short silence.

"You love me, don't you?" Whitney's voice had a strange cadence, like she was forcing words she didn't mean. Which made sense. A woman capable of such treachery didn't have any business using the word "love."

"Yes, but—"

"Just do it!" Whitney urged.

There was a rustling sound, then the recording ended.

"I have no further questions," McJames said, his voice firm and confident.

"Does the defense have any questions?" Lane asked.

Behind him, Marko could hear movement—probably pool reporters rushing to file. Marko looked down at his long list of notes. He had no idea what other evidence the prosecutor might produce. He could question the witness, but there was a very real risk that he could make things worse for his client. The old attorney adage, *never ask a question you don't already know the answer to*, existed for a reason. Lawyers who traversed into the unknown often regretted it.

"No questions," Marko said.

Again, he heard movement. Apparently, Whitney did as well, and they both turned to see what was causing the ruckus.

It was Leo Moore leaving the courtroom, his ears and neck crimson with anger.

What remained of Whitney's fire seemed to extinguish in that moment. Marko understood; they'd heard the testimony and seen the evidence. Whitney would never teach again. Even if Marko could pull off a miracle and keep her out of prison, her degree in education was worthless.

Lane invited no closing arguments—her mind was made up. "I've made my decision," she began. "After hearing the evidence, the court finds that probable cause exists. I doubt that is any surprise to anyone in this room after hearing that recording. This case will be bound over to the district court for scheduling. This hearing is adjourned."

McJames jumped to his feet. Whispers grew to murmurs, which grew to full-throated excitement in the gallery.

Marko did not move. Whitney didn't either. They would wait until the onlookers filed out and the prosecutor was gone, then they needed to talk. First subject on the agenda was honesty. Whitney could lie to everyone else, he didn't care, but not to him. When he obtained information from her, he wanted to stand by it. He would not be blindsided again, or Whitney would be looking for a new attorney. He may not be in the height of his career or in his best mental condition, but he was still an attorney. He had his own problems that had him scraping the bottom of the barrel. He wasn't about to allow Whitney to drag him down any further.

If he withdrew as her attorney, Whitney would be in real trouble. Few attorneys would touch such a loser case.

40

ALLEE

She lied, Allee thought.

That was not surprising to Allee, but she was surprised by her own reaction. She'd been in prison. She'd heard the pleas of the other inmates. *It wasn't me. I didn't do it. They confused me with my sister. I was framed.* But Allee had never believed them. That was the difference. Whitney, she'd believed. She'd thought Whitney was special, better than the rest of the prisoners, jailbirds, and losers Allee had associated with for her entire adult life. But she wasn't.

As Allee came around the partition to the defense table and stood behind Marko, she heard Whitney asking him, "What was that?" They were the only people remaining in the courtroom, aside from the jailer; Marko had asked him to wait at the extreme rear of the courtroom. Allee could hear him whistling the *Rocky* theme song; it was off-key but identifiable.

"I'll tell you what it was," Marko said quietly. "It was your ship sinking."

"That wasn't me," Whitney said, turning in her chair to face Marko and Allee, who was standing a few feet behind him.

"Whitney, everyone heard you talking. It was your voice," Marko said. "Damned sure sounded like you."

"Well, that's not the same thing. Tina Fey sounds and looks a lot like Sarah Palin, but that doesn't make them the same person."

Allee scoffed. By now she thought she'd heard everything, but *someone is imitating me* was the lamest of them all. "You're kidding, right?"

"No. I'm not," Whitney replied. "I heard her. That person on the recording just sounds like me."

There it was. The old "it wasn't me" bit. Allee had used that one herself ten years earlier when she was caught on camera stealing copper wiring from an abandoned house. Copper was worth a fortune back then and the house was empty. Nobody was using it. But abandoned didn't mean deserted. The property owners had been having trouble with vandals and kids using the place for partying, despite the heavy fencing surrounding it, so they'd put up cameras the week before.

It was bad luck, bad timing, maybe a little of both, but Allee had been the first one caught on that fancy camera system. She tried claiming, *that's not me, that's someone who looks like me.* She was much younger, much dumber back then. It was long before she'd gone to prison, before the tattoos, and so it could have been an easier sell, but even back then, no dice. The jury saw through her weak lie and convicted her.

"You realize nobody is going to believe that, don't you?" Allee asked.

Whitney's eyes moistened, the tears building up, ready to spill over. She really was quite striking, even while crying. Allee rarely cried, but when she did, it was ugly. She shed big, intense tears—tears filled with pent-up rage and usually followed by some form of self-imposed pain. Physical hurt to match the roiling mess baking her from the inside out. That was how the tattoos started. She'd been cutting for years, but in prison, she found tattooing. It wasn't counseling that had cured her pent-up rage. It was the tattooing and the discovery of the prison library section dedicated to old horror books.

"Let's take a step back," Marko said, his tone softening.

Whitney's crocodile tears had no impact on Allee. If Bryant's testimony was true—and there seemed to be quite a lot of evidence pointing in that direction—Whitney was a sex offender. There was no worse person in a prisoner's eyes. That was something that had been burned into Allee's mind through her five years of incarceration. *We're bad, but they're worse.* Like every social system, prison had a hierarchy, and sex offenders were the lowest of the low.

"How could someone be impersonating you?" Marko asked, his words slower, softer, absent the disbelief they'd held moments earlier.

"I—I don't know." Whitney's eyes were a deep cobalt blue, wide and wild, like a cornered animal. Her eyes flicked up to meet Allee's, then skittered away.

"You're a teacher," Allee said, walking past Whitney to the prosecution table and placing a hand on the back of a chair. "You're supposed to be smart. Give us a theory. A guess, even." She dragged the chair across the room, the legs making a *thwump, thwump, thwump* sound. She stopped when the chair was in the middle of the table, between Whitney and Marko.

"I've had hundreds of students over the years," Whitney began. "They listen to me talk for a full semester, sometimes more. There's got to be at least *someone* out there who can impersonate me, wouldn't you think?"

If that was the best Whitney could come up with, she was in real trouble. Allee looked to Marko, who was clearly thinking the same thing.

"Do you have any names, anywhere we can start working on your defense?" he asked.

Whitney shook her head. "Sorry. I just...Well, it has to be the Prices, right? Nikki, Benjamin, their boys."

"Have you had a problem with Luke? Did you give him a bad grade or something?" Marko asked.

"No." Tears rolled down Whitney's cheeks. "Luke was a good student. He's been doing well in my class. I've never had trouble with him. Not ever."

She couldn't listen to this. "It's far easier to control young men when you're screwing them, isn't it?" Allee offered.

Whitney's head snapped in Allee's direction. "I wasn't sleeping with him! I don't know why Luke is saying that, but it isn't true."

"So the police officer who had you as a teacher years ago, and Luke Price—they were both lying? You don't take a special interest in the boys in class? Tell me," Allee began, tapping her fingernails against the scuffed wood tabletop, "would any other male students say the same thing?"

Whitney wiped viciously at her eyes. "Fine. I am a flirt—okay? I'll admit to that. I like the attention. My husband works a lot, and I don't get a lot of affection from him. But I would never, *ever*, cheat on him. Especially with a student." Whitney shot the words back at Allee, her voice now coated in venom. "And I don't need to. There's plenty of men who would, you know."

At least she was admitting something, Allee thought. And showing a little spine—she'd grown weary of the Little Miss Innocent bit.

"Okay. We'll take a look at Luke and his family," Marko said, his tone placating. "The question is where we go from here."

Allee stiffened at Marko's words and Whitney did the same. It wasn't what he had said, it was the way he'd said it. They were women, they could read between the lines. What he was really saying was, *now, ladies, calm down.* It had them both ignoring him, their attention focused on one another.

"I don't know," Whitney said, suddenly sounding tired and resigned. "You're the professionals. I know you don't believe me, but maybe you can pretend you do and go through the motions of investigating as though you think I'm telling you the truth? Maybe ask yourself, 'What if she's telling the truth? What if this is a setup?'"

"But we still need a place to start," Allee said. "Who am I supposed to talk to first?"

"All roads lead to the Prices," Marko opined. "But they're not gonna be easy to get to, and it's going to be tough to convince a jury of any wrong-doing on their part."

Allee opened her mouth, but Whitney spoke first. "I know you think that's ridiculous—I get that, but just consider it. I was looking into my brother's death. Everyone else had already accepted he was a troubled man committing suicide. I wouldn't. Nobody could convince me that he hadn't been pushed to that point and I was investigating. The Price family wanted me to stop. They've threatened to call the cops, they've threatened me with trespassing charges. But I was talking to you outside the courthouse. I wasn't trespassing then, and Ben Price knew it. There was nothing he could do about it. Except something like this."

It was far-fetched, but Allee had already conceded to placating Whitney, so she went along with it. "What did you find out about your brother?"

"Nothing."

"You think the Prices want to silence you when you know nothing."

"No. I mean, they don't know what I don't know, but I know they want to stop me before I find anything out and expose them for what they are."

"Which is?"

"I don't know." Whitney shrugged. "But it's gotta be something bad, right? Something where they'd go through all this trouble to create lies and hire an impersonator."

Allee's mind shifted back to the lost thumb drive. She'd had a panic attack looking for it in her truck before, but she needed to suck it up. That drive might contain proof. What kind? Who knew, but she needed to turn her truck inside out if she had to. She couldn't let her fears interfere with her job. She couldn't let her fears result in the incarceration of an innocent person. She had to face her fears and deal with them.

She stood to go. "I think I know where to start."

41

MARKO

I need a drink, Marko thought.

The jailer had taken Whitney to the back elevator, and Marko and Allee were leaving the courtroom, headed to the stairs. Allee said something, but Marko's mind wouldn't process it. He needed a drink. Right now. His notes from the hearing looked like they were taken by his grandmother, trembling words that wormed their way across the page. He could smell himself and it wasn't good. He was sweating bullets while everyone else was wearing jackets and sweaters. His clothes stuck to every place his body had touched the chair.

"Heelloooo?" Allee repeated, waving a hand in front of his face. "Earth to Marko."

"Sorry, what?" Marko asked as they began making their way down the stairs.

"I said, what do you make of it? The things Whitney said."

"The same thing I think in every case."

"And that is…"

"We're in trouble," he said. "But to be honest, that's how the system is created. The prosecutor has all the tools and a head start on the investigation."

"I was talking about Whitney lying to us."

"Everyone lies. Even to themselves." Sure, he was pissed. The recording was a knee to the balls, but that was because he'd been blindsided at a hearing. He was over it. Christ, if he held on to everything a client did to irritate him, he'd be pissed off every second of every day. "It's part of the deal. You ever lie to your attorney?"

Allee ignored the question. "But she's a sex offender."

"*Allegedly.*"

"That doesn't bother you?"

Marko stopped halfway down the stairs and turned to look at her. "No. It doesn't. Listen, that kid is seventeen. He's a high school jock. He's probably been dreaming of getting laid by a woman like Whitney since he was twelve years old. If she'd *allegedly* done it when he was twelve, then yes, I'd think of her as a sex offender, but that's not the allegation here. That Price kid is probably weeks away from his eighteenth birthday. I can guaran-damn-tee you that ninety percent of the men in that courtroom were thinking wistfully, 'How come that never happened to me?'"

"I guess," Allee said. Apparently, it made some sense to her; he could see the hard set of her jaw soften.

They continued down the stairs, neither speaking until they'd reached the front door and stepped out into the whipping Iowa wind. He led the way to his car. She still had the keys and hadn't given them up since the last time he'd had a drink. They got inside, Allee behind the wheel and Marko in the passenger seat. She started the car and eased out of the parking spot.

"Where do you want to go?" Allee said.

Marko used his sleeve to wipe the sweat from his brow. "The way I see it, we've got two things we need to look into."

"And those are?"

"The recording and the kid."

"I thought you said he wasn't a kid."

Marko ignored her. "Whitney is focused on the recording—and I get that. But that's not the main problem. Luke Price is going to testify that Whitney solicited him to kill her husband—that's what is going to get her wrung up," he said. "Sure, he'll identify Whitney's voice on the recording and say that was how the conversation happened, but that will simply serve to bolster his testimony. Because as long as he has credibility, the jury will believe him, and they will use the recording as supporting evidence."

"Do you believe her?" Allee asked.

"It doesn't matter to me, and it shouldn't matter to you."

"Why not?"

"You're on the defense team now, Allee. You need to start thinking like it. This isn't about right and wrong, good and bad. That can be sorted out later in prison, the real world, heaven—or hell, depending on how things turn out—once this is all over. Our focus is not on the truth. Prosecutors worry about that. We focus on process and what they can *prove*. Our goal is to find weaknesses in their case. As I see it, their evidence is solid unless we topple the Price kid. If we can damage his credibility, the recording won't matter. If we can't, well, Whitney better get used to terrible lighting and bland food."

Allee opened her mouth to respond but was interrupted by her phone vibrating against the center console. Once, then twice, three times. Not the cadence of a call, but random, like multiple text messages. Her gaze darted to the phone, then back up to the road.

"Do you want me to get that?" Marko asked. He was trying to explain stuff to her and all she was focused on was her phone.

Allee nodded. "The passcode is 4-5-3-8."

Marko typed in the numbers and the lock screen disappeared. "You shouldn't tell people your passcodes."

"I'll change it tonight if you'd like, but it doesn't matter. There's nothing to see on there."

"Don't you have banking apps?" he asked.

"Hell no. I don't have any money."

She had a point. There was nothing to steal if she had nothing. He needed to talk with the Prices about getting her paid.

"What do the texts say?" she asked.

Marko clicked on the messaging app. "They're all from 'Aunt Linda.'"

He watched Allee's jaw tighten. "Read 'em," she said.

Marko scrolled down to the first message. "I'll read them in order. The first one says, 'Have you talked to Nate?' The second one says, 'I'm worried about him.' Then, 'He isn't returning my calls or texts.' Then, 'Have you seen him?' followed by, 'I hate to bother you.' The last one says, 'I hope he isn't using again.'"

"Me too," Allee muttered.

"This is my Nate, right?"

"Right. Will you send her a text back? Say, 'He's supposed to be working. I'll check on him now.'"

"*Now?* But *we're* supposed to be working." He looked at his watch. 2:09. "We've got hearings in Brine County in three hours."

They were still in Franklin. He watched as she looked at the clock and computer on his dash. "It only takes forty minutes to get there from here," she argued.

Marko wasn't convinced.

"We have time to swing by, don't we? I've got to check on Nate."

"Swing by," Marko grumbled. But then he had a thought. "Nate's working at The Yellow Lark?"

"Yes."

"All right," Marko said. "Let's go." He leaned back in his seat as Allee turned around and headed to The Yellow Lark. Marko didn't expect to find the smoking gun at the restaurant, but there was a possibility they'd find some usable information, and that was enough to quell his doubts.

42

WHITNEY

The nice jailer approached her cell. He was probably about her age, with kind eyes and laugh lines around his mouth. He didn't smile much on the job—there wasn't much to smile about, after all—but he seemed like he was probably happy enough off the job. "You have a visitor," he said.

Whitney stood, moving to the bars. "Who is it?"

"Your husband."

Whitney's heart jumped. "Is he alone?"

The jailer shook his head.

"He has Arlo?"

The jailer nodded. He did smile then, a flash of white teeth that lit up his entire face.

She gripped the bars. "Hurry," she said, pulling at them. She couldn't wait to get out of there, to hold little Arlo in her arms once more.

The jailer unlocked her cage and slid the door open, then produced a pair of shackles. "Sorry, but I've got to put these on you. I'll chain your hands in front, though."

She swallowed hard, not wanting Arlo to see her like this. But she produced her hands, holding her arms with the soft skin of her wrist exposed. They looked like toothpicks, she thought, brittle and weak. He encircled them with the heavy metal chains, then led her down the hallway.

He opened the door to a small meeting room. It didn't have a partition. Leo and Arlo were seated at a desk, Arlo coloring a picture of a giraffe. Blue with pink spots. When the door opened, he looked up, ran to her, and threw his arms around her. She crouched so she was at his level, raising her arms to allow him to slip between her chained arms and her body. He clung to her in a true hug. Not a sideways or backward hug. Tears spilled down her cheeks.

"I miss you, Mommy," Arlo said.

"I miss you too," she whispered into his ear.

They held each other for a long moment, Whitney inhaling the familiar scent of her little boy, trying to lock it into her brain so it would never be lost. She took him for granted, she knew that now. She'd chosen to investigate Jaxson's death instead of spend time with her family. She'd never make that mistake again. If she ever got out of jail, if she had another chance, she would be the perfect mother.

Her gaze shifted to Leo, who was seated with his arms crossed. No indication of warmth there. She stood and guided Arlo over to a chair. He crawled into her lap, and she brought the chain around him so he could snuggle close to her. For a moment, she wondered if he felt trapped, but there was nothing tense about his little body. If he felt trapped, he was trapped in his mother's arms. There were worse places to be. *I know from experience*, she thought, her gaze traveling around the cement room.

Leo slid the picture and the crayons across the table to Arlo, who went back to coloring. "How could you?" Leo asked. When she didn't reply, he pressed. "I was there, Whit. I heard that recording."

"It wasn't me," Whitney said, her voice small.

"It was your voice!" Leo snapped.

"I know. But it wasn't me," she said, looking to the floor. "I can't explain it. I just know I didn't do that. I didn't say those things, Leo. I would never."

He shook his head. "How can I believe that? I want to—I really do. But I don't know if I can." His voice broke, replaced by a muffled sob.

Arlo tensed. Whitney pulled him closer. "You have to," she said, her voice barely above a whisper. "I can't go on if—"

"This is the last time I'm going to come," Leo said.

"What?" Panic fluttered in Whitney's chest. "How will I see Arlo?"

"I'll get a social worker to bring him," Leo replied. "I just—I just can't do this." He gestured around him. "Not when it's me they are saying you wanted to kill."

"A social worker. You're going to leave him with a stranger." It was an accusation.

Leo arched an eyebrow. "You have no right to judge me."

"He is our son!" She kissed the top of Arlo's head. "And I did nothing."

He stood and motioned to Arlo.

"If you leave like this, if you take him..." A sob erupted from her. This couldn't be happening! She couldn't speak. The words would not come. She took a deep breath, then issued it slowly, steadying herself. "When this is all over," she was finally able to say, "when I prove my innocence, this choice of yours could be the end of us."

Leo nodded in understanding. "Fair enough. But if you're convicted, it will be the end as well." Then he took her son and left, shattering what was left of her.

43

ALLEE

This is all my fault, Allee thought as she spun Marko's car around and headed toward The Yellow Lark. She'd been busy focusing on herself, and Marko by extension, and she'd completely forgotten to check on Nate. Now he was...what? Most likely, he'd fallen off the wagon.

"A penny for your thoughts?" Marko was watching her curiously.

"A penny is worthless. My thoughts are not," she said. She could feel his gaze on her, heavy and assessing, but he did not comment. Or apologize. Not that she was expecting the latter.

She drove the speed limit, despite the cloying desire to stomp her foot on the accelerator and speed through town. She couldn't afford a speeding ticket, of course—not with The Yellow Lark holding her paychecks. More importantly, it was a crime and therefore a parole violation. A technical violation, to be sure, but it was a risk she couldn't afford to take.

A traffic light turned, forcing her to slam on the brakes. *Come on, come on, come on!* she thought. She sat there, idling, while no cars passed in the opposite direction. Timed lights were the worst. A waste of time. When the light finally changed, she proceeded, passing a row of dilapidated old buildings, grand in the 1950s, now having fallen into disrepair and crumbling. Then she turned onto Main. She parked in front of the restaurant, and they both exited quickly.

"I'm not going to kiss the ground, but criminy!" Marko said with a wry smile.

Lorna was at the hostess stand. She smiled at Marko while studiously ignoring Allee. "Welcome!" Her voice was too loud, her words overly bright. Looking in each direction, she then leaned forward, lowering her voice. "What are you doing here?" she asked Allee.

"I don't have time for whatever possessive nonsense you have going, Lorna," Allee said. In the short time Allee had worked there, Lorna had kept her distance, but Allee had not forgotten the way she treated her when she'd come to apply for a job. "I'm looking for my cousin."

"A table for two or are you waiting on more guests?" Lorna's voice was too loud again. She glanced left and right. "I'm off in five minutes," she said, her voice barely above a whisper. "Wait for me outside—across the street in the alleyway beside the courthouse—and we can talk."

"You know, on second thought," Marko said, his volume matching Lorna's, "I've got a meeting to catch. Better get something on the go. Thanks for your hospitality." He grabbed Allee's arm and pulled her toward the front door.

"Thanks for stopping in. Come back anytime," Lorna replied loudly.

Once outside, Allee wrenched her arm out of Marko's grip. "What the hell is wrong with you?"

"That hostess," Marko said. "She was trying to tell us something."

"Yeah. Probably that I wasn't good enough to work there."

Marko gave her a hard look, then headed to the crosswalk at the end of the block. Allee followed. "Allee, do you really think that girl—a felon herself—is judging you for also having felony convictions?" he asked.

"Umm, yeah," she snarled. "People can find all sorts of reasons to consider themselves superior. She's younger, prettier, and probably less damaged than me."

Marko was shaking his head before she finished. "Not her."

"How do you know?"

"I represented her father years ago," he said. "A world-class sleazeball. Went to prison for abusing her."

"Physical abuse?"

Marko side-eyed her. "Among other things." The crossing light changed from a red hand to a walking man. Marko stepped into the street.

Allee followed. "If he was so terrible, then why'd you represent him?"

"Everyone needs an attorney," Marko said. "It's a constitutional right. As attorneys, we can't cherry-pick which defendants matter and which don't, or decide which rights matter and which don't. We aren't like cafeteria Catholics. The whole Constitution is equal, including the right to counsel."

"How noble of you," Allee said.

His eyes shifted to her and then away. "I didn't say it was noble. And that's not my point." They made it to the other side of the street and Marko headed for the alleyway beside the courthouse. "The point is that she's got bigger problems. If she's pulling a mean girl routine, there's a reason for it."

"Like I'm too old," Allee said.

"A *good* reason." Marko stopped in the shadow of the courthouse. "And if you're going to work for me, you're going to have to cut the ego and follow leads like this. It could go nowhere, but it might be the lead we need. I can guarantee none of the cops have interviewed Lorna."

Cut the ego. That was rich coming from Marko.

The minutes stretched like hours as they waited in silence, watching the restaurant's front door. A few people entered, but nobody exited. From time to time, Marko looked at his broken watch.

"This is pointless," Allee said after ten minutes. "She isn't coming."

"Psst!"

They turned together to face whoever was behind them. It was Lorna, pushed against the wall at the other end of the alley. They exchanged a look and then walked to meet her.

"How in the hell—" Allee began.

"We didn't see you leave," Marko said.

"I left out the back—like I usually do—so the boss wouldn't suspect anything."

Marko nodded. "So, what's this about?"

"Your cousin is in there." Lorna paused, raking her top teeth across her bottom lip. It was full but chapped and flaking.

Allee studied the younger woman. They were standing closer than they ever had before, and Allee could see the telltale signs of anxiety—and maybe something else. Lorna's long blonde hair had grown stringy at the ends, and her nails were bitten to the quick. There was a shiftiness to her gaze that evidenced paranoia.

"But he's also not in there," Lorna continued.

Allee shook her head. "That doesn't make sense."

"I know," Lorna said. "But it's true."

He's not there, but he is there. It sounded like a riddle. Just the thing a mean girl would do for chuckles, even while Allee was clearly worried about Nate. "Are you messing with me?" Allee growled. "You've been stomping on my foot since we met, and I'm tired of it. I'm sure you know I've done time, and I don't play."

Lorna's gaze flicked to Allee's exposed tattoos, then back to her face. "I was trying to warn you away. To tell you not to apply. I knew Price would hire you. I also knew he'd treat you like the rest of us."

"Which means?" Marko asked.

"Like servants," Lorna spat. "We barely get paid. He only counts a fraction of the hours we are there. He takes any cash tips we earn. It's horrible."

"Why doesn't anyone go to the police?"

"Right. Like they're going to believe our word over the Golden Family's." She pulled a pack of cigarettes from her pocket and shook it, knocking one into her hand. "No way."

The more Lorna spoke, the more her words rang true. Allee had felt the tension inside the restaurant, and she was still waiting for a paycheck.

"Why don't you leave?" Marko asked.

"Where am I going to go?" Lorna asked. "I'm on paper for stealing and drugs. My probation officer says I have to work. I can't quit a job until I have a new one. Who else in this town is going to hire me? Nobody—that's who. And I can't leave town 'cause I'm on paper."

"What about Nate?" Allee said. "What did you mean when you said he's there, but he's not?"

"He came into work, but nobody's seen him leave." Lorna shrugged. "But he's not on the line or in the restaurant. It's like he vanished. It's the same thing that happened to Jaxson," she added. "He'd disappear for days, then reappear all of a sudden. I'd ask him what happened, and he'd get pissed but never come across." She produced a lighter and stuck the cigarette in her mouth, heating the edge to light the filtered cigarette. She closed one eye, took a long drag, then blew smoke straight into the air. "He'd say I didn't want to know. But I did."

"Jaxson Michael. Whitney Moore's brother. Is that who you are talking about?" Allee asked.

"Only Jaxson I know. Then he killed himself, so I'll never know. Unless your cousin starts talking."

"Does Whitney know any of this?" Marko asked.

"Yeah, I told her. I think it was..." She paused to take another drag of her cigarette. "It must have been a few days before her arrest for trying to kill her old man. That's some weird shit, huh? I didn't see that comin'. I didn't think she was the type. She would pick Jaxson up from work all the time. She was one of those "I'm clean, but I'm not judging" people who judge like hell but don't want you to know it. Know what I mean?"

I do, Allee thought.

"Thanks for the information," Marko said, looking at his phone. "I hate to cut this short, but we've got to get going. I've got hearings in Brine County."

Allee had forgotten all about Marko's court that afternoon. She didn't want to go. She wanted to stay and demand to speak with Nate. But where would that lead? Nowhere. If she pressed Adam Price, he'd probably call the cops and find some way to get her arrested. Harassment or something.

Marko handed Lorna his business card. "Call me if you think of anything else."

She stared at the small card for a long moment, then her gaze slowly traveled to meet Marko's. "You represented my—that man."

"Yeah. Sorry about that," Marko said, shoving his hands in his pockets. "It wasn't personal."

"Not to you." Lorna lifted the card so that it was in front of Marko's face and ripped it in half. "I've already said too much." She turned to Allee. "Watch your back with this one," she said, pointing with a thumb toward Marko. "He's as bad as the Prices." Then she turned and hurried back down the alley, away from The Yellow Lark.

They stood there in silence, watching Lorna's slender, retreating form, then headed back toward Marko's car.

"I don't think we'll get anything more out of her," Marko remarked.

"No kidding," Allee said, but her mind was on the flash drive still lost in her truck. What was on it? Was it something that could explain what was happening with Nate? Would it help with Whitney's case? Now she really needed to find it, her addiction be damned.

"A penny for your thoughts?" Marko said, his gaze locked on her.

She had never been sure if she could trust Marko. If Lorna was right, she shouldn't. But Lorna was no choir girl. She had theft convictions, crimes of dishonesty. She might have been fabricating the story about Jaxson and Nate. Still, Allee was going to keep that flash drive a secret. At least until she knew what was on it.

"Already told you, my thoughts are—"

"—worth more than a penny," Marko finished. "I forgot."

"You're learning," she said. "Who says that, anyway? Now get in, hang on, and shut up, and maybe we'll get to Brine County in time for your hearings."

44

MARKO

The drive to Brine County felt much longer than forty minutes. Allee was lost in thought. Every time Marko tried to start a conversation, she'd either ignore him or give a one-word response. In the silence, Marko's mind strayed to his empty liquor cabinet. Would one drink really hurt? This was the longest he'd gone without alcohol since he was twenty-one. He felt strong now, like he had a handle on it. He could admit now that he'd been out of control before his arrest. But now he was feeling much better. It wasn't a problem; it was a slip-up.

"Don't you need to work or something?" Allee asked, looking at him with disarming clarity, like she'd seen into his thoughts and known that he'd been craving a drink.

"Do you ever mind your own business?" he asked. "Or is there something that makes you want to tell me how to run my business or my life? You're like an overbearing mother."

"You *are* my business. You're my boss, and I need you to keep your shit together so you have the money to pay me. I'm not doing this for free," she explained. "And I'm no mother—and never will be."

"Why not?" Marko asked, truly interested.

"Well, for one, I'm no spring chicken, and my life's a mess. Besides, I can't be responsible for someone else's life. Look at Nate's situation—I can't even keep track of him."

"That's different," Marko said. "He's an adult."

"Arguably." She shrugged. "And for the record, I'm not interested in being your mother or anything else. That would require me to focus on *your* needs, what is best for *you*. I'm not worried about *you* except that you keep your law license. I'm worried about *me*. I need to get paid. You need to practice so you can pay me."

"Right," Marko said with a sigh. It was simple enough. He removed his laptop from its bag and balanced it on his knees, waiting as it powered up. Then his cell phone started ringing. It was a restricted number.

"This is Marko," he said as he brought the phone to his ear.

"Marko. It's Nikki. Nikki Price."

"Nikki." His gaze cut to Allee, who shifted in her seat, listening. "What can I do for you?" He wanted to ask why she was calling, but he knew she'd find that offensive and he couldn't think of another way to say it.

"You're representing that—that woman, I hear," Nikki said.

"I represent lots of women, Nikki."

"You know who I mean. That woman who took advantage of..." She made a sniffling sound. "I'm sorry...this is hard." She paused, and he imagined she was dabbing her dry eyes with a tissue.

He waited. She hadn't changed. She was still the same self-centered teenage girl he'd once known so well, wanting him to comfort her. Well, that wasn't going to happen now. He wouldn't; he couldn't. Not that he would if he could. Whitney was his client. Nikki would have to go elsewhere for sympathy.

"How can I help you, Nikki?" he asked at last. "What do you want from me?"

"I don't want you to represent her," she said. Her voice was now strong, like she hadn't been crying at all. She probably hadn't been.

"I can't do that. The court appointed me," he explained. "I've got to see this through."

"But she's guilty. She manipulated my child. My child!"

"I know you believe that, but—"

"She sexually assaulted my son! If that's not enough, she tried to talk him into committing a cardinal sin! Murder! If she'd had her way, my Luke would be in prison for the rest of his life, his soul condemned to hell." The crocodile tears were back, he thought.

"I—"

"And you don't even care," she said accusingly. "You're going to just keep...representing her, trying to get her out of this mess she created."

"Yes," he said with a sigh. "I'm going to do that. It's my job."

"Well," Nikki said, her tone catching an edge, "good luck. By the way, I heard you were arrested for driving drunk."

Marko turned to Allee. His phone was not on speaker mode, but the car was silent enough and the volume was loud enough that she seemed to have been tracking the conversation. She fished in her pocket, pulled out her own phone, and clicked a few buttons, her eyes darting between the road and the little screen. "*Turn it on speaker*," Allee mouthed. "*I'm recording.*"

Marko nodded in acknowledgement and thumbed the button. "I'm not sure where you heard that," he replied to Nikki. Allee gave him a thumbs up.

"It doesn't matter *where* I heard it. The important thing is that your arrest hasn't been reported in the papers," Nikki said. "It's been out of the limelight. Of course, your representation of Whitney might change all that."

"Oh yeah?" This was the Nikki he'd known so well. Equal parts sweet and vicious.

"Yes."

"It's almost like you're saying that my arrest will stay out of the news if I withdraw as Whitney's attorney, but that won't be true if I remain as her counsel—am I hearing that right?"

"I do know lots of people in the media business. And Whitney's case, it's a big one. Another Pam Smart. This case is going to blow up in the media. It's already started," Nikki explained. "Trust me, Marko, you don't want that kind of scrutiny of your life."

That summed it up nicely. "And you don't want me to do this because?"

"Because you're good at your job—at least when you're sober. I'm not sure how often that is anymore, but my guess is that your new arrest has helped to keep your head straight. I can't risk you walking her. I want Whitney to go to prison for the rest of her life, and I'm going to do everything I can to make sure that happens—including seeing to it that you withdraw."

Allee was giving him a thumbs up. "I'm flattered that you think I have that kind of ability," Marko said. "But you know I can't do that."

"Then the news about you is probably going to get out."

"That was going to happen one way or another, Nikki," Marko advised. "Ostlund and Franklin are small towns filled with gossips." His present company included.

"Don't say I didn't warn you," she said. Then the line went dead.

Allee pressed a button on her phone to end the recording as Marko pocketed his own phone. They rode in silence for a moment. "That was... interesting," she said at last.

"Yeah."

"A veiled threat," Allee added. "I think that's what it's called."

"Yeah."

"Do you really think that was all about protecting her son, or was it something more?"

"With Nikki, you never can tell."

"It definitely has me wondering," Allee said.

"Wondering what?"

"If there is any way that Whitney might be telling the truth. Maybe this was all a set-up."

"Let's not get too ahead of ourselves. They've got those recordings," he cautioned. But truth be told, given Nikki's involvement, he was wondering the same thing. But would Nikki really put her son out there like this? Maybe. And the thought of a truly innocent client—a rarity, no matter what people read or heard—had sweat forming on his palms and his heart racing. It added a lot of pressure to an already stressful job. Most clients were guilty of at least *something*. A loss at trial wasn't crushing. If Whitney was innocent, this case could end in catastrophe.

"Maybe I should withdraw," he said. He needed a drink.

"That's what she wants," Allee reminded him. "You're going to give that woman what she wants after she threatened you like that?"

"I don't know…"

"Look, it's early. Give it a week. I'll dig up more information. We'll see where we are then," Allee advised.

Marko nodded. He wanted to do this. For Whitney. For Allee. For himself. He was still the best attorney around, but he had to admit he used to be better. Over the years, he'd lost a little of his edge. Maybe it was the booze. Whatever. It was time he turned his life around. Whitney's case might be the catalyst for that. Of course, if the case went to hell, it could lead to his permanent downfall.

45

ALLEE

The afternoon dragged as Allee sat in the back of the courtroom in Brine watching Marko work. She tried to focus, tried listening to the judge's voice as he guided the attorneys through the afternoon docket, but her mind kept wandering back to that thumb drive. Could there be something on it that tied Whitney, Nate, and Jaxson together?

"Ready?" Marko said.

She hadn't seen him approach and she jumped at the sound of his voice, her head whipping in his direction. "You scared the hell out of me!" she said. "I didn't realize the hearing was over." She'd forgotten to stand when the judge had left the courtroom. She hoped that wouldn't be a mistake that came back to bite her. With luck, she'd never be in front of another judge again, that one included.

"Lost in your thoughts?" Marko said. He gestured for her to lead the way out of the courtroom.

"Yeah, and if you say anything about pennies, one of us is going to be in need of medical attention."

"Is that a threat?" he asked, a smile tugging at the corners of his lips.

Allee pulled down the collar of her shirt, revealing the patch of skin where the words, "Beware; for I am fearless, and therefore powerful," were written along her left collarbone.

"Lovely," he said. He looked at his watch, then glanced at the large ornate clock on the wall. "Not bad."

She walked out the courtroom door and into the open rotunda. "It's from Mary Shelley's *Frankenstein*."

"Also lovely."

"She wrote that book as a bet," Allee said. "Did you know that?"

"I don't think I did."

Marko cut in front of her and picked up the pace. "Yeah, she made a bet with her future husband and another writer—a baron or some other titled dude—on who could write the best horror story. Hers is the only one that has survived for two hundred years."

"Interesting," he said flatly.

"Why are you in such a hurry?" Allee asked as they stepped outside.

"I just...I need to get home."

She didn't like the sound of that. "You're not going to start drinking, are you?"

"No," he said, stopping at the passenger door of his car.

She didn't believe him. "You should go to a meeting," she said, pressing the unlock button on the key fob.

"I'm not religious," he replied.

"Don't have to be."

"So they keep telling me."

"My prison counselor said that, 'Religion is for people who are afraid to go to hell; spirituality is for those of us who've already been.'"

"How profound."

"I would go with you, you know," Allee offered. "If you want. If you think it would help."

Marko slammed his door shut. A sheen of perspiration had formed on his brow. "Just let it go, okay?"

"Okay," she said, starting the car. They drove to Marko's house in Ostlund in silence. When they arrived, she got out of his car, locked it, showed him his keys, and then pocketed them. He was not going anywhere tonight. "You gonna be okay on your own?"

"Fine. I'm fine."

She didn't believe him; she could see it—his need. She understood it. The fight was on. He was getting edgy, moody—what Alcoholics Anonymous' Blue Book aptly called "restless, irritable, and discontented." The bad news was that his fight was triggering her—agitating her own desire to get wasted. She had worked hard to bury her need, but seeing him like this was freaking her out. "If you say so," she finally said. "Just remember, you've got other people depending on you now. More than just clients, even."

She turned and got into her truck, started the engine, and backed out before stealing a quick glance in his direction. He was standing still, watching her. She had to get out of there, away from him and his issues. *He'll be drunk in an hour.*

As she drove, her thoughts turned to the thumb drive. She had to find it. She couldn't keep putting it off, so she'd search for it again as soon as she got home. The drive was long, and as her thoughts raced, her fingers nervously tapped the wheel. She pulled into the driveway.

It was dark out and her mother's street was not well lit, so she pulled as close as she could to the garage door and parked. Hopping out, she tapped in the garage code and watched it trundle open. She flipped the garage light on, illuminating her truck.

"Here we go," she said, trying to verbally urge herself on. She knew she needed to find the thumb drive, but she was still frightened of all the things she might also find. "The only way out is through."

She grabbed a trash bag and began her search again. This time, instead of focusing on the floorboard of the passenger side, she zeroed in on all the small nooks and crannies beneath the seat. She used her cell phone light and saw the shadow of a small rectangular item. *Bingo.* She squeezed her hand beneath the seat and grabbed it. It was plastic and squishy in her fingers—definitely not a thumb drive. She pulled it out to reveal a small package of ketchup that she tossed in the trash bag.

"Come on," she told herself, frustrated. "Focus."

She got down on her knees and looked beneath the seat again. She shoved aside a couple discarded napkins, then saw something that seemed promising, but she didn't get her hopes up this time. Squeezing her large hand beneath the seat, she tried one more time. Her fingers brushed the item. It was solid. She pushed her arm further and grabbed it, pulling it out.

It was the thumb drive. She could hardly believe it. She'd finally found it! She stared down at it. "Now it's time to find out if you are worth all that effort." She pocketed it, closed the garage door, and headed into her mother's house.

46

ALLEE

The tiny home was dark. She flipped the light on and made her way through the galley-style kitchen, stopping short when she reached the small dining area. Her mother was sitting at the table, her fingers interlaced and resting atop the scuffed wooden tabletop.

"Karen," Allee said.

Allee's mother had shoulder-length, curly hair, once dark but now streaked with gray. Years of hard living and bad decisions had left their scars; deep lines cut across her face, making her appear ten years older than her actual fifty-eight. "Where have you been," she asked in her bar-room-developed contralto.

"Work," Allee said without stopping. "Why are you sitting in the dark?"

"Nikki Price called me."

Allee stopped short. *Well, that didn't take long*, she thought. "I didn't know you knew Nikki."

"We go to the same church. She said you left your job at the restaurant."

"I did."

"Why?"

"That's none of your business," Allee said. There was no point in telling Karen the truth; she would never believe it. Allee had been caught in too many lies over the years, and Nikki, well, she was a Price.

"It is my business when you're living under my roof."

"Not if I'm paying rent and keeping my nose clean," Allee countered. "But for the record, I have a new job. I cleared it with my PO before I quit The Yellow Lark. Did everything I was supposed to do."

"I heard," Allee's mother said with a scoff. "You're working for that drunk, Marko Bauer, who represents child rapists." She shook her head, trying to appear disappointed.

It wasn't going to work. Karen had *never* been anything but disappointed in Allee.

"After all you've been through," Karen lamented. "And after all Nikki has done to help people like you and me—is this how you repay her? By quitting her restaurant to work for someone who is out to get her family?"

"That's not how it is, Karen."

"Mom," her mother said, her scowl dipping deeper.

"Karen." Allee hadn't referred to this person as *mom* or *mother* since she was thirteen. She hadn't earned the title. Yes, giving birth bestowed that status upon a person, but only momentarily. Women who gave up children lost the title; so too should a woman who abandoned her daughter for booze and men. "Give me a break. Right now, you're all full of self-righteous opinions because you're acting like a church-going, God-fearing woman," Allee said, her voice low. "But remember who you're talking to. I know different."

"I have confessed my sins and I've been forgiven."

"Not by me."

"One day you will see the error of your ways."

Allee had seen plenty of errors in her past—up close and personal. She'd paid the consequences and done the time. She was the first to admit that. Nobody ended up in prison by habitually making good decisions. Even the innocent ones—if any of those still existed—were tied up in something they shouldn't have been as the result of bad decisions. Drugs. Biker gang boyfriend. Booze. Desires for the people or things they couldn't or shouldn't have. Something. It was always something.

"Have you talked to your cousin?" Karen said.

"No. But I stopped at The Yellow Lark," Allee replied. "I was told he was there, but I didn't see him. Has he been home yet?"

"He came home for a bit this afternoon. Your aunt texted me."

It would have been nice if she'd texted Allee, too. Especially since she had asked her to check in on Nate.

"Then he headed back to work. You know, there is a thing or two you can learn from him. Nate has turned into a hard worker. Nikki's son, Adam, has turned him around."

That little turd didn't turn anyone around. Something was going on. Allee knew Nate. She practically raised him while Aunt Linda spent her time chasing men and sitting on barstools. Nate was a lot of things, but a hard worker wasn't one of them. He never was, and he never would be. Something Lorna said...What was going on in that restaurant? Nate was so much younger than Allee. He had needed her then, and she was there. He needed her again.

"Right," Allee said, gripping the thumb drive in her hand. "If that's all, I'm tired and I've got work tomorrow."

"For an alcoholic."

"Pot, kettle, Karen."

"I do not drink."

"Not anymore," Allee said as she headed down the narrow hallway in long, determined steps to her bedroom.

She closed the door behind her and locked it, sighing at the silence of the room. Suddenly, she froze. She listened, waiting to see if Karen had truly changed. The old Karen would be storming down the hallway right about now, getting ready to pound on Allee's door until she grew tired or Allee relented and opened it. She listened expectantly, but Karen apparently had other ideas, and after a few minutes, she released the breath she hadn't realized she'd been holding.

Maybe Karen *had* changed.

Allee retrieved the laptop from her nightstand. It was old and outdated, one that most would call a dinosaur, but it still worked. She sat on her bed cross-legged with the laptop balancing on her knees. She pressed the power button and reached for the remote as the laptop powered up. It would take a while to load.

Her TV had a small, forty-two-inch screen, and it sat atop an old dresser in her room. It was nothing special, but it was hers, and that made it special. At least to Allee. It was already on the channel for the local news, where the impossibly attractive newscaster forced a grim look on her perfect features and read from the teleprompter: "Marko Bauer, a defense attorney from Ostlund, Iowa, was recently arrested in Franklin and charged with suspicion of drunk driving."

Marko was right about Nikki, for sure. Allee tried to focus on her computer, which was finally up and running. She typed in her password and jammed the thumb drive into the USB port. As she did so, the newscaster continued reading: "Mr. Bauer is the attorney for Whitney Moore, the teacher who allegedly had an affair with a teenage student and then conspired with him to kill her husband. She's been charged with conspiracy to commit murder and sexual abuse and is presently confined in the Wyandotte County Jail awaiting trial."

Allee clicked on the "my computer" icon and chose the thumb drive. Jaxson had labeled it, "The Truth." A small square box appeared on the screen, asking for a password.

Shit, Allee thought. The thumb drive was password-protected. She didn't know Jaxson well enough to guess the password. She tried a few generic options like *Password* and *123456789*, but nothing worked. She'd have to talk to Whitney. She was the only person alive who might know the code.

Allee's gaze returned to the television. Marko's mugshot now was up on the screen. His eyes were dull, his skin pale and visibly clammy, and his mouth was twisted into a frown. He looked like a criminal. Someone who deserved to be behind bars, which was just where he'd end up if he kept drinking. That, or dead. Neither option fit with Allee's plans. She needed him out and sober.

47

MARKO

Alone in the dark, Marko uncapped the bottle and took his first gulp. The liquid touched his tongue, warmed his belly, and he felt relief. He could finally breathe. Allee might have taken his keys and dumped his stash, but she had no control over grocery delivery. Marko had placed his order a few days ago. Thanks to a change in the law, grocery chains were now permitted to deliver booze as well as food—and delivery was free so long as the order was over one hundred dollars.

Now, where to stash it, Marko wondered as he carried four of the seven grocery bags into the kitchen. He needed to find a place where Allee would never think to look. The problem was that Allee, too, was a recovering addict, and that meant she was able to think like him.

While considering his options, he took another swig of whiskey and went through the booze-free bags. Coffee, energy bars, frozen pizzas, chicken wings, potato chips, soda pop...the staples of life as a bachelor. He put them away and turned back to the alcohol, considering his options.

Then his phone rang. It was Allee.

He needed a little time, damn it. "Did she put a camera in here or something?" Marko wondered aloud before picking up. "This is Marko," he said, focusing on keeping his voice neutral. He hadn't had much to drink, but he needed to play it safe. Otherwise, Allee would be back to dump his newly purchased liquor down the drain. He didn't think he could stomach that. Or afford it.

"Are you watching the news?" Allee said.

"No." His gaze shifted to the dark television screen. "Should I be?"

"No," Allee said quickly. "Don't."

"Nikki made good on her threat," Marko concluded. He brought the whiskey bottle to his lips and took another pull. It immediately dulled the knot of panic forming in his stomach.

He'd known it would happen; Nikki Price didn't make hollow threats. She never had. Not even as a child. Words like *you'll be sorry* uttered to a rival girl on the playground resulted in gum stuck in the other girl's hair, a pixie cut and the loss of years of beautifully grown ringlet curls. Nikki had been capable of that kind of revenge in elementary school when popularity was the only thing at stake. This time it was Nikki's son. It was unsurprising that she'd come at him full force.

"You're not drinking, are you?" Allee said.

"Nope." Marko took another swig.

"This is the type of thing that leads to relapse," Allee observed. "And you haven't gone to treatment. You need a meeting."

"When did you become Miss Goody Two-Shoes?" It came out, "two-shoosh."

"You *are* drinking."

"It isn't illegal."

Allee was silent for a long moment, letting the unspoken words hang out there. It was an accusation. Her drug of choice was a crime. His was not. It created distance between their addictions. His was a problem, but it was still better than hers.

"No, but it's a violation of your bond."

It was true. But they had to find out, and with pre-trial services under-paid and overworked, it was unlikely anyone was going to check. So long as he didn't do anything stupid, he was okay.

"I'm going to an NA meeting," Allee said when he didn't respond. "I think you should come with me."

"No thanks. I'll see you in the morning." He took another long pull from the bottle. "And don't dump my stash." His words were starting to blur at the ends, the liquor blissfully shaving the edge off the world. "I'm filing for depositions in Whitney's case."

"Great," Allee said. "I'm not sure those two things have anything to do with each other, but sure. Okay."

"Promise me."

"Fine. Whatever," Allee replied irritably. "You want to give up? Give up. But I'm not. I don't know if Whitney is innocent or not, but something strange is going on in Franklin, and I'm going to figure it out—with or without your help. I just need you to pay me for my work. If you want to spend your time after-hours drunk, then fine. But you better be sober enough to work between eight and five."

"Or what?"

"Or you're going to screw your life up even more than you already have."

He'd been goading her, looking for the threat. He needed to blame someone, needed someone to bear the brunt of his fury. But Allee wasn't that person; apparently, she wasn't going to give up on him.

"Listen, I've got to go," Allee said.

"Go where?"

"A meeting. I already told you. Do you want to come?"

She was bluffing. "You'd drive all the way back here to get me?" Marko asked.

"If that's what it's gonna take, yeah."

Something inside Marko fluttered and stirred. Nobody had ever been so willing to go out of their way to help him out. Allee wasn't the person he'd expected. Marko looked down at the now half-empty bottle, his vision blurring at the edges. "I think I'll get some sleep."

"Okay," she said with a sigh of resignation. "I'll be there at eight o'clock sharp. Be careful, and be ready to work."

"I'll be ready," he said. He hung up the phone and looked down at the bottle of amber liquid clutched in his hand. "Just as soon as I finish this." He brought the liquid to his lips. He wanted to stop, but it was hard. How would he cope with stress? How would he let off steam? He was starting to see the edges of the problem, the loss of control. He just wasn't quite ready to do anything about it yet.

One last hurrah. I deserve it.

48

ALLEE

"Hi. My name is Allee, and I'm an addict. My drug of choice is meth, and uh, I've been sober for five years, one hundred and thirty-two days."

"Hi, Allee!" The small group of addicts clapped in appreciation.

"It's not really that good; I was in jail or Mitchellville for five years and one hundred days of that, so I've really only got a month or so clean on the outside."

This was Allee's first NA meeting on the outside. Like everyone else, she'd seen this kind of meeting portrayed on television and in the movies: a group of people sitting in folding chairs positioned in a circle inside a junior high school gymnasium or a church basement with a stand of bitter, tepid coffee and stale cookies off to the side. She had to admit, Hollywood had gotten it right this time—all the way down to the stale cookies.

"Cut yourself some slack," the moderator advised. He was a middle-aged man, thin with a large bald patch stretching the length of his head. His remaining hair was worn long and pulled back, resembling a skunk's tail. "A lot of us used as soon as we got out."

"Yeah. I wanted to."

"But you didn't," the moderator said. "Can you tell us a little about yourself?"

Allee looked around the room. There were thirteen other people, including the moderator. She didn't know any of them. She hadn't used with them. That struck her as odd. Lots of people used drugs recreationally, but the high-use crowd, those who got into the harder stuff, all knew each other. She was either in a room with marijuana users—which she didn't consider a real drug—or casual users. Either way, she didn't fit in.

"Someone else can go," Allee said, crossing her arms. "I'm done."

"Thank you for sharing," the moderator said, flashing a smile as tepid as the coffee.

The group clapped again, and the meeting continued. Everyone had a chance to speak, and she'd been right. Most of these people were amateurs: marijuana users, two women who had developed an opioid addiction following surgery, a couple of guys who'd got busted with meth and were court-ordered into recovery programs that ordered twelve-step program participation, and three boozehounds who needed to catch extra meetings who were here only because at this time of day NA was the only show in town.

Half-listening to their stories, Allee let her mind wander back to Marko. He was boozing again, which meant it was only a matter of time until he got busted. At least he wasn't driving, so she didn't have to worry about him getting new charges—unless he did something really stupid. Right now, her job was solid, and it was a hell of a lot better than working at The Yellow Lark. But if he screwed up, she was hosed. She'd probably have to go back to the restaurant. She couldn't do that. She had to help—or even force—Marko to get his shit together.

"That concludes our meeting," she heard the moderator say.

Allee stood. Small clusters of people began forming, their voices rising in the gymnasium in a low murmur. There was light laughter and low voices muted by the high ceilings. She headed for the door.

"Allee...Allee, is it?"

She had almost made it. She turned. A short, round woman with an alcoholic's ruddy complexion extended her hand. Fiftyish, she wore her hair in a pixie cut, but not in the same edgy way that Allee did. This woman's hair screamed, "*I'm a mother and a housewife.*"

"I'm Lucy Peterson's mother."

Allee took the woman's small, clammy hand and shook it. "I assume that's not your actual name, is it?"

The woman chuckled nervously. "No. It's not. It's Karen. Karen Peterson."

Another Karen, Allee thought. An unfortunate name. In a world where everyone wanted to avoid acting like a Karen, this woman was a Karen whether she acted like one or not. Allee sensed that very soon she would have two Karens breathing down her neck.

"You're working with Marko Bauer, right?" Karen asked. "The lawyer who was on the news for driving drunk?"

"You saw that, huh?"

Karen nodded.

"Yeah," Allee said. "I am working for him. How did you know that?"

"Well," Karen began, folding her hands as if in prayer. "I heard it from Nikki Price. I go to her church, you see. I ran into her at the grocery store today and she told me about her son and you and that Marko Bauer fella."

Allee was instantly on edge. Oh, no. Not here. "Did Nikki send you?"

"No!" Karen put up her hands in a gesture of surrender. "I'm not accosting you—I promise. I'm an alcoholic—in recovery, thanks to God and Nikki. I just—I just wanted to tell you that my daughter has some information that you might like to hear."

Allee crossed her arms. "If she's going to tell me how *bad* Whitney is, then I'm not interested."

"That's not it. Please. Just talk to her. Will you? We can call her now if you want."

Allee studied the woman for a long moment, looking for insincerity but detecting none. "Fine. We can do it in my truck." If she was going to do this, she was going to control her surroundings. Not the other way around.

"Okay."

Allee motioned for Karen to follow. It had rained earlier in the evening; it was too late in the spring for snow, but the cold sent a chill through Allee's threadbare jacket, sinking into her bones. She motioned for Karen to sit in the passenger side of her truck. They got in and closed the doors, but Allee didn't start the engine. She wouldn't waste the gas.

She looked to Karen expectantly.

Karen got the message. She retrieved her phone, pressed a couple buttons, then held it out, the speaker feature highlighted on the screen. It rang several times, then someone picked up.

"Mom! Are you almost home?" a girl said.

"Hi, sweetie. I have someone here with me. You're, uh, you're on speaker."

"Okay?"

"I'm with Allee—" She looked at Allee quizzically. "I don't think I caught your last name."

"Smith."

"Allee Smith," Karen said, turning her attention back to the phone. "She's working with the attorney who represents Mrs. Moore."

"Oh, okay." The girl's voice was suddenly chipper. "I'm Lucy Peterson. I'm one of Mrs. Moore's students."

"Hello," Allee said.

"I go to school with Luke. Everyone is talking about what happened. What he said Mrs. Moore did."

"How do you know it was Luke?" The complaint had only listed initials.

"Well, duh," Lucy said with exasperation. "Everyone knows."

Gossip still spread through schools like wildfire. Some things never changed. "Fair enough."

"Anyway, I like Mrs. Moore. She's my favorite teacher. I take as many classes as I can from her. She's nice," Lucy began. "I'm also on student counsel, Model UN, and all sorts of other clubs."

"Good for you," Allee replied.

"I don't play sports, though, so I'm not part of Luke's crowd."

"It sounds like you are smart."

"I am. Not only with books, but—" Lucy hesitated. "Are you going to, like, tell on me if I tell you I did something that could get me in trouble?"

"Not if it helps Whit—er, Mrs. Moore."

"Okay. Cool. So, I'm really good with computers."

Allee waited. "And?" she asked at last.

"Well, I hacked into the school's surveillance system and pulled all the video footage."

Allee's eyebrows shot up. That was impressive. A felony, but still impressive. She looked to Karen, who shrugged.

"I've gone through it," Lucy continued. "I can't find a time where Luke and Mrs. Moore were ever alone together," she added excitedly. "Someone said this supposed relationship and conspiracy happened at school, but it couldn't have. They weren't ever together."

"Are you sure?" Allee said.

"One hundred percent positive."

Allee sat back, laying her head against the driver's seat headrest. If true, this evidence was gold. They'd have to find a way to use it without involving Lucy, but that was a problem for Marko to solve. Allee just needed to get the evidence.

"Can you make me a copy?"

"Yes."

"Come by any time," Karen said.

Allee's gaze traveled up to meet Karen's. Her eyes were intense, wide and unblinking. It creeped Allee out, and made her think of the tattoo running along her right forearm. *You are mine, you shall be mine, you and I are one forever*. It was a quote from *Carmilla*, a vampire tale with a possessive villain and an innocent victim. Allee was no innocent, but plenty of people like her—current and former criminals—fell victim to crimes.

"I'll stop by tomorrow morning," Allee said, her gaze locked on Karen. The woman was creeping her out, but the evidence was too important to ignore. Allee just hoped she wasn't walking into a trap set by Nikki Price, because Allee was quickly starting to learn that woman was cunning. She had been outwitted by plenty of higher-class women like Nikki over the years, but this time she was sober, and her reputation was already tarnished. The way she viewed it, she had nothing, so she had nothing to lose.

49

ALLEE

The next morning, Allee knocked on Karen's door. Then she waited. And waited.

"Am I late?" she wondered aloud.

She pulled her phone out of her back jeans pocket. It was seven-thirty sharp, the agreed-upon time. Thirty minutes before Karen's sixteen-year-old daughter, Lucy, would need to leave for school.

Allee looked over her shoulder. Karen and Lucy didn't live in the worst part of Franklin, but she could see it from there. They lived in a traditional two-story house with a sagging front porch and a broken, boarded-up window on the second floor. The street was quiet at this time of morning, but she knew from experience that drugs flowed freely through the area.

I could do it. I could knock on any of these doors and get some dope. It would be nice to get high one last time. But, as her prison counselor had told her, *there's never a last time.* Every time would fuel a desire to use just once more. Then she'd be in full-blown addiction again. And then what? Parole violation. Prison. Starting from scratch yet again. Hell no. She wouldn't, couldn't backslide.

She shook her head and turned, knocking again, harder this time. There was a creaking and thumping sound, followed by a dragging noise. Then the door flew open and a teenage girl appeared. She had shoulder-length, blonde hair, light—almost translucent—skin, and freckles dotting her cheeks.

"You must be Allee. I'm Lucy." She thrust her hand out and Allee took it. "Come in."

Allee stepped inside. There was a stairway to the right—likely the source of the creaking and thumping—and a living room to the left where Karen was lying on the floor, snoring lightly. The room reeked of booze.

Lucy followed Allee's gaze. "Sorry about my mom. She does this sometimes."

"Don't apologize for your mom or her choices," Allee said quickly. Addiction was a bitch. Last night Karen had attended an NA meeting, but it wasn't enough. She probably needed more than NA. Maybe intensive outpatient or even inpatient treatment.

"The videos are this way," Lucy said, leading Allee down a hallway into a kitchen at the back of the house. "Here they are," Lucy said, gesturing to the table where a handful of thumb drives was piled. "There are a bunch of them. I wanted to get every camera from every angle, and those videos burn up a lot of memory."

"This is great," Allee said, grabbing the drives and shoving them into her laptop bag.

Lucy watched. She was silent for a long moment, then said, "*Carmilla.* Cool."

"What?" Allee said, only half listening.

"'You are mine, you shall be mine, you and I are one forever,'" Lucy recited. "It's from the book *Carmilla.*"

Allee put the last thumb drive in her bag. "How do you know that?" Nobody recognized her tattoos. The women at the prison did, but that was only because Allee was always carrying one of the classics around. But nobody had placed them since her release from prison. Most people acted like Marko, thinking the words odd and creepy.

"I'm well-read," Lucy said immodestly. "I like the classics. I think it is interesting to read old books like that, because people never change. Think about it: even in the 1600s, or whenever those books were written, people were frightened by differences. And we still are. In the books, vampires walked at night and drank blood. They were like humans, but they were singled out and murdered because they were different. The same thing with *Frankenstein*. Dr. Frankenstein brought his monster to life, then shunned him for his unnaturalness, and duh! The monster spent his life hunting his creator."

Allee studied Lucy, looking for any hint of sarcasm, but she saw only earnestness in her expression. "You know, you're going to do great things one day," she finally said.

"I hope so. I want to make a difference."

Allee envied her drive. When Allee was that age, all she wanted was someone to love and to get high. "Then don't get too far into this hacking business," Allee advised. "I'm no lawyer, but this can't be legal. And let me tell you, criminal convictions will destroy your chances in life—I know these things."

"I figured," Lucy said. "What's prison like?"

"It's a cage," Allee said quickly. "A very large cage filled with people who are dead inside. You don't want to go there."

Lucy shook her head. "Nope."

Allee was silent for a long moment, then nodded at her messenger bag. "What do I owe you?"

"Nothing."

"Fifty bucks?" The house was clean inside, probably thanks to Lucy, but it was not in good condition. They needed money. Allee could not justify taking the drives without paying something.

Lucy nodded. "That'll work."

"I'll get the money from my boss. Promise. Now, stay out of trouble, and don't tell anyone about this. You could get in big trouble."

"But it's the right thing to do to help Mrs. Moore, isn't it?"

"Of course," Allee admitted. "But there are people sitting in jails and prisons for doing what they thought was right. A crime is a crime."

She thanked Lucy and departed, passing a still-snoring Karen, and drove straight to Marko's house. She'd told him that she would be there at nine o'clock, and she was five minutes early when she pulled into his drive. She got out of her truck and knocked on the front door.

Nothing.

"Marko!" she shouted. "Are you in there?"

She spent a good five minutes calling his cell phone and banging on the door, but there was no answer.

"Whatever," Allee said, turning away from the door. He was probably in the same condition as Karen, passed out somewhere with a bottle in his hand. *Damn it!* She was tied to him now. If he sank the ship, she was going down with him. He needed to suck it up; he wasn't the only person in town struggling with addiction.

She returned to her truck and dialed his number one last time.

"You have reached Marko Bauer, attorney at law. I am unavailable right now. Leave a message and I will return your call when I have time."

"Marko, this is Allee. Get your shit together. I'm going to the jail to meet with Whitney. I'll be back when I'm done. We are going to have a chat."

She hung up, seething with anger. She drove all the way back to the Franklin jail with her hands drumming the steering wheel, taking deep, even breaths. Marko was about to get one hell of a gas bill. She'd feel guilty, but he'd done it to himself. As each moment ticked past, her agitation grew. When she was almost to the jail, she saw a young man walking along the street. She pulled up beside Nate and rolled down her window.

"Nate," she said, stopping at the curb beside him. "Are you just getting off work?"

They were near The Yellow Lark, but it didn't make sense for him to be leaving so early in the morning. The restaurant served customers from eleven in the morning until ten o'clock at night. He should have left at midnight at the latest; alternatively, he should be walking in the other direction.

"Uh, yeah." He had deep bags beneath his eyes and an angry red welt on one arm.

"What happened to you?" Allee asked, indicating the welt.

"I got too close to the stove. That's all," he said defensively. "Don't worry about it."

Allee would worry about whatever she wanted to worry about. Her mind was the only place where she had absolute control. "Do you need a ride home?"

"No." Nate shook his head. "I'll walk."

"Why don't you ever call? And you *work* all the time." She paused, letting it hang out there. "Your mother is worried," Allee added.

"It's none of your business or her business. Got it?" Nate snapped.

She didn't need this. He'd never talked to her like that before, not even when he was using. "Fine." Allee lifted her hands in surrender. "You do you."

She rolled up her window and continued to the jail to speak to Whitney, who might appreciate her help.

50

WHITNEY

True to his word, Leo hadn't come back to see Whitney. It wasn't a surprise. They weren't exactly getting along great *before* her arrest. Her sneaking around to investigate Jaxson's death had put strain on their marriage. And that was *before* he heard those recordings.

But where was Arlo? She hadn't seen her little boy either. As angry as Leo was, he wouldn't harm their child by keeping him from Whitney. Unless...

Unless Arlo didn't want to see her either. The thought tore at the remnants of her heart. She was starting to understand why Jaxson broke. There was only so much one person could take.

"You have a visitor." The jailer with the kind eyes was back. They'd gotten to know one another over the past few days, bits of conversation here and there. His name was Ralph, like *Wreck-It Ralph*, a movie she'd watched many times with Arlo cuddled at her side while they shared a bag of popcorn. Always with candy corn. She and Arlo had experimented and found that eating one candy corn and three popcorn kernels at the same time was the perfect ratio.

"Is it—" She rushed to the bars. She couldn't say her son's name. Like a wish over birthday candles, to say it aloud would ruin it, cause Arlo to flit away, a figment of her imagination.

Ralph shook his head. "No. Sorry. I know you were really looking forward to seeing your son."

She crumpled.

"I know it's disappointing. Really, I do." Ralph was apologetic. "I'll call the social worker again. See if she can bring him out. They're busy, but you should see your son."

Whitney slid to the floor, placing her hands over her face. A beat of silence passed. Then she looked up, wiping away the tears. "Why are you so nice? Nobody else is."

Ralph shrugged. "Innocent until proven guilty. I think that means something."

"Even after everything you've heard about me?"

He shrugged again. "Technology. It lies."

Whitney froze. *Technology!* Was that how they did it? Was that how the Prices framed her? She needed to talk to Marko.

"Are you okay?" Ralph asked. "You're white as a ghost."

Whitney rose to her feet. "I'm fine. I'm fine. Or as fine as I can be in this cage." She looked up. "Who did you say is here to see me?"

"I didn't, but it's Allee. That investigator."

"Oh."

Whitney didn't understand how Allee had gone from a convicted felon to a restaurant cook to an investigator for a lawyer's office. She'd always liked Allee, at least when she was sober, but the cards were stacked against her. Jaxson used to always say, *once you're in the system, there is no way out.* Yet Allee had seemed to find one.

Ralph opened the cell door, clamped chains around her wrists, and led her down the hall to the same meeting room where she'd last seen Arlo. She froze, her heart stopping, her body growing cold. Sweat beaded along her brow. Was she having a heart attack? Was she breathing? She wanted to rip at her jumpsuit. Tear into clothes and flesh. Expose her heart. See her lungs.

"You're okay, Whitney." Ralph's voice was soothing.

She blinked several times. "I'm sorry. I think I..." Was she losing her mind?

"You're having a panic attack," Ralph said, his tone calm, gentle, like he was coaxing a cat.

"I...I can't breathe."

"Yes, you can," he said. "You're just hyperventilating. Slow your breathing down."

She couldn't.

"You can do this," he coached her. "One deep breath in and one deep breath out."

She focused on sucking in one long breath.

"That's it. You've got it," Ralph said.

Whitney blew the breath out and breathed in another, long and slow. The world started to return to normal. "I thought I was dying," Whitney said once she started to feel better.

"A panic attack," Ralph said.

"Really?"

Ralph nodded again. "I see them all the time."

"I'm not crazy?"

"No crazier than the rest of us," he said. "You're under a lot of stress. That's what causes 'em, I think."

"Oh."

"Of course, I'm no doctor." He watched her for a few seconds. "Are you ready?"

She nodded. She wondered if Ralph knew how much each of these small kindnesses meant to the inmates. Simply asking if she was ready in a place where there were no choices meant something. And Ralph wasn't just kind to her. She'd seen the way he treated the other inmates. He allowed them a small amount of autonomy over their body, something few other jailers considered. The others weren't exactly mean; it was more they were cold. Their job was to keep the cages closed and the animals inside. They weren't paid to treat them like human beings. But Ralph did. By choice, not obligation.

Ralph said something into the radio affixed to his shoulder, and the lock on the heavy metal door shifted with a loud *thud*. He pulled the door open, revealing Allee seated at the desk in the center of the room. A large, clunky laptop computer sat on the desk in front of her.

Allee looked up when the door opened. Then she stood, like the lawyers and occupants of a courtroom did when a judge entered. "Hi, Whitney," she said. "You don't look so hot."

Whitney turned back to Allee. "The last time I saw you, you called me a liar and sexual predator." *She's not even bothering to deny it,* Whitney thought. *Why is she even here?* "What's changed?"

Allee gestured to her laptop. "A lot."

51

ALLEE

Allee was startled by Whitney's appearance when she tentatively entered the room. She looked like crap. She already had that sallow look.

"The last time I saw you, you called me a liar and sexual predator," Whitney said.

It was true. But things had changed.

"What's changed?" Whitney asked.

Allee gestured to her laptop. "A lot." She watched as Whitney took a deep breath and then released it. "Don't give up, Whitney. It's not over."

"That's not what you told me the other day."

"I was a jerk the other day."

Whitney lowered herself into her seat gingerly, as if her tiny, birdlike bones might break upon meeting the hard chair. "Is that an apology?" she asked.

"Not exactly; as a general rule, I don't apologize," Allee replied. "But it's the best you'll get."

"Okay, well, I accept your pseudo-apology. Honestly, I can't afford to hold grudges, anyway—not with everyone against me."

There was an alarming heaviness to Whitney's words. Depression, perhaps? That was normal, in Allee's experience, but it had developed quickly.

"What's with the computer?" Whitney asked.

"We have some security footage to look through."

"I don't understand."

Allee quickly reviewed what she had come by without naming Lucy.

"How'd you get it?"

"Can't say." Allee shrugged.

"My money's on Lucy Peterson," Whitney said. "She's one of the few kids good enough with computers to do something like that. How'd she get access?"

"Yeah, well, I will neither confirm nor deny, as they say on TV," Allee replied. Whitney damned sure knew her students. "Let's get started. We've got a lot of footage to go through."

Even though the jailers had given her extra time due to her status as investigator for Marko, Allee set the computer to play the videos at five times the actual speed. There was no accompanying sound, but it didn't matter. What was important was to track the locations of Whitney and Luke in the building throughout the day, if possible. She unrolled a large sheet of paper while Whitney watched the screen.

"What are you doing?" Whitney asked.

"It's a blueprint of the school. I'm gonna track you and Luke while we watch the videos," Allee explained. "You're the big paperclip here. He's this document clip."

For almost two hours, Whitney and Allee watched videos together. Allee took notes and moved the clips around her blueprint.

Lucy had been correct; there was never a point when Luke and Whitney were alone. There were a couple times when he stayed after class to speak with her, but there were always a couple other students also present, hanging around for presumably the same reason. Reviewing the recordings and logging the movements from one week before the allegation through Whitney's last day at school was painstaking work, but it confirmed Whitney's denial.

Allee used her phone to record herself moving the paperclips around so she could show it to Marko later. Assuming he was ever sober enough to understand. Maybe they could even use the recording in court.

When they finished the last recording, Allee turned to Whitney. "Why do you think he's lying? Grades? Is he failing? Does he need a passing grade to play sports?"

"Luke isn't, er, wasn't the best student, but he wasn't the worst either. He had passing grades. Mostly C's. I thought he was capable of much more, of course, but his coaches were happy, and that's what mattered to Luke."

"Then what was it?"

"Jaxson." His name brought a cloud to Whitney's already tormented expression. "And me."

"I don't understand. What does your brother have to do with it? And you? What did you do—"

"His parents put him up to it. This is Nikki's work."

"I get the kid is part of that family, but he's a teenager. Do parents really have that much control over their teenage child?"

"It depends," Whitney said.

"On what?"

"What happens behind closed doors."

Whitney was hinting at child abuse. It could be going on in the home. Allee saw plenty of it in her days as an active user. Sadly, she'd never reported it. She chose drugs over everything else, even helping innocent children. She didn't like to remember herself back then, but it was also a stark reminder of how far she'd come. She was not that person anymore. She hoped to never be that person again. "So, what do we do with that?"

"I don't know," Whitney said. "I suspected that Jaxson knew something. That's why I started investigating."

"I don't understand."

"Jaxson was living with us when he"—she swallowed hard—"jumped off that balcony." She paused. "He'd get calls at all hours of the day and night," Whitney continued. "He was coming and going at strange hours. He'd be gone days at a time. I thought he was using at first, but he was always going to the restaurant."

"How do you know?" It sounded like Jaxson had fallen off the wagon. That kind of sneaky behavior was common for users. They all did it.

Whitney looked in both directions as if others were listening. "I know this sounds bad, but I put a tracker on Jaxson's phone," she explained. "I had to know what he was doing. He was living with us. He was around Arlo. I couldn't have drugs in our home."

"I'm not judging," Allee assured Whitney. It wasn't a bad idea, honestly. She probably should do the same with Nate.

"Anyway, I knew he was going to the restaurant, but he was staying there days at a time. It didn't make any sense," Whitney continued. "And when was he sleeping? He couldn't have been working all that time. Otherwise, he'd have tons of money, and I've seen his bank accounts. They were empty."

It could have been after-hours parties, but the money portion sounded about right. "I'll bet the Prices weren't paying *him*, either."

"You too?" Whitney asked. When Allee nodded, she continued. "I think they were using him like an indentured servant, working off his probation. I was trying to get proof."

Allee thought about the things Lorna had said, among them that none of the felons were getting paid. "You might be right. They work their people like dogs, knowing they won't report it."

"How could they know he wouldn't report it?"

Regular people can't understand. "Because people like Jaxson—and me—don't report things like that. First of all, we don't like authority, because all authority has ever done is to punish us somehow," Allee explained. "Secondly, when you've been involved with drugs and stuff, you find that no one believes *anything* you say. Doesn't matter what it is or what it's about. But then you came along."

"It's...It's my fault, then," Whitney replied, crestfallen. After a few seconds, she shook her head. "So, let's say the Prices might have been afraid of me reporting them. I see that, but the most they would get would be a fine. That's not worth framing me, is it? And it doesn't explain Jaxson disappearing for days at a time. Restaurants close."

Allee reached into a side pocket of her laptop bag, producing the thumb drive that Jaxson had slid toward her just before he jumped over the rail. It was time.

52

MARKO

He was lost, wandering down the halls of the junior high school. He knew he needed to get to class, but he had no schedule.

I'll stop at the office. Get another copy of my class schedule, Marko thought. Except he didn't know where the office was either. The bell was ringing. He was tardy. He spun in the hallway, placing his hands over his ears as the bell grew longer and louder, more insistent.

Wait a minute.

His eyes shot open. Marko was on the couch in his living room. It was a dream. He hadn't had that one since he was in law school. He looked at his watch. 2:09—still broken.

His cell phone buzzed against the coffee table, and he reached for it. What the hell time was it? The screen read, "Restricted." It had to be the court.

He cleared his throat. "This is Marko." He focused on making his voice sound normal, but the clumsiness of sleep still clung to the edge of his words.

"Where the hell are you?" Connor boomed.

"I—"

"You had court today."

"I'm sorry, Your Honor! I must have mis-calendared something." Marko was on his feet and rushing to his bedroom. "I'll be there in ten minutes."

"Don't bother," Connor said. "Your client showed and requested a new attorney. I took you off the case and assigned someone else. Someone who will show up. Someone who still has a driver's license."

"Your Honor, I—" Marko said.

"Don't apologize, Mr. Bauer," Connor said. "I don't want to hear it, and neither does any other judge in this district. We don't need apologies. We need you to figure it out. We understand addiction is endemic in our profession. Lots of lawyers and judges struggle. But help is out there—use it. I'm not going to be so understanding next time. You do this again, and I'm reporting you to the bar and to the lawyer assistance program."

He was threatening an ethics complaint. The bar association was a self-regulated entity, which meant that lawyers and judges reported other lawyers and judges when they witnessed misconduct. The ethics board reviewed the alleged misconduct and made recommendations to the Supreme Court, which meted out punishment ranging from a private reprimand (embarrassing, but not in a public way) to disbarment. Marko had already lost his driver's license. That was bad enough. He could not afford to lose his license to practice law. "Your Honor, it won't happen again."

"It better not." Connor was silent for a long time—long enough that Marko wasn't sure if he was still on the line. When he did speak, Connor's voice had softened. "Can you handle this Whitney Moore thing?" he asked. "If not, no harm—I can appoint someone else if you need to take some time off. You know, the lawyer assistance program can help."

"No, sir. I can do this."

Connor sighed heavily. "I might as well warn you," he began. "The Des Moines and Mason City news stations have all picked up the story. They're calling Whitney the new Pamela Smart. Given your, er, *condition*, are you sure you can handle it?"

Marko bristled. He was struggling a little, but he was fine. He was a better lawyer drunk than most of the nitwits who appeared in front of Connor were on their best day. "I can do it," he assured the judge. "I've hired someone to help with the investigation."

"Is that who is visiting her now?" Connor asked.

"How do you know who is visiting my client and who isn't?"

"The jail administrator called," Connor explained. "He said a convicted felon has been claiming to be an investigator representing your office and visiting Ms. Moore. He didn't know if he should allow the visits."

"He should."

Another long silence followed. "A felon. Marko, really?" Connor asked. "How is that going to help?"

You should focus on your job; I'll handle mine. "She's going to add value. I have a plan."

"See to it that you execute it, then," Connor said.

The line went dead, so Marko opened his recent calls and clicked on Allee's name. She answered after the first ring.

"He's awake," she said.

"I need you to come here."

"Why?"

"Obviously, because I need a ride."

"Are you sober?"

He was moderately sober, but gruesomely hungover. "That's none of your business."

"Au contraire. I remind you yet again, I work for you," she said. "It's definitely my business."

He didn't have the time or the energy for her sarcasm. "I need to talk to you about Whitney's case, okay? Can you just come by here?" He heard himself begging and hated himself for it. But he was desperate. He needed her.

"Yeah. Sure. I just finished up with Whitney. I've got some things to discuss with you, too."

"Be here in an hour," Marko said.

"More like ninety minutes."

"Who's the boss here?"

"You need me as much as I need you."

It was true, damn it. "Why is it going to take you so long?"

"I have an errand to run."

She hung up and he did the same. He tossed his phone back on the coffee table, lay back on the couch, and closed his eyes. He just needed a few minutes to settle his stomach, then he would jump in a cold shower.

53

WHITNEY

Allee produced a thumb drive, holding it in front of Whitney as if it were a precious gem. "I have something else we need to look at, as well."

"What's on it?"

"Not sure," Allee said. "I got it from Jaxson."

Whitney froze. "What? When?"

"The day he...died," Allee began. "I was there."

Whitney gripped the edge of the desktop. "At the courthouse?"

Allee nodded. "My cousin, Nate, had a pretrial conference. His attorney—Marko—was running late, as always. When he finally showed, he came over to talk to us. I didn't notice Jaxson standing in the corner. I don't know how long he had been there. But he ran toward us, toward the balcony."

Whitney closed her eyes, pressing them shut. "I know the rest."

"Right. Well, as he was running, he slid the thumb drive toward me," Allee said. "I was the only one of us to see him do it. Marko and Nate were too focused on your brother to notice. I bent down and picked it up and pocketed it."

"Marko doesn't know?" Whitney forced the words out as her mind reeled. Seriously? There were three other people present the day her brother died. Three. And not one of them even attempted to grab him, to save his life.

"No, he doesn't. It all happened so quickly—a second at most."

His last second.

"There was nothing we could do, Whitney. It all happened so fast."

Allee had been there. So had her attorney, Marko, who seemed to be ghosting her, of late. She rarely spoke to him, and she had only seen him a couple of times. Jaxson's last seconds were spent with three people who didn't even care enough to reach an arm out to grab him. What had gone through his mind in those last seconds?

"He loved rocks, did you know that?" Whitney asked. "All kinds of rocks. He knew where they came from, how they formed. In a different world, a different life, he would have become a petroleum engineer or maybe a geologist."

"I did not know that," Allee replied.

And you probably don't care. You're only interested in what's going on with your cousin. When he was young, before the drugs, before the addiction, when she used to babysit him, Jaxson always wanted to go to a lake or a stream and hunt for rocks. He'd find one and hold it up. She vividly recalled him proudly displaying a sedimentary rock and explaining what that meant. "Did he say anything?" Whitney asked. "In those last moments, I mean?"

"He said something about freedom. 'I'm free,' and 'You don't own me'— something like that."

He was talking about them. The Prices. It had to be. "This," Whitney said, pointing to the thumb drive, "is what I've been looking for. It's probably the reason I'm here. They wanted to stop me from finding out the truth." And the truth had to be on that little plastic drive. "What's on it?"

"I don't know," Allee replied. "It's password-protected. I was hoping you might have an idea what the password might be."

Whitney shrugged. "How should I know?"

"He was your brother."

Whitney watched as Allee plugged the thumb drive into her computer. A folder popped up. It was labeled *The Truth*. Whitney's heart skipped a beat. This had to be it. The key to everything. Allee clicked on the file folder and a password box popped up.

"I tried all the usual options," Allee said. "*Password. Pa$$word. 123456.*

Other number combinations. I knew his birthday was in June, but I didn't know the date."

"It's—it was—the sixteenth."

Allee turned the laptop so it was facing Whitney. "Go ahead. Try whatever you think might work."

"Will it lock us out if I try too many times?"

"Maybe, but what do we have to lose?"

Whitney's fingers hovered over the keyboard for a long moment, then she began pressing keys: *Jaxson*, *JaxsonRocks*, *Rocks*, *Geology*, and dozens more. She kept at it for ten minutes, then finally gave up, the failure hanging heavy in her heart. "I guess I didn't know Jaxson as well as I thought I did," she said, turning away from the computer.

"Or he was good at picking passwords," Allee replied softly.

Whitney sensed Allee was disappointed in her. Well, she could take a number and join the club. There was a whole line of people upset with her.

54

MARKO

From Marko's perspective, the next few weeks with Allee sucked. It started the morning Allee returned from seeing Whitney about the thumb drive.

Marko's nap had somehow evolved into a full-out sleep and Allee had let herself in using the spare key he kept inside a fake rock beside the front door. He'd awakened to a loud *slap*, jolting up on the couch to find Allee standing beside him, her hands on her hips, and a copy of the *Iowa Rules of Court* lying on the coffee table in front of him.

"She's innocent," she had announced, and produced a pile of thumb drives. "I'm not saying she's *probably* innocent or I *doubt* she did it—I'm saying that there is *no way* it could have happened the way that Price kid is saying it did. He's lying, and—if, as you said, their whole case depends on his testimony—you ought to be able to prove it with this."

Marko rubbed his eyes. "What are you talking about?"

"Simple. She's innocent and I'm not going to let you screw this up."

There was a big difference between *not guilty* and *innocent*—a world of difference, really. Maybe it was time they had that discussion. He opened his mouth to protest, but she was already talking.

"You know what? You can dork up your career and your life, and that's fine, but you aren't going to sit around drunk and feeling sorry for yourself and thereby see an innocent person sent to prison—not on my watch,"

Allee said. "And by innocent person, I mean me *or* her. I need this job. Nobody else will hire me. I'm not innocent in the sense that she is, but I haven't done anything that deserves me losing my job and thereby earning a return trip to prison. You need to get it together, and now!"

He nodded. A short, barely perceptible movement of his head. She was right, but he couldn't say it. He had lain back down, intent on sleeping off the hangover when he would have much preferred to have another drink. *Just one.*

Despite the lecture, his hangover won out, and he'd fallen back to sleep. Later, he'd discovered that while he'd been snoring, she had gone around his house for a second time, again finding and dumping all his booze down the sink. He'd awakened to a grilled cheese sandwich and a bowl of home-made chicken noodle soup. "What's this?" he'd asked.

"Hangover food. Eat."

He'd taken a couple of tentative bites and then wolfed down the balance. It was fantastic. "Where'd you get this?"

"I made it while you were passed out," she had said. "I told you I could cook. But don't get used to it," she warned. "I'm not gonna be enabling your drunk ass. I'm only doing it today because I need you to get your shit together. If you can't do that, I'm leaving."

But she didn't leave. Instead, she had stayed with him for two long weeks almost around the clock, leaving only when the bars and liquor stores were closed. Despite her earlier promise not to do so, she had fed him, forced him to go to AA meetings, and driven him to substance abuse treatment sessions with a counselor. She kept his calendar and ensured he didn't miss any client meetings or court sessions.

He hated it, of course. At times, he had wanted a drink more than anything in the world.

Now, two weeks later, he was seeing things through eyes no longer clouded. *Maybe her constant harassment is working.* "What's on the agenda today?" Marko asked. He had poured himself a large cup of decaffeinated coffee and now joined Allee in what used to be his living room—a space that had magically morphed into a real work-from-home office. There were two desks, one for Allee, the other for him. *Where the hell did the second desk come from?* He must have bought it. Two desktop computers were up and running. He did recall Allee convincing him to purchase client management software that would digitize the files, handle billing, track time spent on cases, and—most importantly—manage his court calendar.

He didn't even want to know what all that cost him.

Allee was already at her laptop. She was an early riser and a hard worker. He hadn't expected that of her. He had expected slacking and blackmail and threats to expose him if he didn't raise her wages or whatever—the usual felon-type stuff.

"Did you grab a cinnamon roll?" she asked without looking away from her laptop or slowing her keyboarding.

"I'm not a breakfast eater."

"You better learn," she replied. "I am. I like to bake, and I don't bake for one."

Marko returned to the kitchen and saw a pan of homemade cinnamon rolls atop the stove. She'd basically moved in. He vaguely remembered her telling him, "I will be there when you go to sleep; I will be there when you wake up. You cannot escape me. So don't even try to drink."

It was annoying. He was used to his own space, but he was starting to adjust, his habits softening and bending to allow room for hers. Everyone had their quirks. Hers was late-night baking. He selected a cinnamon roll and took a bite. The roll melted in his mouth, and he groaned.

"Good or bad?" Allee called from the living room.

He took another bite, this one larger, and joined her. "Amazing. Everything you make is amazing. I'm going to gain one hundred pounds with you around."

Allee shrugged. "Whatever keeps you off the sauce."

"You should sell these things, you know that?" Marko said, taking another bite.

Allee swung around in her chair. "Great minds think alike," she said. "That's one thing I wanted to talk to you about."

"Opening your own business?" Marko asked. He was just getting back on his feet, starting to understand life as a sober person, and it was because of Allee. He didn't want to admit it, but he needed her. If she left, he would go back to drinking. Two weeks of sobriety was nothing, a raindrop in the ocean, when compared to the rest of his life.

"No," she said.

Marko's body relaxed; he felt the tension in his shoulders lessen.

"This." She clicked a button on her laptop and turned it so he could see the screen, which showed an advertisement for a vehicle—a large panel truck with *Rob's Burgers* written on the side.

Marko was perplexed and admitted as much. "I don't follow."

"I know Rob—the owner of this truck. We ran around back in the day—before I got sent off. She nodded to one of the tattoos on her arm. "He sobered up and started a food truck. He's done well enough that he is opening a storefront in Brine and is selling his truck."

Marko's heart sank. "So you *do* want to start your own business."

She was almost smiling. He didn't see that often. "Sorta. I want to expand *our* business."

Our business? "Food trucks have nothing to do with the practice of law."

"Not yet," she admitted.

She was running some kind of con. He could feel it. He knew it was too good to be true. Marko sighed and dropped into his chair. "I'm almost afraid to ask."

"You work in all the rural counties. Each day you're in a different county. I drive you and then I just sit there in the courtroom or on a bench in the courthouse, waiting for you to finish. It's a waste of time for me."

"That's our agreement," he countered. "And you'll remember I pay you while you're sitting."

"Yes, you do. But think about it: you're always griping about limited or no meeting space with clients when we're on the road. You've told me a dozen times how these old courthouses have few, if any, available attorney-client rooms."

He couldn't remember complaining about that to her, but he had made the complaint many, many times. "I'll bite," he began. When she didn't return his smile, he continued. "How does a food truck solve that?"

"Hold on a second. The other thing is, those small towns, they've got nowhere to eat—all the cafes are closing down. So here's my idea: we buy that truck, paint some law-related name on it, and I set up shop outside the courthouse on days you are practicing there. We set up the canopy and a table and you meet with your clients. If someone is waiting, they can order something to eat. That'll occupy them—especially when you are running late. It solves a lot of problems for us. Plus, I would have something to do during the day. We'd make some extra money, you'd have a place to meet with people, and it might bring in some clients."

Marko was thinking about fetching another cinnamon roll. He had to admit, he didn't hate the idea. It was definitely different, new and strange, but that was how all innovation started, wasn't it? "How much is the truck?"

"Forty thousand dollars," Allee replied tentatively, wincing.

"How would it work? Who pays for what? What food would we make? I mean, I have questions, you know?"

"I don't tell you how to practice law," she replied tightly.

"Well, kinda," he replied. He sat back in his chair, thinking. "You really think you could pull it off?" he asked at last.

"I could—with your help."

She clearly respected that it would take his money to get things started. And it wasn't a fortune, in the big scheme of things. Not all that much more than purchasing a used car, and it might actually work. "I'll think about it," he said. "But I'm gonna want to look at the truck first, of course."

He didn't know squat about trucks, but it seemed like the thing to say. Allee's face lit up. She must have expected an immediate, hard no and got a maybe instead.

"Okay," Allee said. "I'll message him and see when he is free."

"One more thing, Allee," he began. "If we do this, you can't leave the firm. I'll need your help. I mean, we might need a noncompete agreement."

"If we do this, it'll be because you're fronting the money," she observed. "So, I can't leave. I'll sign whatever you want. You might be a drunk, but you're a relatively honest one."

"Relatively?"

"You lie about your drinking," she said. "But that's addict stuff. I get it."

"Thanks, I think."

Allee nodded, a smile spreading across her face. That made for two smiles in one day—a record. It looked good on her. They were silent for a long moment.

Allee folded her laptop. "Depos."

"What?"

"Depos. That's what's on the calendar for today. You are deposing the State's witnesses in Whitney's case."

"Right," Marko said. It was nearing eight o'clock. "We'd better get going if we want to get to Franklin on time."

"Put on a tie—a clean one," Allee ordered, producing his keys from her pocket. "I'm ready whenever you are."

55

ALLEE

"Is it really necessary for you to talk to my Luke?" Nikki asked, pulling her shoulders back. She was wearing a form-fitting black dress, her large breasts threatening to break free of the thin fabric. It was no accident.

"He's listed as a State's witness," Marko replied. "So yeah. I need to depose him."

Marko, Allee, Nikki, and Luke were in the courthouse, awaiting the arrival of McJames, a court reporter, and—eventually—Whitney. They were on the third floor, steps away from where Jaxson had jumped. Allee wondered how Whitney would react when she arrived on scene. The plan was to have the jailers bring her up when everyone else was present.

"I just don't see that it's necessary," Nikki continued. "Lucas made a statement—he swore to it! We are God-fearing people. It should be enough for him to place his hand on a Bible and swear he's telling the truth." She crossed her arms and pushed her bottom lip into a pout.

Allee dropped into one of the chairs lining the hallway. *Oh, please.* This woman was insufferably transparent. What did anyone see in her?

Marko sat next to her.

"Well, that's not enough—as a matter of law. And that's the thing, Nikki," he said, producing his phone and unlocking the screen with his thumb. "We're going to follow the law. I know you think you are running the show, but we're going to operate within the confines of the law."

Her pout dipped into a scowl. She looked like she was going to cry.

"It doesn't matter what *you* want," Marko continued. "Your son has accused my client of committing serious crimes. *I'll* determine what's necessary, and *I'll* do it according to the rule of law."

"I liked you better when you were drinking," Nikki mumbled.

Allee bristled, but Marko appeared to ignore her. Allee watched him closely, gauging his reaction to the presence of an old girlfriend and present foe. His sobriety was hard-won and tentative, at best. She knew he could easily revert back to his old ways. Allee fought to avoid snapping at Nikki; it wasn't her fight. She was tempted to tell Nikki her comment was not very Christian for a supposedly "God-fearing" woman.

Allee received a text from her aunt. Without looking, she recalled their earlier discussion. *"He says he's working, but he hasn't been paid. They can't do that, can they?"* she had asked.

Allee's gaze drifted to Nikki. Her clothing was always new and expensive, her hair a bright, unnatural blonde with no roots showing, and her nails were perfectly rounded and polished. She was making enough to maintain her own appearance. She should have enough to pay her employees.

What did her aunt want now? She snuck a quick peek. *"Can you check on him?"*

Allee almost typed, *"You do it,"* because she was tired of dealing with Nate's problems, but she didn't. He was family. She would not abandon him. *"I will stop by the restaurant after work."*

"You can't go sooner?" Linda replied.

"No. I'm tied up in a court thing," Allee typed. She sent the message, then locked and pocketed her phone.

When she looked up, the elevator across the atrium opened and McJames and the court reporter stepped off.

"Oh, thank goodness," Nikki said as McJames approached. "A better class of people."

McJames smiled broadly. "You mean you don't like Marko and his..." His voice trailed off as his gaze locked pointedly onto Allee.

"Investigator," Allee said, rising to her feet.

McJames' gaze swung to Marko, his eyes questioning.

Marko nodded. "This is Allee. She works for me."

McJames shifted his stare back to Allee, and she held it. She wasn't facing charges. She would not back down to him anymore.

Tiring of the game, he looked away. "That's fitting," he said. He turned to Nikki and Luke. "Are we ready to get started?"

"Do we really have to do this?" Nikki asked, her tone turning to a whine.

Yes, Allee thought. How many times was Nikki going to ask the same question in a different way?

She stood as McJames opened the door to a tiny courtroom with "Equity" written on the door in scripted, faded gold lettering. Allee and Marko hung back, awaiting Whitney.

They exchanged a knowing look as Nikki placed a hand on her son's shoulder and Luke jumped in—what? Was it shock? Fear? Either way, her touch caused him to snap his head toward Nikki, allowing Allee to see the terrified expression on his face. He was taller than his mother, broader in the shoulders, and far more muscular, but his lip quivered when his gaze met his mother's cold green eyes. *That touch was not a comfort; it was a warning.*

She had an idea, and she pulled Marko to the side and quickly suggested a couple of questions that he could ask Luke during his deposition. Marko looked at her questioningly. "From your books?"

"Trust me. I think it's important."

Marko shrugged. "Well, it can't hurt."

She watched as he wrote down the titles. Moments later, the elevator in the back end of the building chimed. The rattle of chains followed, and seconds later Whitney rounded the corner, led by a middle-aged jailer with a face creased with deep laugh lines. He wasn't smiling. As Allee watched, Whitney's eyes darted about, taking in her surroundings before settling at last on the gold railing.

"Good morning," Marko said.

Whitney slowly looked away from the railing and lifted a hand, her chains clanking in greeting.

"Are you ready for this?"

"What do I have to do?"

"Nothing," Marko assured her. "Just watch."

Whitney's gaze shifted to Allee, questioning. Allee understood the hesitation; she'd been the same way all those years ago, before she'd gone to prison. Depositions were not easy on anyone, but especially not the accused. They had to sit there and listen to witness after witness tell their version of events without saying a word. In Allee's case, they were giving mostly true statements peppered with lies and exaggerations. In Whitney's case, of course, it would all be lies.

"You'll be fine," Allee said. "You have us." She gestured from herself to Marko. *And you have the truth*, she thought.

Whitney nodded and took a deep, steadying breath. "Okay," she said, "I'm ready."

56

MARKO

When the court reporter indicated she was ready, Marko began. "Have you ever given a deposition before?" he asked Luke.

Luke looked to his mother for help.

"He's just a boy—of course he hasn't," Nikki interjected.

Marko was seated across from Luke. Nikki was to her son's right, with McJames to her right. Across the table, Whitney was seated to the left of Marko. The court reporter was at the end of the table, her fingers flying across her miniature keyboard. She'd already had Luke raise his right hand and he'd sworn to tell the truth.

Allee was in the corner. Marko's eyes settled on her in time to see her tap a few times on her phone screen, then flip it over face down with the microphone facing Luke. She was recording.

Good.

He turned his attention to Luke, ignoring Nikki. "These questions are for you," he said, fixing the younger man with his stare. "Not your mother. You're a minor, so she can be here, but she's not permitted to speak— understand?"

Luke swallowed hard. "Umm, yeah."

Nikki shifted her weight.

"I mean, no. Or..." Luke wiped his hands on his jeans. "What was the question?"

Marko smiled. Depositions were not just about pinning down the person's testimony; lawyers also used them to measure the strength of the witness. Luke was about to cry, and Marko hadn't even started yet. "Will the court reporter read the question back to the witness?" he asked.

The court reporter was a woman in her mid- to late-fifties with small, birdlike bones. She removed her fingers from the small keyboard, then leaned forward to read the tiny words. "Have you ever given a deposition before?" she read. Her fingers returned to the keys of her steno machine, poised and waiting.

"No," Luke said, tugging at his collar.

Marko was surprised to see him in a suit. It was an uncomfortable outfit for a teenager who had placed himself—or been placed?—in an uncomfortable position. He'd better loosen that tie; it was about to get a lot more uncomfortable. "Today, I'm going to ask you a bunch of questions. All I want is the truth. I am not trying to trick you," Marko began. *At least not yet.* "If I ask a question that is confusing, will you ask me to reword it?"

"Yes," Luke said, his gaze darting to his mother, then back to Marko.

"All right, then, let's get started. State your name for the record."

"Lucas Adam Price."

"How old are you?"

"Seventeen."

"Who do you live with?"

"My mother, father, and my brother."

"How old is your brother?"

"Twenty."

"What is his name?"

"Adam Lucas Price."

"You have matching names," Marko observed.

"What?" Luke said.

"Your brother's middle name is your first name, and your middle name is his first name."

Luke shrugged.

"You can't do that. The court reporter can't take down body movements. You have to answer out loud."

"You didn't ask a question," Nikki interjected.

Marko raised an eyebrow. "These questions are for your son, not you."

"Then ask a question," Nikki said curtly.

"Mrs. Price," McJames said, his tone soft. "I know this is hard for you and your son, but it will go a lot faster if you refrain from interjecting." His eyes shifted back to Marko, and he gave a small nod. "She's right," he added gratuitously.

"Where do you attend school?" Marko asked.

"Franklin Senior High."

"What grade are you in?"

"I'm a senior."

"Do you know my client, Whitney Moore?" Marko placed a hand on the back of Whitney's chair and waited to no avail for Luke to look at his former teacher.

"I know her," Luke replied.

"How do you know her?"

"She was my English teacher. Then we started having an—" He swallowed hard, his gaze flicking to Nikki and then back to Marko. "We were having sex."

"Do you play any sports?" Allee knew Marko would probably come back to the alleged relationship later. He was guiding the questioning, not Luke.

"Yes."

"What sports do you play?"

"All of them."

"You play every single sport?"

"Yes."

"You play football?"

"Yes."

"And tennis?"

"Well, not tennis."

"That's a sport, isn't it?"

Luke shrugged. "I mean...I guess."

"Okay. So you don't play *all* the sports," Marko said.

"No."

"Are you playing a sport now?"

"Yes. It's baseball season."

"So you play football in the fall and baseball in the spring. Do you play any sports in the winter?"

"Yes. I'm on the basketball team."

"Is it fair to say that while you are in school, you always have after-school practices?"

Luke was nodding in agreement. "Yeah, I don't get a break," he said. "The sports overlap, so I start practices for basketball and baseball later in the season than other players because I'm still playing the sport before that."

"I see." Marko looked down at his notes, tapping his pen against his legal notepad. "You had Mrs. Moore as a teacher, is that right?"

"Yes."

"She was your English teacher?"

"Yes."

Marko looked to Allee, who nodded slightly. It was time. "Do you read books in that class?" he asked.

Luke looked around the room as if that was the dumbest question he had ever heard. "It's English, so, like, yeah."

The answer was perfect—for Allee's purposes, at least.

"What was the last book you discussed in Mrs. Moore's classroom?"

"*The Count of Monte Cristo.*"

Allee made eye contact with Marko. She nodded imperceptibly.

He continued to stare at her, then shrugged and changed the subject. "You mentioned you were having sex with Mrs. Moore."

"Whitney? Yeah." Luke's gaze shifted around the room, but he didn't look at his former teacher.

"When were you doing that?"

"We'd find time."

"I'm going to need you to be a little more specific than that," Marko replied levelly. "When?"

"During the day."

"When 'during the day?'"

"Like between classes and stuff," Luke said. "Is that even important?"

Yeah, it was important. It was going to sink Luke's little ship, Allee knew. "Where was this happening?"

"In the bathroom."

"Girls' or boys'?"

Luke looked quickly toward his mother. "Umm...both."

"At the same time?" Marko said, lifting his eyebrows.

"What?" Luke asked, confused.

Marko put his elbows on the table and leaned forward. "I'm trying to find out when and where you and my client had sex. You're telling me during the day and in both the boys' and girls' bathrooms—is that right?"

"Yeah." Luke sat back, folded his arms, and nodded his agreement.

"And when did this start?" Marko asked.

"I can't remember."

"Months ago? Years?"

"I just said I can't remember!"

"Was it before Christmas, or after?"

"After."

This kid was so full of shit, Allee thought.

"So you *can* remember." Marko smiled and leaned toward the younger man. His eyes met and held Luke's before he abruptly changed the subject. "School safety is important, don't you agree?"

Luke was trying to meet Marko's stare, but the question had him off-balance. "I—I guess."

"Did you know there are cameras covering every inch of the high school?" Marko asked.

"Yeah. We all know that."

"Well, I'm going to represent to you I've seen all of the footage from all those cameras going back several months."

Allee watched as Luke looked to Nikki for help. Nikki, in turn, looked to McJames, who appeared confused but didn't do or say anything to assist Luke or Nikki.

"S-So?" Luke stammered.

Marko smiled, showing even white teeth. "Would it surprise you to know that there are no recordings of you and my client ever entering a bathroom together?"

Allee was thrilled to see Luke's eyes were now resting on his mother. He was busted.

"Those recordings are not released to the public," Nikki interjected. "I checked with the school."

"Nikki, I have no doubt you did—and I have to wonder why," Marko said. "But right now I'm more interested in your son's answers, and I'll remind you one last time that you are not allowed to interrupt my questioning." He flashed another fake smile. "As I recall, I asked a question your son has so far failed to answer. Luke?"

Nikki's interruption had given Luke time to think. "We didn't go together. She'd go first and I'd come in a few minutes later," he offered, then sat back, self-satisfied.

Allee almost smiled. Marko had anticipated the response. "Would it surprise you to know that there are no recordings of that either?"

Luke wiped at his brow. "How do you know? Do you have the recordings?" he asked.

"Of course not," Nikki said, watching Marko closely. She shifted her body so that she was facing the prosecutor. "He's bluffing." She turned her attention to McJames. "They don't have anything like that, do they?"

"I don't know," McJames replied. "Do you?" he asked Marko.

"Doesn't matter. I'm still waiting on discovery from the State," Marko began, "which is taking longer than usual, I might add. I don't have to produce reciprocal discovery until I get yours."

"See, he's lying!" Nikki said, turning to her son with a satisfied look.

"It seems like the idea of school recordings has you alarmed, Mrs. Price," Marko said. "Could it be that they might show something different than you and your son—two God-fearing people—are saying?"

"Don't answer that," McJames instructed Nikki. "Can we get back to questioning the witness?"

"Certainly," Marko said. "Did anyone see you go into the bathroom?" he asked Luke.

"I was usually with one of my friends."

"Which friend?" Marko lifted his pen, placed it against his legal notebook, poised and ready to write. It was an act, though, a ruse. Luke didn't have a witness. He knew it. Marko knew it. Even Nikki seemed to know.

Luke sat quietly, and then began to shake his head. "I...I can't remember. But I didn't lie—I don't lie. That's a sin." He was talking to Nikki.

"I think we should take a break. He's just a boy," Nikki said. She turned to McJames. "Can we take a break?"

McJames looked to Marko, who nodded his approval. "Let's take a ten-minute break," McJames said.

When all but Whitney, Allee, and Marko had left the small room, Allee spoke up. "Can they do that? Can they interrupt you like that?"

"Not under the rules," Marko replied. "But I think we've already got what we needed."

Normally, he'd be annoyed with the interruption when he was in the flow of questioning, but he'd already gotten what he needed out of the witness. He'd sworn under oath to something that video surveillance could easily disprove. McJames didn't know it yet, but Marko had already won. When it came time for trial, Marko would destroy Luke's credibility in minutes—especially now that he was sober.

"He's lying," Whitney said cautiously.

"We know," Marko and Allee said in unison. "We have enough to go to trial, but it really shouldn't go that far," Marko said. "I need to convince McJames to dismiss the charges before we even get to that point, but I'm not sure we have enough."

Allee held up her phone. "I might be able to help with that."

57

ALLEE

When McJames and the others returned, Allee stood, taking that as her cue to leave the room. The questioning would resume soon enough, but she had enough to try and prove her theory. She didn't want to spend the rest of her afternoon listening to a teenager spin tales.

Whitney grabbed her arm, her long fingers encircling Allee's tattoo—the one that said, "You are mine, you shall be mine, you and I are one forever."

"Where are you going?" Whitney's eyes were wide, pleading. "I need you."

It was the first time in Allee's life that she was wanted, let alone needed. "I'm going into the hallway to work on a...project."

"Now?" Whitney asked.

"Yes." Allee met Whitney's eyes and softly intoned, "Trust me."

Whitney released her arm, but she didn't look convinced.

"Trust me on this, Whitney," Allee said again. She was watching McJames, who was in his seat, opening his laptop, pretending like he wasn't listening. "It'll be worth it."

McJames' head snapped up when he heard Allee's promise. She could see the thoughts as they passed behind his eyes. Interest followed by dismissal.

Go ahead and judge, Allee thought. *I'll prove you wrong in less than an hour*. She stepped out of the deposition room in time to catch Nikki and Luke in a heated discussion. They were in a corner, the same secluded area where Jaxson had stood shortly before he ended his life. The heat was coming exclusively from Nikki. Luke loomed large over her but was clearly terrified. As Allee watched, Nikki jabbed her son in the chest with a long, manicured fingernail. He flinched, his body crumpling in on itself. The conversation continued until Nikki—perhaps aware of Allee's presence—froze before turning her full attention (and wrath) toward Allee.

Allee had dropped into one of the seats, produced her laptop and a pair of earbuds, and pretended she'd seen nothing. She opened her laptop and pressed the power button, willing it to boot up quickly. She kept her gaze on the dark screen, listening to the *click-click-click* of Nikki's heels as she approached. Allee didn't look up, even when the sound of Nikki's heels came to a stop immediately in front of her.

"You saw nothing, little felon! You of all people should know snitches get stitches."

Allee almost laughed. Had Nikki heard that on TV? Was this church-going, PTA-attending, public official seriously threatening her? It didn't make any sense. And if this was how she treated her kid in public, what was going on at home? She didn't respond; instead, she focused on her laptop.

Nikki remained for a long, tense moment, then turned on her expensive heels and clicked into the deposition room, with Luke's shuffling feet following.

The door slammed, and in the heavy silence that followed, Allee issued a sigh of relief and got to work, first opening an artificial intelligence application. Then she plugged her phone into her computer, downloaded the recording of Luke's deposition, and fed it into the AI application. She typed in thirteen words.

Then she waited.

An hour passed. The courthouse was still, silent, almost eerie. It was a large building and a public one, but with no court scheduled for the day it was largely uninhabited. The sound of someone trudging up the stairs caught her attention. She eyed the staircase warily, waiting for the person's face to emerge.

When it did, she had to fight the urge to run.

It was Adam Price. Seeing her, he sneered openly. She looked from Adam to the corner where Jaxson had hidden before he jumped. Before he slid the USB drive toward her.

Maybe she did know the password after all!

Just then, the conference room door swung open and everyone but the court reporter filed out, with nary a glance in her direction. Whitney and Marko were the last to leave, with the jailer trailing close behind.

Allee stood. "Are you taking another break?" she asked Marko.

"No. Luke's deposition is done," Marko explained. "I'm deposing Adam next." He nodded to Allee's former boss and tormentor.

"Why?"

"Because I want to know if Whitney's snooping around the restaurant had anything to do with these charges," he said. "That's what you've been insinuating, isn't it?"

"I don't know what that means, but if you're asking if I think the family is involved, my answer is hell yes!" Allee replied quickly. "But they'll all just lie."

"I know," Marko said, and winked at Whitney. "I'm counting on it."

Allee looked around her, noting that everyone had remained in the atrium. Surprisingly, no one had left to use the restroom, stretch their legs, or make calls.

It was now or never. Showtime.

Allee unplugged her earbuds and cranked the volume on her laptop to the maximum. Then she pressed play.

Luke's voice burst from the speakers, bouncing off the ceiling and walls, amplifying, and shooting back in an echo. It sounded like he was all around them, speaking like an omniscient narrator. "No," Luke's voice boomed. "I did not have sex with Whitney. I lied. That's a sin."

Nikki, Adam, and Luke had been huddled, with Nikki again doing the talking. Upon hearing Luke's voice, they turned to face Allee. She watched as Luke, hearing his voice, went pale. He'd said every one of these words during his deposition, just not in that order. That's where the AI application had come in.

Allee had set the recording to repeat. Nikki headed straight for Allee.

"My son did not say that!" she shouted over Luke's voice coming from the computer, over and over.

"Well, actually, he did," Allee said. She stopped the recording. Silence descended over the courthouse. Every eye on the third floor was on her. "AI's a bitch, isn't it?"

Nikki's eyes widened. "You took Luke's words out of context!"

"There's a lot of that going around." Allee closed her computer and stood, towering over the smaller woman.

Nikki took an involuntary step back, but her expression remained hard, hateful. "What is your point?"

"I spent thirty minutes in that deposition recording your son. Thirty minutes. Your son had Whitney as a teacher for almost a year. A year! He had hundreds of hours to record her, including a class where they were discussing *The Count of Monte Cristo*. I don't know if you've read that book, but I have. There's a lot of free time in prison. That book is about greed, sex, violence, and revenge—all words Luke needed Whitney to say in order to make a recording just like this one." Allee tapped the laptop with her index finger.

"What are you saying?" McJames asked.

"I think you know exactly what I'm saying."

Nikki reddened, anger flashing behind her eyes. "You're going to be sorry." She turned to McJames. "Are we done here? Can Luke go back to school now?"

McJames nodded slowly, his gaze glued to Allee's laptop. He had under-estimated her, she knew. He'd viewed her as invisible and unimportant merely because of her past. Well, an unimportant felon had just pulled the pin and thrown a hand grenade into the middle of his case.

Underestimate that, she thought.

58

WHITNEY

If Whitney hadn't heard that recording with her own ears, she wouldn't believe it possible. Allee had not only figured out how Luke had made the recording of her, but she'd turned it around and done the same thing to him.

"Daniel," Marko began, walking toward the prosecutor with a wide grin. "Looks like you've got some problems with your case."

"Your...*investigator's* little trick doesn't prove shit. The case is still solid," McJames replied, trying to remain poised. But Whitney could hear his words didn't carry their usual gusto. "Luke will describe the relationship. He will say that she said those things. He's trustworthy. I believe him—so will a jury."

Whitney felt the jailer's hand touch her lightly. It was time to go. But she wanted to hear this.

Marko smiled broadly. "You'll recall we don't have to prove anything," he said. "And when you add Allee's theory to the video from the school, well..."

McJames narrowed his eyes. "You're bluffing."

"I'm not," Marko assured him.

"Where'd you get the recordings?"

"Doesn't matter," Marko replied. "What does matter is that I can authenticate them and that they show Luke and Whitney were never alone. Ever. Not in the classroom. Not in a bathroom. And just between us, when I get him on the stand, it will get ugly. Quick. I mean, I'll smile and all, but it'll be ugly. You have to know that."

Whitney was watching Marko, fascinated.

McJames' gaze flickered toward Whitney. She was standing in the hallway, halfway between Marko and Allee. She held his gaze. A challenge. *See, I told you*, she willed her eyes to convey. *I didn't do it*. He hadn't believed her. He'd believed Luke instead. And now Luke had made him look like a fool. *Good*, Whitney thought. He'd destroyed her family. Even if she was released, even if they removed her chains now and said, "*Whoops! We made a mistake*," it wouldn't undo the damage they'd caused to her career and her marriage. They couldn't rewind time and unarrest her in front of her young, impressionable son. They couldn't give her back the days she'd been gone from the home, unable to read Arlo bedtime stories or tuck him in at night. The damage was done.

"Let's go talk in private," McJames said, motioning for Marko to follow him into a separate meeting room. With a quick wink, Marko followed.

"Hang tight," he whispered.

"Whitney, come here." Allee beckoned. "I thought of something."

Whitney had Allee to thank for everything. All the evidence that supported her innocence had come through Allee's hard work. Even if the prosecutor took her to trial and somehow got a conviction, she'd be forever grateful to Allee. The jailer nodded his approval, and Whitney shuffled toward Allee, the chains weighing her down. "Yeah?"

Allee shifted her gaze to a man standing in a corner. Shadows engulfed his features, but Whitney recognized him as Adam, Jaxson's former boss. "What's he doing here?"

"He's Marko's next deposition," Allee replied. "But that's not what I wanted to show you." She sat and opened her laptop, then reached into her laptop bag, produced the thumb drive that Jaxson had created before his death, and plugged it into the port. When she clicked on it, the password box popped up. "I think I know what the password is."

"You do?"

"Watch." Allee's fingers flew across the keyboard, then she pressed "enter" and sat back. The cursor turned into a whirling bar, then the computer indicated a successful download of the thumb drive's contents.

"You're amazing!" Whitney exclaimed. "What was the password?"

Allee's expression turned grim. She nodded toward Adam. "It was *Mr.Price*, with no spaces."

"What? Why him?"

Allee's gaze shifted to the screen. She moved the cursor so it hovered over the first video. "You'll see."

59

MARKO

"Show me the recordings from the school," McJames demanded. Sweat beaded along his brow. He knew he was in trouble.

"What's in it for me?" Marko asked. "Will you dismiss the charges?"

"Whose? Yours or Whitney's?"

In all the chaos with his sobriety and Whitney's case, he'd nearly forgotten about his operating while intoxicated arrest. "I'm not talking about me. But since you brought that up, when are you going to file the Trial Information?"

"I've got forty-five days."

"Well, it's all over the news, thanks to Nikki, so the sooner the better. I'd rather not have things calm down just to flare up again when you get around to filing the TI."

"I'll see what I can do."

That was lawyer-speak for *your emergency is not my emergency.*

"I'd appreciate it. Will you dismiss her charges if the recordings show there is no way that the kid was ever alone with his teacher?"

McJames sighed, his bravado leaving along with his breath. "It's just not that simple," he said. "You know that."

"What's complicated about dismissing a case against an innocent woman with no criminal history?" The conference room was the size of a walk-in closet. There were four chairs and one small table. No other furni-ture could fit. Marko lowered himself into one of the blue plastic chairs and leaned back, placing his hands behind his head, interlocking his fingers.

Despite their being unaccompanied, McJames looked around the room before he spoke. "Look, uh, Marko. How can I say this? This is a…political case. It's caught national attention. And then there's the Prices…" He dropped into the chair across from Marko. "I'm just saying I have to tread lightly."

"You can't tread lightly when you are holding Whitney in jail for crimes she didn't commit. That's wrong. You know it."

"I can't just dismiss the charges," McJames explained. "How about I agree to release her before trial?"

"I'm listening," Marko said, bringing his hands down and leaning forward.

"Give me the recordings. I'll listen and look at them. If they are consis-tent with what you're saying, I'll agree to her release before trial, but only with supervision."

Release with supervision meant that Whitney would be assigned a pretrial release officer who would keep tabs on her. *That's like probation without a conviction.* "No," Marko said, shaking his head. "She doesn't need supervision. Release her OR and we've got a deal." OR was short for "own recognizance," meaning a straight release, no strings attached. People out on OR bonds didn't have to post a bond or keep in touch with anyone other than their attorney.

"Fine," McJames said, running a hand through his bright red hair. "This isn't going to go over well with the public. Or my boss."

Marko shrugged. "Sometimes doing the right thing isn't easy." He reached into his laptop bag and produced a high-capacity thumb drive. He'd saved all the recordings on two separate drives, one for the State and one for himself. He handed the small object to the prosecutor. "Watch it now. I want her released by the end of the day. Of course, I could give it to one of those media wolves you called in."

McJames stood and closed his thick hand around the small object. "This better hold what you say it does," he said.

Marko left the meeting room, a spring in his step. He couldn't wait to tell Whitney the good news. She was getting out. Well, probably. He turned the corner and found Whitney and Allee in the hallway, hovering over Allee's computer. The horrified expressions on their faces leached all the excitement out of him.

A pleading voice, unrecognizable to Marko, burst from Allee's speakers. "No! No! No! Not again, Mr. Price. I will be good this time."

Marko felt a tingle run up his spine.

"I swear I'll be good! I swear it!" A scream followed, one so filled with agony that goosebumps popped up along Marko's neck and arms.

What the hell were they watching?

60

ALLEE

The screen was black, as if something covered the camera, but Allee could sense movement. Whoever had the camera was in complete darkness. There was a loud bang and a shuffling noise. It felt sinister, but she didn't know what she was seeing or hearing. A harsh voice cut through the darkness, as raw and broken as a wounded animal, but Allee easily recognized it.

"Is it working?" he whispered. The screen shook with the sound. He was striking the camera.

"That's Jaxson!" Whitney whispered.

She reached toward the computer screen like she could somehow go back in time and yank him out of the room of horrors that he'd apparently been held in. Her manacles jangled, and she startled, pulling her hand back. "Why is he in the dark like that? Where is he?" Whitney asked.

Allee shook her head. Wherever it was, it was worse than Mitchellville. She couldn't see it, but she could feel it in her bones. Jaxson was in living hell.

"I'm going to put the camera down," she heard Jaxson whisper. "I don't want him to catch me."

"Who is 'him?'" Whitney's voice rose by several octaves.

"I don't know yet," Allee said. She did, but she needed a minute. "Hush for a sec."

A light carved through the darkness, emanating from a peephole built into a wooden door. Even on video, the light was so powerful it temporarily blinded Allee. She didn't want to imagine what it had been like for Jaxson, kept like that in total darkness for no telling how long. As Allee and Whitney watched in horror, two eyes filled the space. Allee couldn't tell what color they were.

"Please let me out," she could hear Jaxson beg. "I won't do it again. I promise."

The person at the door didn't respond.

Jaxson swallowed hard. "My apologies, sir. I won't do it again, *Mr. Price.*"

Mr. Price. Two words, so innocuous on their own, turned sinister together.

"It's Adam Price," Allee said.

"Adam?" Whitney's eyes widened. "The manager at The Yellow Lark?"

Allee nodded. They each looked at Price, who remained pressed into a corner across the room. While they watched, McJames approached Adam, whispered in his ear, and the two of them left quickly.

"It was a setup—wasn't it?" Whitney asked rhetorically. "I told you!" She raised her wrists, displaying the shackles. "I was getting too close to the truth. That—that *monster* abused my brother until he killed himself. I wasn't going to give up until I found out what happened, so they set me up."

"They found a way to get rid of you," Allee agreed. "Or so they thought."

"I won't forget to wipe down my station, Mr. Price! I won't! I swear it!" On the recording, Jaxson was growing more desperate by the second. "Will you let me out? Please. It's been days. Please. I won't do it again. I swear," Jaxson pleaded, and then paused, adding, "Mr. Price."

A lock clicked. The door began to open. Jaxson did not move toward it.

"He's letting him out," Whitney said excitedly.

There was a sliding noise, then the door slammed shut again.

No. He's not, Allee thought.

"Eat that," Price said. "And I'll let you out."

Whitney and Allee struggled to see Jaxson as he shuffled toward the door. Retrieving whatever was on the floor, he groaned.

"Eat it and I'll let you out. Every. Last. Bite."

"But it has maggots!"

"You said you were hungry earlier. I recall you begging for food. That is food."

"No, it's not!" Whitney cried. She was interacting with the recording like she could somehow change the outcome.

"Eat it or you aren't coming out," Price said.

Whitney and Allee watched in horror while Jaxson obeyed. Thankfully, the video was dark enough that they couldn't see clearly, but the groaning and gagging they heard was sufficient to make Allee's stomach churn.

"Are you done?" they heard Price ask.

"Yes."

Allee could hear Whitney's intake of breath when Price opened the door again, and with an object of some sort in his hand, he demanded, "Let me see." As Adam stepped into the room, the light caught the object. It was round, long, and metallic-looking. A pipe? A night stick?

Allee shivered as Adam used the object in his hand to tap the cement floor. It made a chiming sound instead of a thud.

Metal, then, Allee thought.

"You missed a piece," Price said.

"It was dark, Mr. Price. I couldn't see. I meant to eat it all. I swear."

They watched in horror as Price stalked toward Jaxson, smacking the end of the metal pole into his palm. "That's a punishment."

Then Jaxson started screaming. Every hair on Allee's body stood on end.

"Stop it! Stop it! Make it stop!" Whitney was backing away from the computer screen. "I can't see any more!"

Allee scrolled through the drives she had downloaded, counting. "There are thirteen to go," she finally said.

"Oh, my God!" Whitney placed a hand over her mouth. "He killed him! Adam Price killed my brother!"

"What the hell are you watching?" Marko said, arriving at Allee's side.

"A nightmare," Allee said.

61

WHITNEY

He's here, Whitney thought, her gaze traveling around the open atrium. She'd seen him before Allee started the recordings, in the very place where he'd driven her brother to commit suicide.

"Where is he?" Whitney demanded. "I'm going to kill him."

"I don't know who you are talking about, but I would advise against murder," Marko said. "Especially in a courthouse." There was a positive, almost joyful lilt to his words.

What the hell was wrong with him? How could anyone or anything in the world hold any joy when those horrible things had been done to Whitney's brother. How had she not known? Why didn't he tell her? "Oh, it'll be worth it. Where is Adam Price?"

Marko sobered. "Hold on," he said. "What's going on?" He looked from Allee to Whitney. "You're watching a blank screen and screaming; I feel like I showed up at halftime and the scoreboard is broken."

"Adam Price," Allee said softly. Her voice was bleak, haunted. "He tortured Whitney's brother." Her gaze remained on her computer. "It's all right here."

"He's the reason Jaxson killed himself," Whitney said. "He'd been tortured, tormented."

"You're sure?" Marko said.

"Yes!" Allee and Whitney said in unison.

Allee nodded vigorously. "We only watched one of the videos, but it's obvious that's what was happening." Allee's phone chirped, and she reached into her pocket. She unlocked it and looked at the screen, her eyes switching between the computer and her phone. She was silent for a long, tense moment. "And I think he's doing the same thing to Nate."

"What?" Whitney hissed. "Why do you think that?"

Allee turned her phone around, showing a text message from her aunt, which read, "Please check on him. I haven't heard from him in days."

"Now I'm really going to kill him," Whitney said.

"Allee, I don't understand what Nate's disappearance has to do with Adam Price," Marko said. "I mean, I know he's not paying on time and working people ridiculous hours, but—"

Marko was not keeping up, and it was pissing Whitney off. If he'd been paying attention; if he'd bothered to try and put the pieces together, he wouldn't be so far behind.

"You have to go forward with the deposition," Allee said, standing and shoving her laptop into its bag. "You need to buy me some time so I can get Nate out of there."

"I'm going," Whitney said.

"Even if you could, I don't think that's a good idea," Marko advised. "It could be dangerous."

"Do you have a better idea?" Allee asked.

"Not really, and there isn't going to be a deposition."

"What?" Whitney asked. "Why not?"

"Don't need it." Marko shrugged. "That's what I was so excited about. You're getting released, Whitney! It's likely McJames will dismiss your case. It'll take a while for them to process you out." He ran a hand through his dark hair. "But it's going to happen today."

"That's fine, but I can't wait," Allee said, slinging her bag over her shoulder. "Not after seeing that video. I'm going over there now. I'll force my way in if I have to."

"Whoa!" Marko raised his hands, palms out. "Let's pump the brakes here. We should go to the cops. This isn't a problem to solve ourselves."

"No, that'll take too long," Allee said. "First, we'll have to talk to someone, do a full interview, which will be, what? An hour? Then they'll want to watch the videos, do some investigation into that. You know they'll doubt their authenticity just because I'm a criminal. That'll take another hour. Then they'll want to get a search warrant and arrange for backup, and all the while...all the while"—her breathing had grown heavy, her tone intense—"Nate is in there *eating maggots!*"

"What?" Marko said.

Allee shook her head. "There isn't time to explain. You can watch the video—that'll show you what's going on if you don't believe me—but I'm not waiting while you do it."

"No. I'll go with you," Marko said with a sigh. "If for no other reason than to try to keep you from committing any felonies while you do whatever it is you plan to do."

"Break his legs," Whitney said. "Every. Single. Bone."

The words and the vehemence behind them surprised even Whitney. She'd never been a violent person. She was always a *turn the other cheek* type. But she found that, at least in this instance, she had changed. She didn't want him dead; she wouldn't go that far, but only because she wanted him to face lady justice. He didn't have to walk into a courtroom to face her, though. He didn't have to walk into his prison cell either.

62

MARKO

"What's the plan?" Marko asked. He put a hand on Allee's shoulder to try to slow her. "You can't just walk inside and demand to see a secret torture room."

"Watch me." Allee shrugged off his hand and balled her hands into fists as she stalked toward the back door of The Yellow Lark.

Marko had seen her angry, but he'd never seen her like this. The heat and intensity radiating from her frightened him—and it wasn't directed at him. He'd come along to keep her level-headed, to talk some sense into her before she did something that would land her in a jail cell, but he could now see that was fruitless. Allee was a five-foot-ten-inch mass of muscle and fury.

"Allee, wait!"

"No, I'm going in. You can do what you want."

Stopping her would be like calming an enraged mother bear. Impossible. "And then what?" he asked. He was having to hustle to keep pace with her long strides.

She didn't slow down. "I strangle Adam until the life leaves his worthless eyes."

"And then you go back to prison," Marko said. "This time forever."

"No," she said through gritted teeth. "Not this time."

"Allee!"

She stopped at last. They were steps away from the restaurant's back door.

"You don't have a plan," Marko began, breathing hard. "You don't even know where Nate is. Do you think Adam is just going to point out the cell or chamber or whatever the hell, and then bare his neck so you can assault him? If he's doing everything you say he is—"

"He is!"

"Then he'll have a way to protect himself—alarms, weapons, who knows what?"

"Okay." Allee sighed heavily. "Then what's your idea?"

He motioned for her to follow him. They moved until they were flush with the side of the building, where they were concealed but could see anyone who would come out the back door.

"We wait," Marko said.

"For what? He doesn't use that door. He never does."

"I'm not talking about him. I mean anyone else. Does anyone use that door?"

"Yeah. All the other employees. They use it to come and to—"

As she spoke, the back door swung open and Lorna stepped outside, producing a cigarette and a lighter. She put the cigarette in her mouth and struck the lighter, placing the flame to the end as she stepped down the steps and into the alley below.

Unseen by Lorna, Marko cleared his throat loudly as he and Allee stepped away from the wall.

"What the hell?" Lorna swung around, taking a defensive stance. "Oh," she said when her gaze fell on Allee. "It's you again. Where's the princess? And what are you doing back in this hellhole?" She took a deep drag from her cigarette, then tilted her head back and blew the smoke in the air.

"Is my cousin here?"

"Cousin?"

"Nate Shore."

"Oh, Nathaniel. We call him Nathaniel. *Mr. Price* likes it better." Lorna uttered her boss's name with disdain.

"Whatever," Allee said. "Is he here?"

"I think so." Lorna took another drag. "Nobody has seen him, but nobody saw him leave either." She shrugged and exhaled. "I tried to warn you about this place."

We've heard that before, Marko thought.

"Yeah, well, what can I say? I don't scare easy," Allee said impatiently. "And what do you mean, nobody has seen him? He's a cook."

"Nathaniel is Mr. Price's new favorite," Lorna said. "I've never been so thankful to be a woman. His favorites are always men."

"What does that mean?" Allee's words were clipped.

Lorna shrugged, seemingly unbothered. "It's not my business, so I don't get involved."

Allee stepped forward, but Marko put an arm in front of her to protect Lorna. "But?" he asked.

"But," Lorna said, taking another drag from her cigarette and blowing the smoke out agonizingly slowly, "I know he takes them to the basement. And then they just...disappear for a day or two."

"And Nate is down there now?" Marko asked.

Lorna nodded. "I think so."

Marko watched her closely. She might have some stuff in her record, but she was a kid, scared shitless and trying to act tough.

"You've got to get me in there," Allee said. "I need to get him out."

"Nobody goes in the basement," Lorna said, her tone flat. "Mr. Price's rule."

"Lorna, I need your help!" Allee pleaded.

"I'll show you the stairs," Lorna said with a shrug. "That's as far as I'll go." She dropped the cigarette and crushed it beneath her heel. "You ready?"

"Yes," Allee said with determination.

Marko wasn't so sure. The look of abject terror that had crossed Lorna's face had him hesitating. Lorna was young, but she had seen the dark side. People like her—people who had been through the things Lorna had—didn't scare easily.

If she was afraid, he and Allee probably should be, too.

63

ALLEE

"Stay hidden," Lorna said as she led the way into the building. "I'm not going to prison over this."

Like every other employee at the restaurant, Lorna was on probation or parole. If Adam Price caught them, the best-case scenario for Lorna would be termination from her employment and a warrant for violation of probation.

"I hear that," Allee said. If Adam caught her, she'd likely end up with a felony burglary charge and an automatic parole violation. Once again, that was the best-case scenario. Allee didn't even want to consider the worst. Nate was probably living it.

Lorna headed into the open area of the kitchen, her head on a swivel. Allee and Marko hung back, waiting beside a large piece of kitchen equipment.

"Come on," Lorna indicated with a wave. "It's clear."

The kitchen still had people working the line, washing and chopping meat and vegetables. Nobody looked up. Like most criminals, they minded their own business. As she walked through the kitchen, a sense of dread overcame Allee. She had promised herself that she'd never come back. Yet here she was.

Lorna led them into a long and narrow hallway that appeared to run the entire length of the restaurant. When they came to the end, Lorna turned to the left and gestured to a large steel door.

"That'll take you to the basement," she said.

Allee studied the door. It was heavy like the door from Jaxson's video, but it didn't have a peephole. Allee reached forward, pulling on the handle. It twisted, and the door swung open on well-oiled hinges. She'd expected it to be locked. *This is too easy*, her mind cried out. *It's a trap*. She pushed the thoughts aside. Nate was in danger. In her attempts to keep him safe from himself and free of prison, she'd pushed him into a much worse situation. Now, she needed to help get him out of the trouble she'd caused. She took a step toward the door, but Marko again caught her shoulder, holding her in place.

"Are you sure about this?" he asked.

Allee looked down the dark staircase. The air was still, quiet, sinister—a mustiness mixed with sweat and something faintly metallic. *Blood, perhaps.* "Come on," she said, removing her phone from her pocket and clicking on the flashlight, then aiming it into the darkness. "We are out of time and out of options, and I'm out of patience."

"We've still got options," Marko cautioned. "We could go to the cops."

"We already discussed that," Allee replied, placing her foot on the first step that led downstairs. "You can go to the cops. But I'm going in."

Marko sighed heavily, but it was a sigh of resignation, not irritation. She felt him on the steps behind her as they descended slowly.

"If you get caught," Lorna whispered into the darkness, the light from the hallway surrounding her small figure, "I had nothing to do with this." She abruptly closed the door, plunging them into complete darkness. A burst of anxiety shot through Allee. She had to fight the urge to dash up the stairs and check to make sure the door was still unlocked.

"You still there?" she asked Marko.

"Of course," he replied. "I'm too scared and too stupid to be anywhere else."

She smiled in the darkness. "Okay. One step at a time." She led them carefully down the stairs in total silence, aside from the soft sounds made by the soles of their shoes against the cement steps. The air grew thicker and heavier with each step. She'd expected to find a room when they reached the bottom, but instead they found a small landing and a second steel door.

"What's with the doors?" Marko whispered. "What are they storing in here? Solid gold bars?"

"Prisoners." Allee's stare settled on the peephole. It was the door from Jaxson's video.

Allee handed Marko her phone and approached the door. Should she knock? Should she call out? Was Nate even behind it? Was Adam in there with him? One wrong move could result in disaster. For Marko. For Nate. For her.

"What are you waiting for?" Marko whispered.

Strength. She'd been dying to get here, to force her way inside and wrench this very door open so she could usher Nate to safety. But now that she was here, she didn't want to see what awaited her.

He's living it, you fool, Allee chastised herself. While she stood here hesitating, Nate was living through the horrors locked behind it.

She took one last breath, released it slowly, then gripped the doorknob and turned it as quietly as possible. The door opened and she felt stale air rush past her, followed by the unmistakable stench of blood and urine.

Marko coughed. Allee gagged.

Then they entered.

64

MARKO

Marko's brain screamed for him to run. The basement was pitch black and deathly quiet, but it felt and smelled like death and despair. They should leave while they still could.

"We should get the cops," Marko whispered. "I think we've seen enough."

"I'm not leaving without Nate," Allee replied. She surveyed the room with the small light that issued from the back of her phone.

He had his phone, too, but he didn't produce it. It would draw attention to him. They were not alone in the basement. He could sense the presence of someone else, watching, waiting. *For what?* He couldn't be certain.

Maybe for them to leave. Maybe for the right time to strike.

"I don't see anyone." Despite himself, he allowed his eyes to follow the light. The walls, floor, and ceiling were bare cement. A bucket sat in a back corner next to a drain that reeked of urine. Boxes were stacked along the side walls, all appearing to be untouched and dusty with thin spiderwebs connecting them.

"There's another room," Allee said, moving her light to a small, crude opening in the wall.

The sides of the opening were jagged, like someone had ripped into the wall with a crowbar. It was only about four feet high and two feet wide. They'd have to crouch to get through.

"Let's check it out," Allee said, taking a step toward it. "Come on."

There was no way he was following her. He stood stock-still as Allee made her way through the opening. Darkness enveloped him when she was through to the other side. He shuddered, uncertain of where to look or what to do. He could follow her, follow the light, produce his own light and become a potential target, or remain standing in the dark, closer to the exit, closer to freedom. In the end, his body chose for him. It locked up, freezing him in place like a rabbit sensing the tiny disturbances of a snake in the grass.

Someone was in the room with him. Marko could sense the change in the air, movement from somewhere other than Allee's direction. It was slow, cautious, stalking.

"He's here!" Allee cried from the other side of the wall. "Nate! Wake up! Nate!"

Even from where he was, Marko could hear Nate groan.

"Allee," Marko heard Nate rasp. "What are you doing here?" He sounded half awake, like someone emerging from the fog of drugs, or sleep, or a concussion. "You have to leave."

Marko heard a thump and a loud crack. The light that had been trickling through the opening in the door disappeared.

Someone is here, Marko thought. A predator. And Marko and Allee had become his new prey.

65

ALLEE

"What the hell?" Allee swung around, her hand stinging. Something had hit her. Hard. But the darkness was so total that she could not see directly in front of her face. She'd been holding her phone in her left hand, and she reached up to feel it with her right. There was no wetness or stickiness, so she wasn't bleeding. But it was starting to swell. A broken bone was a strong possibility.

"You shouldn't be here," Nate said.

"That makes two of us. Three with Marko." She looked around in the darkness. Wherever the hell he was.

"He isn't going to let you leave."

"Screw that," Allee said. "This ends here." She heard an odd pair of sounds from the room she'd just departed. A cry followed, one of pain and agony. Then the unmistakable sound of a body hitting the unforgiving concrete floor.

"*Marko!*" Allee whisper-shouted. He didn't respond.

"Go check on him," Nate said. "I can't move anyway."

"Why not?"

"I think my ankle is broken."

"How?"

"I don't know," Nate said, his breath hissing through his teeth. "Adam hit me. Now, he's hitting your friend."

"It's Marko."

"He's the one who got me into this mess."

Nate had burglarized Ben Price. He'd gotten himself into this mess, but there was no point in arguing. If they didn't figure something out quick, they were all going to die. Or something far, far worse. They'd be stuck down here while Adam Price tortured them.

"I'll be right back," Allee said.

"Be careful."

Allee turned and, keeping her hands protectively in front of her, felt for the entryway to the next room. Finding it at last, she ducked under it and moved forward with small, shuffling steps. One step. Two steps. Three. Her foot struck something.

Marko groaned.

She crouched down, feeling his body in the darkness, trying to find his injury.

"What happened?" Marko said through gritted teeth. "And why are you feeling me up?"

Allee's hands found his pressed into what felt like his stomach. She pulled his hands away and felt a large wet patch around a hole in his shirt. The blood was warm and sticky on her hands. "I think you've been stabbed," Allee said.

"By you?"

"No."

Allee pressed Marko's hands back to his stomach. He was losing a lot of blood. Someone needed to apply pressure to the wound, but she couldn't stay. She could not see Adam Price, but she could sense him. He wasn't using light; he was moving around in the darkness like a phantom. She had no idea how he could see in the inky darkness, but it didn't seem to be hindering him.

A weapon, Allee thought. She needed to find something she could use to protect herself. But what? Her cell phone was gone, smashed on the floor somewhere in the room with Nate. She couldn't call for help. She felt around in her pockets, her hands encircling Marko's key ring. She pressed a key between each knuckle, creating a makeshift set of brass knuckles.

She stood cautiously to her full height. Adam might have a weapon, but he had no experience with people like her. He'd never been to prison. He'd never fought to establish himself as someone not to screw with inside the prison walls.

She hadn't faced the possibility of serious violence since her first year in Mitchellville. The first month of her first year, in fact. But as she tried to see her assailant in the dark, she felt the familiar adrenaline rush that facing death brought. She took a deep breath and held it, steadying herself, fixing her resolve. *If this is how it's going to be, then let's get it on.* Allee was no target. Not in prison. Not in this hellhole.

66

WHITNEY

It had taken an hour for the jail to process and release her. Every second she'd waited was excruciating. Her mind raced from Arlo and her desire to see him to Allee and Marko and her concern for their safety. She'd heard nothing, but then, she hadn't really expected to hear anything.

Had they gotten into the basement of the restaurant? Was Nate okay? Were any of them okay?

"You've got forty-eight hours to meet with your pretrial release officer," Ralph said. He palmed a business card from the counter and handed it to her. It read, "Pamela Banks, Probation/Parole Officer, Second Judicial District."

Whitney attempted to hand the card back. "I'm not on probation or parole."

Ralph shook his head. "I understand, but they do the supervising for pretrial stuff, too."

"Okay," Whitney said, pocketing the card. Marko had said she'd be released OR, but this was no time to argue. She was back in her own clothing, which was ridiculous. She'd been arrested late in the evening, after she'd put on her pajamas—a pair of ratty plaid pants that she'd owned since her second year of college and a T-shirt so thin and faded that it had holes along the bottom.

"Is someone coming to get you?" Ralph asked, genuine concern in his eyes.

Whitney shook her head. She felt betrayed by Leo. He hadn't believed her. Sure, nobody else did either, but at least Allee and Marko had eventually listened. Leo hadn't. He'd heard one piece of evidence and he'd bailed with their son. She didn't want to ask him for any favors. Not now. Not ever again. Not even a small one, like picking her up. "I'll catch a ride with someone."

"Like who?"

"I'll figure it out," she said with far more confidence than she felt. She literally had nobody. Only Marko and Allee, and who knew where they were. She couldn't follow them. She wasn't allowed at the restaurant anymore. The Prices had said they would file trespassing charges against her if she returned.

Ralph was watching her while she weighed her options. At last, he opened the back door to the jail, gesturing outside. "Your freedom awaits."

For now, she thought. She might just beat Adam Price to death. She doubted she could stop herself if she got started. Then she'd be right back here. Adam's abuse of Jaxson would not justify homicide; that, she knew. But that was only one possible outcome. She could become his next prisoner.

Either way, freedom was not on her agenda. At least not yet.

67

ALLEE

From somewhere behind her, Allee heard Marko cough, thick and wet. *Not a good sign.* She'd had to make a split-second decision—stay or go—and she'd left him. Part of her regretted leaving him; she wanted to run back to him and protect him, but another part of her was exhilarated.

She was hunting a hunter.

She'd been in the dark long enough that her senses were starting to adjust. It was just like solitary confinement—"complete auditory and ocular deprivation," someone once called it. In her lingo, she couldn't see or hear shit.

Her stint in solitary had been short but well worth it—that guard never touched her again.

Hearing replaced vision as her primary sense. The slightest of noises was now amplified.

Even so, she felt, rather than heard, a soft swish in the heavy air. *He's right here!*

Earlier, he'd been silent and invisible, free to move unseen at will. But now he had to act, and his location was slowly being revealed. She turned, pressed her body against a wall, and froze. She knew how to disappear. All she had to do was stay still.

Do. Not. Move.

He grunted and the air moved around her. He was lunging blindly.

She dodged, twisting her body away from the sound and the movement. She felt another rush of air near her head and heard a click and a snap as his knife struck the cement wall and broke.

The playing field was leveling.

He was closer now, moving in for the kill, intent on getting his hands on her. She could smell his sweat. She waited, crouching, listening, estimating his body position.

When she knew it was right, she straightened and threw a punch, putting all her strength behind it, aiming for his unseen face. Two of the keys struck something hard. Skin wrapped tightly over bone. *A nose or forehead.* The others hit something softer, sinking in easily.

An eye.

He screamed.

She tried to pull her hand back to throw another punch, but her makeshift weapon was seemingly stuck.

The screaming continued. Something clattered to the floor.

She released the keys. Her hand was slick with something. Blood, perhaps, but it didn't feel quite like blood. She dropped to the floor and felt around on the concrete, her fingers cold and wet against it. *There!* Closing her fingers around the object she'd been searching for, she rose and crept back through the opening, intent on getting away from the wounded Price and locating Marko.

Adam continued screaming, and she had the handle of his broken knife in her hand, just in case.

68

WHITNEY

Whitney rushed through the back door and strode purposefully through the kitchen. No one paid her any attention, let alone tried to stop her. *Nobody asks questions. Nobody cares.*

She saw a knife next to a half-sliced tomato on a table as she passed. She wiped the blade on her thigh and pocketed the knife. It wasn't large, but it was better than nothing. She wandered about until she found a hallway that appeared to run along the back of the building.

A pretty young woman with dead eyes and long blonde hair intercepted her. "Who are you?"

"Jaxson Michael's sister."

"I thought you were in jail."

Whitney gestured to herself, her ridiculous outfit. "Not anymore."

"Are you looking for the others?" Lorna asked. "The big chick with super short hair and a defense attorney?"

"Yeah."

"They went downstairs. They've been there a while."

That didn't sound good.

"Follow me." Lorna led Whitney down the long hallway, stopping in front of a heavy steel door. "They're down there."

Whitney slid her hand into her pocket, gathering strength from the heel of the knife. She had no idea what she would find, but it probably wouldn't be good. She slid her hand into her other pocket and removed her cell phone. The jailers had turned it off while she was in custody. She powered it back on. It still worked, but it was at ten percent power. She clicked on the flashlight and opened the heavy door.

No time like the present.

69

ALLEE

Allee had just located Marko again when a door slammed somewhere in the distance, the loud steel sound reverberating around the room. "Marko!" she hissed as she shook her boss's shoulder.

He groaned. He was on the ground, curled into the fetal position.

"Can you move? We need to get out of here." Allee had no idea who had just entered the basement, but more than likely it was someone who knew Adam. It could be Luke, or Nikki.

Adam was no longer screaming, but he wasn't quiet either. He was issuing whimpering noises from the opposite corner of the room. "Come on." Allee shook Marko's shoulder.

The second door opened, and a light entered the small basement chamber, illuminating the room.

"Allee!"

"Whitney," Allee said. Relief flooded through her, but they weren't out of danger yet. Adam was still there somewhere; Marko was barely clinging to life; and Nate was hurt and unable to move. "Call 911!"

Whitney's phone flashlight swung around the room, landing on Adam cowering in the corner. "You!" she said through clenched teeth.

Price had an object protruding from his left eye, held in place by his blood-soaked hands. *Marko's keys.*

"Whitney! Make the call now! We need help," Allee said. She was crouched beside Marko, who had grown eerily still.

"No," Whitney said.

Allee ran her fingers along Marko's arm, settling at his wrist, searching for a pulse. It was faint, barely there. "No, Whitney! We don't have time for this."

Whitney pulled a knife from her pocket. "I want to talk to *him*," she said as she approached Adam.

Marko needs help now! Allee thought. And so did Nate. He was in far better physical condition than Marko, but he was weak and in pain. But Whitney had the only working phone. Or did she? Allee began feeling around, searching through Marko's pockets. *It has to be here. Lawyers never leave their phones.* Her hand closed around a small, rectangular object.

"It isn't self-defense at this point," Allee said as Whitney took another step toward Adam. She had to talk sense into the other woman. If Whitney continued, everything she and Marko had done for her would be for naught. "The cops will take care of him," Allee said, switching tactics. "There is plenty of evidence."

"Not if I take care of him first," Whitney said, taking another step toward a cowering Adam.

70

WHITNEY

"Why? Why Jaxson? Why did you do it?" Whitney's voice did not sound like her own. It was like she'd been possessed, like someone else was speaking through her mouth. She could hear herself, see herself, but she wasn't in control.

"Do what?" Price pushed himself further into the corner.

"Don't. Don't play dumb." She tapped the blade of the knife against her leg. "Not with me."

"He was...bad."

"Bad?"

"When you're bad, you get locked up." Price said it as though he'd uttered the words a thousand times.

"What the hell does that mean?" Whitney took another step closer, gripping the knife tighter in her hand.

Behind her, Allee had her phone on speaker mode. "911. What's your emergency?"

Whitney swung around, facing Allee. *Not yet!* She wanted Allee to let her finish with Price.

"We need help," Allee said quickly. "We're in the basement of The Yellow Lark."

Whitney turned back around. *Do it! Do this now!* She imagined herself dragging the knife down his gut, opening a wound to match the invisible wounds he and the entire Price family had opened inside her heart.

"That's what happens," Adam said, curling into a ball. "In my family. The favorite gets punished."

"What are you talking about?" Whitney demanded through gritted teeth. *Time to finish you off. I'll argue self-defense. Allee won't say anything.*

"The favorite child must live up to expectations," Adam replied tearfully. "Or be locked up. Jaxson was my favorite."

She brandished the knife. But for whatever reason, she now saw only a pathetic little man in front of her, curled in a ball, helpless, holding his face with both hands. All the fury and violence rushed out of her.

She felt Allee beside her now. "Whitney, what are you doing?"

What am I doing? Finish him. She raised the knife.

Allee was pleading with her. "If you ever want to see Arlo again, don't."

Whitney heard sirens, then footsteps hurrying down the stairs, then voices crowding the small space. Soon, dozens of people in uniform streamed past her. Paramedics. Cops. Firefighters. Someone hit her arm as they rushed past and she dropped the knife. It clattered to the floor. Whitney dropped to the floor as well.

The very floor where Jaxson had been tortured.

71

ALLEE

"Tell me the story again. Just one more time," the female officer ordered. She had introduced herself as Officer Walters, and she was the only person in the interview room with Allee. They were at the police station, separated and isolated in that way cops always did during investigations.

Allee ignored the question. "Have you heard anything from the hospital about Nate or Marko?"

Walters shook her head. She looked to be nearing middle age and did not pretend to be anything other than herself. She didn't wear a bit of makeup and her hair was pulled back into a tight ponytail. "I'll let you know as soon as I hear something. But as far as I know, nothing's changed. They are both in surgery. Marko is critical and Nate is in fair condition."

She might be the first cop Allee had ever met that she didn't instantly hate. "Okay. So, what exactly do you want to know?"

"Just repeat it all from the beginning."

Allee did. For the first time in her life, she was completely honest with law enforcement. She told Walters about her short stint working for Adam Price, how Nate became an employee, how Allee got a new job, and how Whitney became her client. She explained her ties to Jaxson, how she knew him before she'd gone to prison. She spoke about her investigation and the depositions, ending with the thumb drive and her desire to save Nate from Jaxson's fate.

Walters scribbled notes as Allee spoke, her strong hand flying across the page. When Allee finished, Walters stared down at her notepad for a long moment. "Explain a little more to me about the interaction you saw between Nikki Price and her son, Luke."

"Well," Allee began. "It was just...odd. He's physically much larger than she is, of course, but he's afraid of her. Physically. It didn't seem right. Not for a kid that age. Boys that age are full of testosterone and bravado. They think they are bulletproof."

"I see," Walters said.

"You don't believe me." Allee's heart sank. She'd never been able to trust law enforcement, but this officer had seemed different. She had treated Allee like any other person rather than focusing on her past. Maybe it was all a ruse to get Allee talking.

"That's not it. Everything you've told me checks out," Walters said. "He is here, you know."

"Luke?"

Walters nodded. "He's in another interview room."

"Nikki Price is here?"

"No. Luke came with his father, but he insisted on talking to us without his parents present. Benjamin Price is out in the waiting room, pacing like a cat inside a dog pound."

"Okay." Allee didn't know why the officer was telling her all of this. What did it mean?

"Would you like to watch some of the interview?"

"Absolutely. Can I?"

"I don't see why not," Walters said. She stood and led Allee out of the interview room and down the hall. "By the way," she said, nodding to Allee's arm, "I like the tattoos."

"They're from books."

"I know."

Walters came to a set of doors positioned adjacent to one another, produced a set of keys, and unlocked the door to the right. It opened into a small room with a large window. The window overlooked the room next to it, which was occupied by a young male officer and Luke.

"Yeah," Luke was saying as Walters and Allee watched, his voice coming through speakers that piped sound into the small room. "I made it all up."

Walters gestured to the row of chairs lined up in front of the window. Allee chose the one nearest to the door. Walters closed the door and sat next to her.

"Made what all up?" the male officer asked.

"All the stuff about Mrs. Moore."

Oh, so now it's "Mrs. Moore." In his deposition, he'd always referred to Whitney by her first name. This kid had either been coached to use his words to manipulate or he was naturally good at it.

"The affair?"

"Yes."

"Yes, it is true, or it isn't true?"

"It's not true. I didn't have an affair with her. She's not like that."

The officer nodded in understanding. "And the stuff about her husband, her asking you to kill him—that wasn't true either?"

"No. It wasn't."

"So, why? Why did you make that up?"

"I had to. I mean"—he sighed heavily—"I have no idea what is happening with Adam. My friends have been sending me stuff about cops raiding the house and the restaurant. I hear he's in the hospital. I hear he has done...some things."

The officer nodded but kept silent.

"If he did the things people are saying, if he locked people in the basement of the restaurant, that's only because that's what Mom did to *us*."

"Your mother?" the cop asked. "Nikki Price?"

"Yeah," Luke said. "I mean, she only did it to me a couple times, but she did it to Adam all the time. He was her favorite. It was her form of punishment."

Favorite. Punishment. Those were both words Adam Price had used.

"Locking you somewhere, you mean?"

"Yeah. She'd lock us in a room in the dark in the unfinished basement."

"For how long?"

"It depended on what it was for," Luke replied. "Whether it happened on a weekend or during the summer, for one thing."

Involuntarily, the cop looked at the mirror where Allee and Walters sat, observing. "Why did that matter?" he asked.

"School," Allee said aloud.

"Because we couldn't be absent from school," Luke explained. "That would look bad. And my mom is all about keeping up appearances. My dad, too."

"Was your father part of this?"

"Not directly."

"Did he know about it?"

"He had to know. I mean, I hope I'd wonder what happened to my five-year-old son if he disappeared for days—even a week."

"You were being locked up for a week when you were five?"

"Even younger," Luke said. "For as long as I can remember."

Allee stood and walked out of the room. She'd heard enough. Walters followed.

"So, what now?" Allee asked. "Adam gets away with it because he's been abused, and nothing happens to Nikki because she was only punishing her kids?"

"Well, no," Walters said. "She's already been placed under arrest."

"For what?"

"False imprisonment. Child endangerment, to start."

"So, misdemeanors."

"Yeah."

Allee shook her head. She hated the criminal justice system. Nikki had created the monster in Adam, who had tortured Jaxson until he saw no way out and killed himself, and Adam had planned to do the same with Allee's cousin. And all Nikki would face were misdemeanors. It made her sick.

"But Adam will go to prison for the rest of his life," Walters added.

"Great," Allee deadpanned. She started making her way toward the door.

"Where are you going?" Walters asked.

"To the hospital." There was no point in staying. She'd just get angry at the unfairness of the system. Intellectually, she understood that no construct as large and looming as the criminal justice system was perfect. There were benefits and drawbacks. But emotionally, all she could see were the glaring flaws. There was nothing she could do to change it. She was a tiny player. An ant crawling across a football field. Nothing she did would make any difference.

EPILOGUE
MARKO

Three months later

"Where are we going?" Allee asked.

She was in the passenger seat of Marko's car. He was finally driving again. He'd never thought of a license to drive as freedom, but it was. After losing his license, he now understood why his grandmother had fought so hard when his parents tried to take her car after she'd hit that telephone pole.

"You know, you shouldn't be driving," Allee said, turning her attention from the window to focus on him. "You've got a temporary restricted license—not a full license. You can drive for work purposes and medical appointments. That's it."

He smiled. "And just when did you become such a stickler for the rules?"

"When I started working for someone who flagrantly disregards them." She crossed her arms and turned her attention back to the window. "You'd better not get pulled over," she warned. "I'm not bailing you out of jail."

She was right, of course. If they were out on a joy ride he'd be looking at driving under revocation—a serious misdemeanor under Iowa law, one that could result in a year-long jail sentence. But they weren't on a joy ride. He was taking her somewhere on business. She didn't know that.

"I'm serious," Allee said.

"You always are."

As he drove, the silence lengthened. *Normally, it would bug me, but it won't last. When we get there, things will change.* Ten minutes later, he pulled into a dirt parking lot. The sign above the business door read, "Custom Cars, Detailing and More."

"Where are we?"

"Gonna see a client."

As he spoke, Whitney exited the front door of the business. Before they'd stopped fully, she was approaching, Arlo by her side. He was clutching her hand like she was full of helium and dropping it would cause her to float away.

Marko got out of the car and watched as Allee cautiously did the same.

"What's going on?" she asked, her irritation giving way to confusion.

"We've got a surprise for you," Whitney said. Arlo hid behind his mother, beaming.

"Okay...I guess," Allee replied uncertainly. Marko knew she didn't like surprises. That was part of what was making this so enjoyable.

"Follow me," Whitney said, and headed for a large, pre-fabricated metal building located next to the business office. She entered, then stopped beside a vehicle parked just inside the entryway. Marko and Allee followed.

Allee stopped and gasped aloud when she saw the large truck with a window at the back and a business name painted along the side.

"The truck you originally had your eye on sold, so we thought we'd splurge for a brand-new one," Whitney said, a smile spreading across her face.

"I don't understand," Allee replied.

"Your food truck law firm idea," Marko explained. "Whitney and I have decided to go into business. Would you like to join us?"

"As what?"

"As head cook. And part owner, of course!"

Allee shook her head. "I don't know what to say."

"That's not a no, is it?" *Every no is a yes in progress.* "Because we are really going to rake in the money. Especially in Franklin now that The Yellow Lark has shut down," Marko said.

Adam was in jail. Nikki had bonded out but was lying low, trying to salvage her reputation. Ben had tried to keep the business afloat, but it turned out that people didn't like to eat somewhere when they knew there had been a torture chamber in the basement.

"Oh my gosh." Allee shook her head again. "It's a yes!" Her eyes teared up. "Just one thing—"

"What?" Marko asked.

Allee bit her lip. "Nate needs a job. Can he work here, too?"

Marko looked to Whitney. She had hired Marko to sue the Prices for civil damages—real and punitive—resulting from the false accusations that had been made against her. The case was still pending, but between the criminal evidence that would be available, statements made by Luke, and Whitney's loss of wages, the case was as close to a slam dunk as Marko had seen. Whitney would never be able to teach, but she probably wouldn't have to work for a long time, either. She and Leo were still trying to work things out, but the possibility of divorce was out there, as well.

"Marko and I are planning to focus on the law practice," Whitney said. "I'll be his office manager. He, obviously, will practice law."

"I see," Allee said.

"You will manage the food truck when you're not investigating. You've got a knack for it," Whitney said.

"And driving. My license is limited, you know," Marko added. "You'll be busy, so you'll need help running the food truck." He shrugged. "And you're the boss, so if you want to hire Nate, have at it."

Allee nodded.

"All right," she said, her face lighting up in a wide grin. "Let's do it." She put her hands on her hips and gazed at the name on the truck. "'Justice Bites,'" she read. "Perfect!"

Bodies of Proof
Smith and Bauer Book 2

A shocking confession. A prolific killer. A legal minefield.

Mark Bauer and Allee Smith thought defending James Innis on a simple charge would be straightforward. But when he confesses to a murder, it's clear that this case will be anything but easy. Bound by the law, they can't expose him, even when he leads them to the body. Desperate to escape the ethical trap they've fallen into, Mark and Allee search for a loophole to report him, weighing the options of dropping the case or outright defying the rules. But every move they make seems to pull them deeper into his sinister game, and Innis's chilling arrogance shows them just how dangerous he truly is.

When another victim mysteriously disappears, their ethical dilemma escalates. With each disturbing clue, the full scope of Innis's plans becomes clear: he's orchestrating Mark and Allee's every move, and no one in their lives is safe.

Upholding their professional ethics may come at a price too steep to pay, as the cost begins to threaten not only their careers but the lives of those they love.

Will they break the law to stop a murderer... or risk becoming his next victims?

ABOUT JAMES CHANDLER

Wall Street Journal bestselling author James Chandler spent his formative years in the western United States. When he wasn't catching fish or footballs, he was roaming centerfield and trying to hit the breaking pitch. After a mediocre college baseball career, he exchanged jersey No. 7 for camouflage issued by the United States Army, which he wore around the globe and with great pride for twenty years. Since law school, he has favored dark suits and a steerhide briefcase. When he isn't working or writing, he'll likely have a fly rod, shotgun or rifle in hand. He and his wife are blessed with two wonderful adult daughters.

Sign up for James Chandler's newsletter at
severnriverbooks.com

ABOUT LAURA SNIDER

Laura Snider is a practicing lawyer in Iowa. She graduated from Drake Law School in 2009 and spent most of her career as a Public Defender. Throughout her legal career she has been involved in all levels of crimes from petty thefts to murders. These days she is working part-time as a prosecutor and spends the remainder of her time writing stories and creating characters.

Laura lives in Iowa with her husband, three children, two dogs, and two very mischievous cats.

Sign up for Laura Snider's newsletter at
severnriverbooks.com